P9-APQ-635

"Why don't you tell me what has you running scared every time I touch you?"

Trey suggested.

"I don't have a lot of experience," she said in a low voice.

Her words, not totally unexpected, sent a curl of satisfaction through him. "That can't be from lack of opportunity."

"I've dated, but I couldn't...I could never..."

"Is that what happens with me?"

"No. It's so different," she whispered honestly.

A primordial surge of possessiveness arrowed through his gut. He doubted she recognized the significance of her confession, but *he* did. "There's something between us, Jaida. And after we find Benjy, when we're sure he's safe..." He paused meaningfully until she raised her gaze to meet his. "Then you and I will finish it."

Dear Reader,

The weather may be cooling off as fall approaches, but the reading's as hot as ever here at Silhouette Intimate Moments. And for our lead title this month I'm proud to present the first longer book from reader favorite BJ James. In *Broken Spurs* she's created a hero and heroine sure to live in your mind long after you've turned the last page.

Karen Leabo returns with *Midnight Confessions,* about a bounty hunter whose reward—love—turns out to be far different from what he'd expected. In *Bringing Benjy Home,* Kylie Brant matches a skeptical man with an intuitive woman, then sets them on the trail of a missing child. *Code Name: Daddy* is the newest Intimate Moments novel from Marilyn Tracy, who took a break to write for our Shadows line. It's a unique spin on the ever-popular "secret baby" plotline. And you won't want to miss *Michael's House,* Pat Warren's newest book for the line and part of her REUNION miniseries, which continues in Special Edition. Finally, in *Temporary Family* Sally Tyler Hayes creates the family of the title, then has you wishing as hard as they do to make the arrangement permanent.

Enjoy them all—and don't forget to come back next month for more of the best romance fiction around, right here in Silhouette Intimate Moments.

Leslie Wainger,
Senior Editor and Editorial Coordinator

Please address questions and book requests to:
Silhouette Reader Service
U.S.: 3010 Walden Ave., P.O. Box 1325, Buffalo, NY 14269
Canadian: P.O. Box 609, Fort Erie, Ont. L2A 5X3

BRINGING BENJY HOME

KYLIE BRANT

Silhouette®
INTIMATE MOMENTS®

Published by Silhouette Books

America's Publisher of Contemporary Romance

If you purchased this book without a cover you should be aware
that this book is stolen property. It was reported as "unsold and
destroyed" to the publisher, and neither the author nor the
publisher has received any payment for this "stripped book."

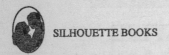 SILHOUETTE BOOKS

ISBN 0-373-07735-1

BRINGING BENJY HOME

Copyright © 1996 by Kimberly Bahnsen

All rights reserved. Except for use in any review, the reproduction
or utilization of this work in whole or in part in any form by any
electronic, mechanical or other means, now known or hereafter
invented, including xerography, photocopying and recording, or in
any information storage or retrieval system, is forbidden without
the written permission of the editorial office, Silhouette Books,
300 East 42nd Street, New York, NY 10017 U.S.A.

All characters in this book have no existence outside the imagination of
the author and have no relation whatsoever to anyone bearing the same
name or names. They are not even distantly inspired by any individual
known or unknown to the author, and all incidents are pure invention.

This edition published by arrangement with Harlequin Books S.A.

® and TM are trademarks of Harlequin Books S.A., used under license.
Trademarks indicated with ® are registered in the United States Patent
and Trademark Office, the Canadian Trade Marks Office and in other
countries.

Printed in U.S.A.

Books by Kylie Brant

Silhouette Intimate Moments

KYLIE BRANT

married her high school sweetheart over sixteen years ago, and they are raising their five children in Iowa. She spends her days teaching learning disabled students, and many nights attending her sons' sporting events.

Always an avid reader, Kylie enjoys stories of love, mystery and suspense—and insists on happy endings! When her youngest children, a set of twins, turned four, she decided to try her hand at writing. Now most weekends and all summer she can be found at her computer, spinning her own tales of romance and happily-ever-afters.

Kylie invites readers to write to her at P.O. Box 231, Charles City, IA 50616

With love, to Jill, Kevin, Jeff, Joel and Kelcie.
Here's to the next reunion!

Chapter 1

He found her in a field of wildflowers.

Trey Garrison narrowed his eyes against the glare of the midmorning Arkansas sun. The lone woman sat amid the brilliant blues, reds and golds in the meadow. She had her back to him, and the rich bouquet of color surrounding her provided a vivid backdrop for her hair. The shade was such a startling blond it was obvious even to the most untrained eye that it derived its origin from a bottle.

He left the rented four-wheel-drive on the side of the narrow gravel road and began making his way carefully across the meadow. As he drew closer he was able to see that she was seated on a large rock, scribbling in the notebook she held on her lap.

"Jaida West?"

His approach had been silent, and at the sound of his voice the woman went utterly still. Then she turned toward him, gracefully maintaining her perch. He felt an actual physical jolt when she met his gaze. Her eyes reminded him of the sample of lapis he'd picked up in Afghanistan. They were a startling dark blue, with flecks of gold tracing through them. The golden glints appeared molten in the sunlight, bathing him with heat. The effect was undeniably disquieting. And then she spoke.

"What can I do for you?"

Her drawl would enchant some Northerners. There was more than a trace of "y'all" in her words.

Trey's mouth twisted. That magnolia-and-honey voice was undoubtedly meant to charm. Instead, it seemed another affectation, like the hair color.

Like her so-called gift.

"My name is Trey Garrison. Your grandmother told me where to find you."

"She did?" Jaida looked him over, ignoring the incongruous sight he made wearing what appeared to be an Italian silk suit and leather shoes in the middle of a meadow in the Arkansas Valley. The initial wariness she'd felt at having her solitude interrupted by a stranger ebbed. If Granny had trusted him enough to send him after her, there was definitely more to the man than met the eye. Although what met the eye was impressive.

He was tall, about a half foot taller than her own five-eight height. His close-cropped hair was as black as a crow's wing, his eyes a deep forest green. There was a cleft in his chin, which accentuated the determined set of his jaw. He was not from around here, certainly. If she didn't miss her guess he was big city. In that expensive double-breasted suit, he could be a banker or a lawyer. The corners of her mouth tilted. She'd never have Granny Logan's talent for sizing people up, but even she could tell that this man was neither. "She must have liked your voice."

His eyes slitted, the dark lashes on the top nearly meeting those on bottom. "Who?"

Jaida patiently explained. "Granny. She never would have sent a stranger out here otherwise, unless . . ." She cast a speculative glance at his chin. "She didn't invite you into the cabin, did she?"

"No," he replied, his voice clipped. "She did not."

"Hmm." Her eyes crinkled with laughter. It was apparent that Trey Garrison was not a man accustomed to being kept waiting outside while he stated his business. "Yep, she must have really liked your voice. So . . ." She shrugged and gave a beguiling smile. "Here I am. Tell me, Trey Garrison, what can I do for you?"

Trey surveyed her for a moment. Her reaction to meeting a stranger out in the middle of nowhere was visibly nonchalant. "Ms. West . . ." he began smoothly.

"It's 'Jaida,'" she informed him, her mouth quirking again mischievously. "I hope you're not going to expect me to call you 'Mr. Garrison.'"

His affable smile bespoke a formidable charm. Most people wouldn't notice that it wasn't reflected in his eyes. "You're right, Jaida. Please call me 'Trey.' Do you know why I'm here?"

She closed the notebook she held on her lap and folded her hands neatly on top of it. "Am I supposed to?"

"I thought you might. I thought—" his voice was meaningful "—that was part of your 'gift.'" He noted with satisfaction that his words had her amusement abruptly fading. Wariness made a belated appearance across her countenance. So, she wasn't completely without defenses.

Let the games begin.

"You came here to consult a psychic?" she asked disbelievingly.

A slight inclination of his head was her only answer.

"I don't believe it."

"Why not?"

"Because," she replied coolly, her gaze clashing with his, "you strike me as an eminently practical man, Trey Garrison. And not a particularly desperate one. A man like you doesn't come across the country to request the help of a psychic. A man like you," she added deliberately, "doesn't believe in them."

"A man like me," he repeated in a soft tone, "doesn't come across the country without a damn good reason."

"Exactly," she affirmed, her voice as quiet as his. "So why don't you tell me what it is?"

He felt the strength of her gaze. It was unwavering, unblinking, and he knew she was searching for something, some clue that would give his motives away. He understood that was how these charlatans worked. They depended more on observation than on any real mystical power. If he'd been so inclined, he could have told her that an attempt to read him would meet with failure.

He wasn't so inclined.

"I've heard you've had some success with locating missing persons. I'm hoping you can help me."

There was something about this man that didn't ring true. It was more than the mask that he seemed able to draw across his features at will. She'd met other people who hid their emotions. Few people were able to keep their true feelings from showing in their eyes, though. His were as mysterious, as impenetrable as the forest of their hue.

Baffled, she pushed her hair off one shoulder, an unconscious, nervous gesture. Mixed messages exuded from the man before her, and she found him difficult to appraise. He'd come quite a ways to talk to her, that was clear. It would suggest that he needed her help, that he *wanted* it.

But Trey Garrison didn't really want her assistance; she knew that intuitively. She'd never met anybody so guarded. He was as buttoned up as the cream-colored dress shirt he wore. It was doubtful such a man would share his true reasons with a stranger. With a chill, she recalled another time she'd been sought out by a man whose stated purpose had warred with the speculation in his eyes. He'd turned out to be a reporter, intent on writing an exposé of people claiming psychic abilities. This man seemed infinitely more threatening to her, though she couldn't yet tell in what way.

The realization infuriated her. "You're lying."

Though she couldn't detect even a flicker of expression, an air of menace seemed to settle over Trey at her words.

"Pardon me?" His words were measured, the tone silky.

Jaida ignored the chill skating over her arms. Her chin jutted out as she continued hotly, "I don't know what brought you here, Garrison, but I'm not a sideshow freak. Amuse yourself at someone else's expense." She scrambled down from the rock.

Her long, gauzy skirt tangled with her legs, sending her off-balance. He stepped forward involuntarily, reaching for her. His movement was sudden, and totally unavoidable. When his hands closed around her waist, a gasp escaped her. Sparks jumped wildly beneath his fingers through her thin blouse. An electric frisson chased down her spine. She was pulling away from him before her toes met the ground. When he let go of her, she put a few more feet between them for good measure. Then she stopped and looked at him, barely disguised panic on her face.

Trey returned her regard assessingly. His hands still tingled from the shocking connection that had leapt between them. It wasn't based on the physical chemistry of two people attracted to each other. No, he definitely had other things on his mind when it came to Jaida West. And she hadn't seemed like a woman overcome with sexual awareness, either. She looked almost . . . *scared*.

"Listen, Miss West . . . Jaida . . .' His voice was soothing. "I didn't mean to frighten you."

"You didn't." She shook her head fiercely, willing the words to be true. "I was . . . startled." Her chin came up again then, and she matched him look for look. "You made me angry when you lied to me and I didn't want you touching me. That's all."

"I did not lie to you." He bit the words out precisely.

She shrugged carelessly. Already the unexpected current of electricity was fading, although the memory of it wasn't. "Didn't tell the whole truth, then. My granny always taught me it was the same thing."

Her drawl was more pronounced now. There was something about listening to the slow, dulcet cadence of her speech that made her insults sound especially provocative. He would have liked to share a few succinct sentences about what he thought of her and her granny, but his usual control exerted itself.

He couldn't afford to let his distaste for this assignment drive her away. At least not yet. After promising his sister that he would ask for Jaida's help, he wanted to be able to tell her, with at least some degree of honesty, that he'd done as she'd requested. He didn't give his word lightly. And there was precious little he wouldn't do for the only family he had left.

The woman before him looked poised to flee. But he knew how to get what he wanted. He'd cultured the manners, the small talk, all the nuances that would put others at ease. He used his deliberately acquired veneer of civility the way some men wielded a weapon. And he got better results with it.

He manufactured a rueful half smile. Jaida stared dumbly for an instant as his whole countenance was transposed. No longer was he the man who had come here intent on his own purposes, who'd caused her nerve endings to riot.

"You're right, and I apologize," he said. "I haven't told you the whole story, but I haven't really had much of a chance yet." His gaze was direct. "Can we start again?"

Shaking her head in admiration, Jaida murmured, "You're good."

"Pardon me?"

"I said, this better be good."

Trey studied her silently for a moment before speaking. "My sister, Lauren, remembered hearing of you and insisted on asking for your help."

Jaida looked beyond him, startled. "Your sister is here with you?"

"No." His voice was terse. "She's under a doctor's care. It's impossible for her to travel at this point. I agreed to approach you on her behalf."

Jaida's gaze returned to his. "What kind of help does your sister need?"

"My eighteen-month-old nephew was kidnapped nine days ago." His bleak words seemed to echo the desolation he'd lived with since Benjy's disappearance. Benjy had been only minutes old the first time Trey had held his tiny body in his hands. He'd looked down into his nephew's face, curiously wizened in the manner of newborns, and felt an immediate, irrevocable bond. He'd vowed at that moment to keep Benjy safe from all harm.

Never had he failed so miserably.

His voice harsh, he added, "The police were called in immediately. A few days later the FBI joined the investigation. But they haven't turned up any real leads." And Lauren was growing desperate, he could have added, teetering on the brink of physical and emotional collapse. Until she was willing to clutch at straws to help find him.

Until she was willing to put her faith in any circus swami fake who professed psychic powers.

Jaida studied him, trying to read what he wasn't saying. That he was here under duress was plausible. That would account for the sense of certainty she'd had that he wasn't being completely honest at first. *He* hadn't been the one to decide to ask for her help. No doubt he'd done his best to talk his sister out of the idea. She felt a grudging respect for the man. She had no doubt that he let few people sway him from his opinion.

"You must love your sister very much," she murmured.

"I'd do anything for her," he said flatly.

She wrapped her arms around her middle. "What's your nephew's name?"

"Benjy."

Her eyes slid shut. She was prepared for the flood of emotion that filled her at the mention of the lost child's name. From long practice she didn't try to suppress it; there would have been no point. The emotions rolled over her, swirling about inside like a dervish. There was nothing from the turbulence within that would be useful yet. She would be unable to pick out any relevant information until she held something of Benjy's to bring it into focus.

And yet…the sensations were clearer, more vivid than usual. That was uncommon.

Her eyes opened to see that Trey had moved to stand before her once again. His face was unreadable. She had a sudden urge to put some distance between them. *He was dangerous.* It was innate, primal instinct rather than psychic ability that told her so. And the memory of the unexpected electric reaction to his touch made her uneasy. She wasn't reacting normally around him, and she couldn't trust herself to make a decision in this jittery state.

Jaida turned and started making her way across the field.

"Wait a minute," he said, a hint of command entering his voice. "Where are you going?"

"Back to the cabin," her voice filtered back. "I'll meet you there."

Trey looked after her in frustration. "Don't you want a ride?" he called.

She picked up her long skirt in her free hand and started running. Forgetting his impatience for a moment, he watched, bemused, as she dodged patches of dogwood and leaped over a small stream. Her familiarity with the area was apparent. She was as surefooted as the meadow creatures.

Shaking off his momentary inertia, he turned and strode back toward the Jeep. He'd somehow frightened Jaida West, and he was going to have to be more careful. At least until he'd proven her for the fraud she was.

Then perhaps she would have a very real reason to fear him.

Bursting into the cabin, Jaida said automatically, "It's me, Granny."

"I know it's you, child," the old woman answered imperturbably. "Who else would be tearing up the path like her skirts was on fire?"

Jaida set her notebook down and crossed to the table where her grandmother was vigorously kneading bread dough. Sniffing, she filched a tiny bit of dough and popped it into her mouth. "Sourdough?"

"You know durn well it's sourdough, and I'll thank you to keep your mitts out of my bread, missy. Les'n you want to give me some help, that is."

Undaunted, Jaida snuck one more piece and ignored her grandmother's invitation to help. She knew well that the woman would be horrified if another pair of hands appeared in the dough. Granny Logan was fiercely, stubbornly, independent. Old age was relentlessly approaching, but she still took pride in "doing just fine for herself."

"Trey Garrison found me."

Granny's hands never faltered. "He's the one I been seeing," Granny explained calmly. "Been nigh on a week now. I knew it was him soon's I heard his voice."

Jaida nodded. She accepted Granny's visions unquestioningly. They complemented Jaida's own gift and were one of the reasons she'd always felt more comfortable with her grandmother than she ever had with her own mother.

At her granddaughter's silence, Granny paused. "Well?" she questioned sharply. "Was I right? He needs your help, don't he?"

Jaida wrapped her arms around herself, suddenly cold. The memory of the disturbing welter of feelings he'd elicited was still fresh in her mind. "He says he does. There's just something about him," she murmured. "He wasn't telling me everything. He didn't want to come down here—I did get that much from him. But it was more than that."

"What more?"

"He made me uneasy almost from the first," Jaida admitted. "And then he touched me...."

"Ah," Granny said wisely. "Did you see anything?"

Jaida knew her grandmother was referring to her psychic eye, but she wasn't sure how to respond. "No, at least not in the way you mean. It was...different than usual," she answered slowly. "Everything jumbled up inside and it was like touching a bare wire and getting a shock. It startled me and I reacted badly." She wrinkled her nose, remembering how she'd been unable to keep her panic from showing. "He thinks I'm a fruitcake."

The old woman looked satisfied. "Mebbe, mebbe not. In any case, you'll find out more shortly. If I don't miss my guess, that's him coming up the drive."

Jaida opened the door. What Granny had described as a drive was barely that. Little more than a rutted path, it was barely wide enough for a vehicle to pass. Trey had apparently abandoned the Jeep less than halfway up the drive and elected to walk the rest of the way.

A wise move, Jaida mused. She'd often cussed the path herself, especially when her four-wheel-drive pickup would hit a new rut with bone-jarring force.

He surveyed her for a moment with those enigmatic green eyes before asking, "Is your granny going to let me in this time?"

"I expect so," Jaida said, standing aside in silent invitation for him to enter. "She'll want to get a look at your chin."

Trey paused. "My chin?"

"Voices and chins," Jaida informed him mischievously. "Granny can tell a lot about a person's character from them. She'll have a time with that one of yours, too. It looks like you slept on a button."

He stared hard at her, then continued through the door.

A little smile played across her lips as she closed the door after him. Trey Garrison was a bit disconcerted, and something told her that was rare indeed. It was only fair. Her world had been set atumble at his appearance.

"Well, no need to keep the man standing in the doorway, Jaida."

Granny's voice snapped her from her reverie.

"Have him come in and sit down."

Trey sank gingerly into the cane rocker Jaida indicated, surprised when it held his weight. He relaxed a little and examined the cabin's interior. It was larger than it appeared from the outside. The room he was sitting in had a kitchen at one end, equipped with modern appliances, a wooden table and chairs. A stone fireplace was on the opposite wall. A few chairs and lamps were grouped around it. The furniture bespoke craftsmanship and gleamed with polish. There was nothing overstuffed in the entire room. He noted three doors leading away from this room. All of them were closed.

Jaida's grandmother placed a towel over the dough she'd been working with. She walked to the sink and washed her hands thoroughly. Then she made her way to where Trey was sitting. He watched her careful approach. It was difficult to guess her age, but he'd estimate it somewhere around seventy. She walked with the slightest hint of a limp, her left leg dragging a fraction. A stroke, he concluded immediately, looking at her face. It had left its ravages there, as well. He noted a plain stout cane leaning against one wall, but the woman didn't go toward it.

His eyes went to Jaida. She didn't hover, but neither did she seat herself until her grandmother had sunk into a rocker. Then she sat on a straight-back chair next to her.

Transferring his attention back to the older woman, he found himself subjected to an intent regard. He sat silently, allowing her the time to measure him. When she spoke it was with the accent of the Southern hills. But her voice was strong, unwavering. "Well, Mr. Garrison, exactly what is it you're wantin' with my girl?"

"My nephew is missing, Mrs. Logan. My sister has heard of Jaida and asked me to come and see if she could help."

The old woman nodded, as if having strange men come here making such requests was not at all unusual. Age had dimmed eyes that surely had once been the same color as her granddaughter's, but a keen intelligence radiated from them.

"What is it you do, Mr. Garrison?"

"I run a security firm, ma'am. My partner, Mac O'Neill, and I started it almost six years ago."

"Security." The old woman snorted. "You mean alarms and bells and all that nonsense you need to keep people out because y'all build too close to each other?"

Real amusement touched Trey's eyes. "Yes, ma'am, that's about it."

"And your sister sent you here?"

"Yes."

"Why didn't she come herself?"

He hesitated a few moments. Then he finally said, "Lauren was strolling Benjy in a park on the day he was kidnapped. Someone came up behind her and jabbed a needle in her arm. The drug she was injected with was probably intended to render her temporarily unconscious. The dosage was so high it almost killed her."

Jaida's gasp was audible.

"She was just released from the hospital yesterday. Her physician wouldn't hear of her traveling. I agreed to come in her place." His gaze moved to Jaida. "You've heard the whole story now. Will you help?"

Jaida and her grandmother exchanged a long look. "It's your choice, child," the old woman said in a quiet voice.

Her choice. Jaida considered the words wistfully. There had never been any choice involved with this strange paranormal knowledge she'd been born with. It couldn't be controlled or ignored. It had always been there, setting her apart from others, making it impossible to lead a normal life. The *knowing* was always lurking, dormant at times, but ready to spring out. It could be elicited by the most innocent human touch. And it could leave her devastated for hours.

Her grandmother had been referring to her decision about whether to help find Benjy, she knew. But that, too, had ceased to be a choice. She'd stopped resisting her fate long ago. She would never be normal. And if she refused to help Trey, his life and Lauren's might never return to normal, either. The decision, if one could call it that, had been made the moment Lauren had sent her brother here.

"Yes," she answered quietly. "I'll help."

His eyes gleamed at her acquiescence, but he only inclined his head slightly.

"I'll need something of Benjy's to hold," she went on, mentally preparing herself for the ordeal ahead. "Did you bring anything with you?"

"What for?"

"Because that's the way I work," she explained patiently. "I have to hold one of his belongings, one that he kept with him much of the time. Then I may be able to sense something about Benjy that can help you find him, or at least give you a clue to his whereabouts."

"I didn't bring anything of his," he responded slowly. His eyes were trained unblinkingly on her face. "I thought I could tell you about what happened and you would—" He stopped abruptly. Actually, he'd figured she'd pretend to go into a trance, then give him some information that would be so vague and open to interpretation as to be totally worthless.

"What exactly were you expecting?" she inquired.

He shrugged. Although tempted, now was not the time to truthfully answer that particular question. He mentally examined his options. He had deliberately chosen to arrive here without a preliminary phone call because he hadn't wanted to give Jaida West time to prepare a flamboyant psychic pretense for him. He was perfectly willing to scrap this visit for the waste of time he'd known it would be, but his accounting of these events would never satisfy Lauren. She'd insist he return to Arkansas, this time bringing something of Benjy's with him. Even then, he wondered just what it would take to convince his sister that Jaida was a fake.

Unless Lauren herself saw Jaida in action.

He considered the possibility, rapidly reformulating his original strategy. It would be several days, perhaps weeks, before his sister would be able to travel. But that didn't preclude taking the so-called psychic to her. Lauren was obstinate, but she was no fool. Once she witnessed the sideshow Jaida would put on for their benefit, surely she would lose that stubborn hope that Jaida, or someone like her, could help find Benjy.

He studied Jaida thoughtfully. His only problem lay in persuading her to accompany him home.

"I'm afraid I've wasted a lot of valuable time," he said, sounding chagrined. "By the time I fly home and back with something of my nephew's..." He sighed. "I don't like to think of how much farther away he could be by then."

Jaida looked at him helplessly. "I'm sorry, Mr. Garrison. I wish there were something else I could do."

"Perhaps there is." His answer came quickly. Maybe too quickly. "You could come back with me to Benjy's home. You could talk to Lauren. And then you could try your..."

She wondered if she imagined the slight hesitation she heard before his next words.

"Ability, with one of his belongings."

Jaida was surprised into silence by his suggestion. She glanced at Granny for help, but her grandmother was studying Trey, a serene look on her face. "I don't think that would be possible," she said faintly. She'd gone before to victims' homes, but only when she'd known them. A few times when she'd helped the local sheriff, she'd even traveled to crime scenes. But this man was a stranger. And one whom she was loath to spend any more time with than necessary.

"I understand your reluctance, but I have to remind you of what my family has riding on this, Jaida." His voice was persuasive, his face intent. "My sister's health is extremely precarious. Her mental state isn't much better. You might be our only hope. Can you really turn your back on us, not knowing if you could have helped?"

She stared at him, something about his manner disturbing her, but she was distracted by the truth of his words. She had no trouble imagining the picture he'd painted. Her gift had always been a liability for her. The only thing that made living with it bearable was the occasional chance to use it to help others. She didn't know if she could forgive herself if she refused even to try. On the other hand, something about Trey's still air, his shrewd assessing gaze made her every sense scream caution.

Granny took her hand then, and at once the woman's blend of wisdom and strength flowed to Jaida, calming her, providing comfort.

"You'll be all right, child," Granny whispered in a low voice. "You do the right thing now."

Jaida looked into her grandmother's eyes for a moment, and what she saw there reassured her. Turning back to Trey, she said, in an almost inaudible voice, "All right, I'll go."

"Great."

A wealth of satisfaction was contained in that one word, and Jaida shivered suddenly.

"Is it all right if I use your phone to make the arrangements?"

Granny nodded, never moving her gaze from his face. After several moments, she rose from her chair. "Come, Jaida, I'll help you pack. Mr. Garrison will be wantin' to get back to California soon's possible."

"California?" Jaida echoed. She looked at Trey. His face was expressionless.

"Yes, California. That's where I live. That's where Lauren is."

Granny walked slowly past Jaida toward the bedroom. Troubled, Jaida followed her without another word.

Trey moved over to the phone and dialed the Little Rock airport. Quiet triumph filled him. Jaida was accompanying him home. Once there he would have very little further use for her. He'd quickly prove to Lauren that the woman was a fake, and she'd give up the idea of enlisting the aid of Jaida West or someone else like her. Chasing these wild ideas took valuable time away from the investigation for Benjy. His biggest concern was the emotional toll the disappointment would have on Lauren once she realized she'd pinned her hopes on a fraud.

He spoke to the airline desk and was able to get an extra seat on his flight for Jaida. He hadn't expected any difficulty. He was traveling first-class and the section was rarely full. Then he made a second call to Lauren's home and gave a brief explanation of the change of plans to Mac. He and his wife, Raine, had been staying with Lauren in Trey's absence. He was the one man in the world Trey could entrust Lauren's safety to. Mac was also the only one in Trey's acquaintance who would agree to follow without question the instructions Trey proceeded to give him.

A slight frown marred his brow as he looked in the direction of the bedroom the women had disappeared into. He'd expected Jaida to ask their destination, but how the hell had her grandmother known? Obviously there was something about him that had given away the state he'd called home in recent years, but he was at a loss to explain what that might be.

"Granny, don't lift that thing. Let me do it." Jaida hurried into her bedroom. Granny had dragged the big suitcase from her closet and was preparing to lift it onto the bed.

"You'll do no such thing," the old woman said tartly. "I've told you before, Jaida, I'm no invalid. Now, get your clothes out and fill this bag up. That Mr. Garrison don't strike me as the patient sort."

Jaida made no move to obey her grandmother. "Just how did he strike you, Granny?" Despite her faith in Granny's visions, something about Trey bothered her. A lot.

"He has a strong chin," she muttered. And then in a louder tone she added, "He's a determined one. That's a fella who gets what he wants. But you'll be safe with him. I seen enough to know that."

"But he doesn't really believe in my ability, Granny. Didn't you read that from him?"

Granny turned to face her only grandchild. "No, he's here for his own reasons—that's a fact," she agreed. "But them reasons can't stop you from finding the boy, now, can they?" Not waiting for her granddaughter to reply, she continued, "And whether that man knows it or not, he needs you. He's got a powerful big void inside him that's eating him alive, but he's a stubborn one. You'll have your work cut out for you this time."

She moved to the closet again, and Jaida rose to help her. Certainly she'd help Benjy in any way that she could. Now that she'd met his uncle and heard of the little boy's plight, her conscience wouldn't let her do otherwise. But she was troubled by what else her grandmother was intimating. If there was an emptiness in Trey Garrison, it was hidden far deeper than she could see. And what could that possibly have to do with her, in any case? Her gift sometimes enabled her to help find missing persons, but it didn't extend to helping people find pieces missing from themselves.

"I don't understand," she finally murmured. "What else can I possibly help Trey Garrison with?"

Granny Logan carefully placed a homemade sachet in the suitcase, between the neatly folded clothes. It was filled with bits of dried flowers and herbs, and its aroma would be a lingering reminder of the hills of home. Jaida went to the drawer of the small table next to the bed and took out a bottle of pills. Exchanging a glance with her grandmother, she dropped the bottle into her purse.

"Trust me, child. That man needs you, in more ways than one. Jist . . ." The old woman hesitated, peering at her granddaughter. "Jist you be careful, girl."

Jaida gave a quick laugh. "Granny, don't be silly. Trey might be maddening, but I've dealt with ignorance and disbelief before. I can handle it."

Her grandmother gave her a sad smile. Her precious child, so full of talent and energy, was much too innocent. Life had hammered her once before, sent her running back to this safe valley, but the girl couldn't hide here forever, no matter what she thought. She followed Jaida out the bedroom door and joined the man in the living room.

Granny walked up to Trey, who was standing at the window. He turned at her approach. Standing very near him, she surveyed his chin again. Whatever she saw didn't disappoint her. This might be a hard man and a stubborn one, but he wasn't evil; he still had a soul. He just needed a little help remembering that.

"You take care of my girl, Mr. Garrison."

The woman's tone was fierce, and Trey felt a hint of respect. Whatever shortcomings Jaida West might have, her grandmother's love was apparent. He gave her a short nod and reached to take the suitcase from Jaida. His fingers collided with hers, and again he felt a strange spark at the touch. She snatched her hand away from his as though she had been scorched.

Turning away from the electric contact, Jaida embraced her grandmother. "I'll call you as soon as I reach California," she promised.

Granny Logan snorted. "I don't need no checking up on, young lady. I've been doin' for myself since long before you was born."

Jaida rolled her eyes. "So you've said," she replied mildly. "Take care, then, Granny. I'll be back soon."

The old woman stood in the doorway, watching them leave. They were halfway down the drive when she called, "Garri-son."

Trey turned inquiringly.

Granny pointed an arthritic finger at him. "You hurt my girl and you answer to me. Understand that?"

Jaida watched the two stare at each other, their gazes clashing. Then Trey turned away without answering and continued toward the Jeep. Jaida blew her grandmother a fond kiss and joined him.

The Jeep was long out of sight before Granny Logan closed the door of the cabin. Despite her faith in her sight, she couldn't shake the feeling that she'd just thrown her lamb to a very hungry lion.

Jaida pushed her heavy sheaf of straight hair away from her face, reached forward and turned the air conditioner on. "The Jeep was a good choice," she told the man driving silently beside her. "How'd you know that a car wasn't going to be much use where I lived?"

"I'm always prepared," he told her shortly.

She'd bet he was. He looked like someone who would plan for every eventuality. He was, as her granny had said, a man used to getting what he wanted.

Those had been the first words he'd spoken since they'd left the cabin. Jaida had pointed out landmarks in the town they passed through, Dixon Falls. The small school building, lone bar and two stores hadn't elicited a comment from him. Nor had the gorgeous countryside they'd passed through for the next hour and a half.

Now, as she recognized the city limits of Little Rock, trepidation filled her. The turnoff for the airport was nearing. "Why don't we stop and get something to eat?" she suggested hopefully, delaying the inevitable. "I didn't have lunch."

"You can eat on the plane," he answered.

"I don't think so," she mumbled. She knew from experience that all traces of her usually healthy appetite would disappear at first sight of the airport. "I don't suppose you ever use the train?"

Trey looked at her oddly. "Do you have a problem with planes?"

Only while they're in the air, she replied silently.

They turned the vehicle in at the rental agency at the airport and checked their bags. "Come on," he said, reaching for her elbow. "Our plane is loading now."

Jaida took a step backward, avoiding his touch. "Wait a minute," she said, stalling. "Let's talk about this."

"On the plane," he said firmly. "Hurry up or it will leave without us."

"We should be so lucky," she muttered. She took a deep breath and reluctantly followed him through the airport, onto the plane and into a seat. She immediately put on her seat belt, rechecking it for secureness several times. The luxury of the first-class cabin was lost on her. As the plane taxied up the runway, her fingers clenched the armrests.

Trey settled his large frame into a seat comfortably. Once they were in the air he turned to Jaida and remarked, "You can tell the flight attendant what you want to eat when he comes by."

"I don't want anything," she mumbled.

He raised an eyebrow, noting her white knuckles and pale cheeks. "You aren't by any chance afraid to fly, are you, Jaida?"

Afraid? "Certainly not," she lied, tilting her chin up. She instinctively knew that it would be a mistake to show weakness in front of this man. He didn't trust her. And any hint of vulnerability she showed could be used against her if he so chose.

But her body conspired against her. She waited for the plane to level off and the seat-belt sign to disappear. She practiced her deep-breathing exercises, but the moment she saw the attendant come toward them with an assortment of food, she knew the battle was lost. Unbuckling her belt with frantic hands, she headed for the rest room.

She locked the door behind her and leaned weakly against it. She was a nervous flier at the best of times. Her stomach was doing jumping jacks, and her heart was hammering from the strain of being confined in the first-class cabin with a stranger in the seat beside her. A seat that, despite its extra roominess, was too close to hers for comfort. *He* was too close for comfort.

She closed her eyes, mentally drawing on all her energy. The only way she was going to make it through this plane ride without disgracing herself was to avoid even the thought of food, and under no circumstances could she glance out a window.

Of course, it would also help greatly if she could ensure that Trey Garrison didn't touch her again.

Chapter 2

The plane's landing was a little better than its takeoff, but only barely. Jaida had, however, managed to control her stomach's inclination to rebel. Trey eyed her white face and unsteady composure as they disembarked and headed toward the LAX luggage-claim area.

"You never did eat anything," he observed. "Are you sure you're not hungry?" She looked as though she could collapse at any minute. And though he was impatient at the thought of further delay, he didn't want to deal with a fainting female, either. Especially this female.

"Make a note, Garrison," Jaida muttered. Her eyes met his. "The only places on the face of this earth that I'm *not* hungry are airports and planes."

Trey dismissed the unnecessary information. Her obvious discomfort on the plane almost made up for the times today that she had really annoyed him. But his use for her would soon be over. Then she'd be free to choose any mode of transportation she wished to return to Arkansas.

Their rapid pace through the airport was halted by the crowd gathered around the luggage belt. Jaida eyed the mob of people and swallowed. "I'll wait back here," she murmured to Trey, and he nodded.

Now that he was so close to home, to Lauren, impatience was eating at him. From his brief conversation with Mac earlier he'd learned that his sister was still confined to bed. In light of the damage that damn drug had done to her system, she was lucky to have been sent home so soon. She'd lain in a coma for the first two days, and when she'd awakened he'd been faced with telling her of Benjy's kidnapping.

He still wasn't convinced that her wild idea to consult Jaida West wasn't the result of remnants of that drug in her bloodstream. He'd tried to gently dissuade her from the idea, and then, confronted by her stubbornness, had been less than gentle. His efforts hadn't altered the outcome in their contest of wills. He'd spent years in military intelligence, had faced down terrorists bent on destroying entire cities. But he'd never mastered the art of denying Lauren something she wanted.

Trey picked out their baggage and strode over to Jaida. There was something almost forlorn about the picture she made, sitting well away from any other people, her purse clutched on her lap. He pushed away the unwilling tinge of sympathy. He should reserve the feeling for the gullible people she preyed on.

"Let's go," he said brusquely.

She rose. "I'll carry my suitcase."

He shot her an impatient look. "Don't be ridiculous."

Her chin jutted mulishly. Her face was finally beginning to regain its former color. I can pull my own weight."

When her hand reached for the bag, he felt that unfamiliar electricity again as their fingers barely touched. He watched her snatch her hand away, as she had earlier that day. "I'll get it," he said tersely. "From the looks of you, just not fainting will be enough of a chore."

His long legs ate up the distance to the parking lot, leaving Jaida to trail after him. The thought came to him then that if he ever needed to curb this woman's unfortunate stubborn streak, all he had to do was touch her. That seemed to have the effect of scaring her off. For some reason, the knowledge was inexplicably annoying.

* * *

The drive to Lauren's helped restore Jaida's equilibrium. And when they turned onto the Pacific Coast Highway, she was completely enchanted. She rolled her window down and inclined her head to catch the balmy ocean breeze.

Trey cast her a glance. For once she'd fallen silent. She'd bombarded him with questions about his nephew and his sister, none of which he'd had the slightest intention of answering. Now she seemed content to feel the wind in her face. Her eyes were closed and a half smile tilted her lips. A strand of her pale-blond hair drifted across her shapely lips, and he was disconcerted by the impulse to brush it away for her.

His fingers tightened on the wheel, and he returned his gaze to his driving. Just another hour or two, he promised himself grimly. And then he'd send this woman back to the Arkansas hills where he'd found her.

Jaida opened her eyes when she felt the car slow down. They were pulling up to an ornate wrought-iron fence. Trey stopped the car and got out. Approaching the gate, he flipped open a box mounted on the side of one of the concrete pillars and punched in several numbers. Red lights winked from the box, and he punched in another series of numbers. He repeated the process once more before the gates swung open. He closed the lid of the box and got back into the car.

"'Open sesame' would be a lot easier," she quipped. After they drove through the opening, Jaida turned in her seat to observe the gates closing silently behind them. "Do you install operations like that?"

Trey's gaze never moved from the private drive he was maneuvering. "We installed that one, yes."

"Pretty fancy. But I can't imagine people wanting to live this way. It would make me feel like a prisoner, like I was the one locked in."

"It usually works the other way," he responded dryly. "With the owners of the property feeling more secure."

Jaida's eyes widened when she saw the large beachfront home they were approaching. A thought struck her then and she winced. "This isn't . . . I mean, you don't live here, do you?"

The private drive forked then, and Trey turned away from the house. She didn't sound impressed, he reflected. Her tone was almost horrified. "No, I don't live here. Why does the thought of that bother you?"

Jaida was craning her neck to get a better look at their destination. "I just don't like the thought of you inside here, I guess," she replied absently. "You're already locked up too tightly as it is."

He glanced at her sharply. But her attention was reserved for the guest house they were approaching.

"Oh, this view is marvelous! And this little house is cute, isn't it?"

"Lauren's employer owns the property. This is where Lauren and Benjy live."

"Trey..." Jaida hesitated as the ordeal ahead of her loomed abruptly. She shot him a tentative look. Then, shoring up her nerve, she continued, knowing it had to be said, "You've mentioned that your sister isn't very strong right now. Is she going to be strong enough to hear the truth?"

His eyes met hers then, and they were so cold she could feel an icy shiver skate down her spine, despite the balmy California air.

"And what truth might that be?"

"Sometimes what I 'see' isn't what people want to hear. Is your sister going to be able to accept it if I have to tell her that Benjy—" Her voice caught, before she forced herself to go on. "That he may not be... alive?"

Pure, deadly rage crossed his countenance. In the next instant he deliberately blanked his expression again. She didn't know which made her more wary—his first evidence of fiery emotion or his iron control over it. The command he spoke next was cloaked in velvet.

"Under no circumstances... will you tell her that."

"False hope is cruel, Trey."

Her words so accurately described his feeling about her presence here that he could feel his jaw clench. "At least we agree on something. But you aren't getting out of this car before promising me that you won't say anything to upset her."

Their gazes clashed, battling silently. Finally, she nodded. She knew from experience that just being the bearer of such bad news would be excruciating. She didn't want to be responsible for the impact such information would have on Lauren's already precarious health. "You can be the one to decide how much to tell her," she said.

He stared hard at her, but she seemed to be sincere. Nodding, he got out of the car and left her to follow him up to the small house. He wasn't trusting enough to take her at her word. He'd be watching very carefully to ensure that Jaida had no opportunity to further upset his sister.

Mac met them at the door. "We didn't expect you for a while yet."

"The plane was actually early for once," Trey replied. He let Jaida precede him into the house. Then he inquired in a low voice, "Did you have time to do as I asked?"

His partner nodded. "All the pictures of Benjy have been removed. And I made the purchase you requested."

"Thanks." He noticed that Jaida had turned to eye them quizzically. He raised his voice. "Jaida West, this is Mac O'Neill, my partner."

"My wife, Raine, and I have been taking care of things on this end while Trey tracked you down, Miss West."

"Mr. O'Neill," she acknowledged faintly. She didn't particularly care for his choice of words. The idea of being *tracked down* by Trey Garrison made her feel a bit like prey. She studied the man. He was at least as tall as his partner, and his shoulders had almost filled the doorway he'd walked through. His blue eyes were as hard as twin chips of ice. She sighed inwardly. Apparently Mac shared something with his partner. Neither of them had trusting natures.

"Well, Lauren is still asleep. I guess that's the best thing—" The woman who'd entered the living room stopped in midsentence. "Hi, Trey. Glad you're back. And you must be Jaida. We're so excited you're here."

Mac walked across the room and slipped his arm around the newcomer. "This is my wife, Raine," he said.

"It's nice to meet you," Jaida said sincerely. Raine's was the first genuine welcome she'd received since arriving, and she couldn't help responding to it.

Mac's massive arm looked heavy around his tiny wife's shoulders. But somehow, when he was standing next to Raine, one noticed his size less than the expression he regarded her with. He was a man clearly entranced by his wife.

Raine's smile lit up her wide, golden eyes. "Can I get you anything? Airline food can be pretty unappetizing, I know. Or maybe you'd like something to drink?"

"No need," Trey said dismissively. *She won't be here that long,* he thought. At that moment, Jaida's gaze met his and held it. When she looked away, he was left with the uncanny notion that she knew exactly what he'd been thinking.

"How's Lauren doing?" Trey asked Raine once they'd all sat down.

"She's getting stronger. She seems to think she should be getting out of bed and on her feet, but so far I've managed to dissuade her of that idea."

"Thank God," Trey muttered.

"She should be awake shortly, if you're ready—that is, if Jaida wants to begin."

Trey flicked a look at Mac and then shook his head. "I don't see any need to wait for Lauren to wake up. And I'm sure Jaida wants to get on with this. Don't you, Jaida?"

Jaida returned his gaze equably, wondering if she was the only one to hear the challenge in his voice. "I'm willing to try, yes. I'll need one of Benjy's belongings to focus on, preferably something he kept with him often. A favorite toy or book, perhaps."

"I'll get it," Mac offered, disappearing from the room. He reappeared a moment later, carrying a stuffed bear.

Raine frowned. "Mac..."

"Hush," he said, effectively silencing her. "Let Jaida concentrate."

The bear was soft in Jaida's hands, its plush fur showing no signs of wear. In another year or so, the rigorous life of being loved by a toddler would be apparent, but right now the bow on its neck was still saucy, its fur as yet unmatted. Jaida let her eyes close. She had to fight the familiar instinct that would have her shoring up barriers against the accompanying emotional onslaught. She needed all her defenses lowered, her senses completely open. Only then would she feel the full force of the psychic sensations.

But the familiar sensory overload was different this time. It was present, but the elements were muted, and jumbled badly. Jaida frowned unconsciously, clutching the bear more tightly.

Try as she might, she was unable to pick through the frag-
mented scenes for one clue of Lauren's missing son.

Long minutes later, admitting defeat, she slowly opened her
eyes. "I'm sorry," she said almost inaudibly. "I didn't see
anything."

Her sense of failure grew as the silence in the room stretched.
"I'm sorry," Jaida said again. This had happened before. Not
often, but when it did it never failed to make her feel helpless.
"I'm willing to try again. Maybe there's something else of
Benjy's I could use . . . an article of clothing, perhaps?"

"I don't know which of you two I want to kick harder."
Raine addressed both men scathingly. "Sometimes you're both
as dense as granite."

Jaida stared at Raine in surprise, and then comprehension
began to dawn. She looked down at the toy in her hand again,
reassessing its condition. No wonder it had seemed so
fresh . . . so new. Anger bloomed within her. She rose from the
couch and stalked toward Trey. He hadn't moved, and he was
still watching her with that shuttered, assessing look that told
her exactly who was behind this charade. She shoved the soft
bear hard at his chest. His hands came up to take it from her.
"I assume that you were behind that little test," she said.

"Test? Your psychic powers seem to have escaped you, Ms.
West. Maybe you need a new spell."

"If I had one," she informed him. "I'd use it to turn you
into a human being."

"Trey, what have you done?" All heads turned in the direction of the softly worded question. There was no doubt about
the identity of the woman standing in the doorway of the bedroom. Her pretty face was a softer, more feminine version of
Trey's, minus a cleft in her chin. Her eyes were the same dark-
green hue, her hair just as dark. Right now a mask of weari-
ness and worry marred her attractiveness. As she began to make
her halting way toward the group in the living room, Trey
sprang to his feet.

"Lauren, you're not supposed to be out of bed." Upon
reaching her, he took her by the elbow and led her gently to the
love seat, where she sat down next to Raine.

"Don't fuss at me, Trey," she responded a little breath-
lessly. It was clear that the short walk had winded her. "And

don't change the subject. From what I overheard you've offended our guest. That isn't like you." Her attention switched to Jaida then, and she offered a shy smile. "You must be Jaida. You don't know how much I appreciate your coming like this. I know it's a terrible imposition."

"I'd like to try to help, if I can," Jaida returned. "I am a little curious, though, about how you heard of me."

"You helped a relative of a friend of mine several years ago. I believe it was in New York City. Do you remember Shannon Davis?"

Jaida nodded. "Her teenage daughter had run away," she replied quietly. "We found her after she'd been missing for three months."

Nodding, Lauren said, "I worked with Shannon's sister after college. She told me the whole story. After I . . ." She swallowed, then continued with difficulty, "After I regained consciousness . . . Trey told me what happened to Benjy." Her eyes closed tightly for an instant, as she visibly strove for control. "I was dazed at first. I couldn't believe this had happened. In the days that have passed, every lead the police have followed has gone nowhere. And then one night I thought of Shannon. I remembered you and the part I heard you'd played in her daughter's return." Her gaze met her brother's. "I badgered Trey unmercifully until he promised to go and find you. I have a great deal of faith in his word, you see."

Jaida was fascinated by the trace of visible discomfort that crossed Trey's face. Obviously the man did have a conscience, though he kept it deeply hidden.

"I apologize for the inconvenience you've undergone on our behalf," Lauren went on, addressing Jaida. "But I can't honestly say I'm not excited about your being here. We've tried more conventional means for locating my son. You might be our best hope of getting him back." Her voice faltered a little. "You might be our *only* hope."

"I want to try. I was just telling . . . your brother . . . when you came in that I would need something of Benjy's to focus on."

The smile Lauren turned on her then was tremulous and full of expectancy. "Of course. Trey can—" She broke off, frowning a little when she spotted the stuffed bear that had fallen, forgotten, to the floor. "What's that?"

The room grew unnaturally still in the wake of her question. Mac finally answered in a strangled voice, "It's just something I bought. For Trey. I mean...for Benjy." He crossed the room rapidly and scooped it up. "I'll put it away." He hurried out of the room.

Lauren studied the expressions on the faces of the room's occupants, but said nothing. Mac returned, carrying a toy.

"I thought we could use this," he said, holding it up for Lauren's approval.

She swallowed and clasped her hands together, before nodding jerkily. "That's Benjy's favorite," Lauren said huskily. "Trey brought it to the hospital the day he was born. Remember, Trey? You swore he smiled at you for the first time. I tried to tell you that wasn't possible but you insisted...."

"I remember," Trey said gently.

"He slept with it every night," Lauren whispered. "Every night until—" Her voice broke.

Trey crossed swiftly to his sister and sank down in front of her, taking her hands in his. "And he will again," he told her firmly. "I need you to believe that. We both have to believe it. Lauren?"

She raised her eyes slowly to meet his gaze, and her fingers tightened in his.

The look the pair exchanged was so anguished that Jaida shifted her gaze, shaken by the raw emotion. Whatever else she thought of Trey Garrison, she couldn't deny the evidence of his love for his family. She focused on the toy. It was a stuffed elephant, a whimsical creature wearing a pair of red corduroy overalls. It was not adorned with buttons or small items that a baby might swallow, but its cloth trunk looked as though it had endured several vigorous chewings from a small mouth.

"Mac?"

Jaida's voice had all eyes turning in her direction. She reached for the toy, and Mac glanced at Trey. The other man nodded almost imperceptibly.

As she took the toy, Jaida was immediately rocked by the sensations she'd expected the last time. Reality receded, and her inner world seemed to stop for a moment, before speeding up to surreal rapidity. Images flooded her mind, snippets of visions that made a brilliant collage. Then the mental barrage slowed, and she was able to view the images more as she would a movie being played inside her head.

A dark-haired toddler was huddled in the middle of a bed that seemed much too large for his small shape. A neon light flickered outside the window. The light fascinated the boy, drew him closer and closer to the edge of the bed, as he craned his neck to look at it. Then a woman walked before him, blocking his view as she gazed out the window. The little boy crawled down from the bed, making his way over to where the bright colors lit the night so invitingly. A large hand yanked the boy backward. The toddler jutted out his bottom lip mulishly, his chin quivering.

Jaida caught her breath sharply, and the familiar pain started in her temples, the muscles in her back and neck knotting painfully. Aching tendrils radiated across her back and shoulders. She squeezed her eyes more tightly closed, blocking out the pain, beckoning more of the scene to unfold.

The woman turned back toward the room, letting the curtain fall into place. A child's cry split the night. Jaida trembled, feeling the boy's fear and loneliness. Her empathetic reaction to Benjy's plight made her head ache unbearably, until the images began to blur and fade, leaving only the hammering at her temples in their wake.

"Did you see anything?"

Lauren's anxious voice sounded as though it were coming from a great distance. Jaida opened eyelids that seemed weighted, and even that small motion was enough to turn the pain into a snarling beast.

Blinking several times, Jaida brought the room into focus. Lauren's face was a contradiction of hope and despair. Trey was watching her, openly sardonic. "I saw a little boy," she said, her voice sounding rusty. "He has dark hair and..." Her breath shuddered with aftershocks. "And his uncle's chin."

"Benjy." Lauren's voice was a reverent whisper. Her hands went to her brother's shoulders, and her fingers clenched there. "Oh, my Lord, it's Benjy. She can help us, Trey. I knew it. I *knew* it."

"Slow down, Lauren." His voice was soothing. "This doesn't really prove anything."

"Doesn't prove anything?" Lauren's voice was incredulous. "It proves everything—everything I told you. You have to let her help, Trey. You *have* to." Several moments ticked by. Then Lauren looked away. "Would you help me back to my room, Trey?" she asked weakly.

He sprang immediately to his feet and helped her rise. "You never should have gotten up in the first place," he scolded her. "This was too much for you."

She declined to argue, leaning against him until he settled her in her bedroom. She reached for his hand, preventing his departure. "Stay, please."

He sat on the side of the bed. "You should take one of the sedatives the doctor ordered."

She made a face. "I don't need a sedative. I need to talk to you."

"Take the pill first," he replied firmly.

Lauren's lips tightened and then she gave an exasperated sigh. "Trey Garrison, you'd bargain with the devil himself."

He smiled slightly. "Only about the living arrangements." He welcomed the return of Lauren's strong will. For too many days she'd lain listless and unresponsive, scaring him half to death with the alteration in her personality. She might be more difficult to handle when she regained her stubbornness, but it was a welcome change nonetheless.

She snatched the pill, downed it with the water and raised her eyebrows. "Satisfied?"

"Yes," he responded imperturbably.

Lauren's gaze dropped, but she didn't relinquish his hand. He waited, knowing she wouldn't rest until she'd had her say. But he wasn't prepared for the subject she broached.

"It's funny what we remember from our childhoods. I don't have any memory of our mother at all, and what I remember of Dad..." She shrugged. "Isn't pleasant. But though I was only three when we were removed from our home, my strongest memory is of you." Her voice grew softer. "Only of you." When she looked at him again, her eyes were filled with tears. "You were my hero then and that hasn't changed. I don't know what I would have done if you hadn't come back into my life when you did."

"Don't, Lauren," he said dismissively. It wasn't her emotion he shied away from, but the patent untruth of her words. He was nobody's hero. Benjy's disappearance was proof of that.

"You have to accept the fact that you aren't responsible for the whole world, Trey. Benjy's kidnapping wasn't your fault. Stop heaping blame on yourself for things you have no control over."

He returned her look steadily. "I never wanted to be responsible for the whole world, Lauren. Just our little part of it."

She sighed, fighting a losing battle with the medication, her muscles relaxing as they succumbed to sleep. "I have to believe that Benjy will come back to us," she whispered. "And I have greater faith in you and your efforts than I do in those of the police. I think you can find him, Trey, just as you found me." Her voice was beginning to slow. "I want you to promise me something."

"You need to rest...."

"No!" Her objection was not above a murmur, but its lack of volume didn't affect its intensity. "Not...until...you promise."

"All right." He took her hand in both of his and held it comfortingly.

"Promise...you'll let Jaida...help you." She saw the shuttered look come over her brother's face and could have wept with frustration. "Please...for me."

The minutes crawled by, and still Trey remained silent. Lauren eventually lost the struggle with the medication. When her breathing was deep, he released her limp hand and rose from the bed. But it was several more moments before he left the room.

The headache had increased in intensity until Jaida's head felt ready to shatter. Her eyes burned with strain, and it was an effort to keep them open. She fumbled with her purse, putting it on her lap and opening it. She shook two capsules into her hand and swallowed them dry.

Sighing, she dropped her purse to the floor. She was dimly aware of Raine's concerned voice, but couldn't summon the energy to concentrate on her words. She let her head rest against the back of the sofa and closed her eyes. Several minutes passed as she waited for the pills to work their magic, but she knew from experience that only sleep could make the headache abate completely. Twelve or fifteen hours of deep, uninterrupted sleep. And she couldn't afford that yet. She still needed all her wits about her to face Trey. She didn't fool herself into thinking he had changed his mind about her. The clamoring ricocheted inside her head, echoing and reechoing until thought was almost impossible. The pain was relentless. As relentless as—

She opened her eyes. She was not surprised to see Trey standing in the hallway, although he'd made no noise. She surveyed him blurrily, her vision affected by the headache. He moved toward her, and without conscious decision she sat up straight. Despite her less than clear state after the session, something inside her gathered all her resources to face him. The realization would have frightened her if she'd been thinking more lucidly.

He sat down next to her, keeping a careful distance between them. "Your little production earlier put my sister on the verge of hysterics. She isn't a great judge of character at the best of times, but right now she's incapable of being sensible."

"Meaning she refuses to let you send me packing."

His jaw tightened at the accuracy of her statement. "She's frantic at the slow progress of this case, and she's clutching at straws."

"Haven't you forgotten something, Trey?" Raine interjected. "Jaida described Benjy to a tee." She indicated the room around them. "How did she know what he looked like, when you had Mac remove all the pictures of him?"

"I'm sure Ms. West has a great deal of experience with situations like this. And the resemblance between Lauren and me is pretty startling. She made an educated guess, that's all. But she really didn't tell us anything we didn't already know."

Jaida blinked rapidly, trying to keep Trey in focus. But her vision refused to cooperate, and his image blurred and doubled. One Trey Garrison was more than enough to handle. The agony in her muscles and inside her head were settling into a howling chorus. She knew from experience that she didn't have much time before the pills she'd taken would have her body sinking into the unconsciousness it demanded. "He's in a motel room, sitting on top of a bed," Jaida said. Thinking was an effort, talking even more so. "There are two people in the room with him. One is a woman."

"You said there were two people," Raine reminded her. "Was the other a man?"

Jaida hesitated, sifting through the images that had sped across her mind. "I'm not sure. I think so. All I saw of the second person was a hand pulling Benjy back up on the bed."

Trey muttered a curse, and his friends looked at him in surprise. "You can't possibly believe this, Raine. I'd expect it from Lauren—she's out of her mind with grief. But you're usually more rational."

Raine's eyes flashed when she replied. "I know that there aren't always rational explanations for human behavior, Trey. I've learned from experience that people do some pretty horrible things, things psychiatrists can't even explain, because those acts aren't *rational*. Why do you accept the reality of evil in the world and not accept the possibility that there are people who possess powers that science can't completely understand?"

"It really doesn't matter," Mac soothed his wife. "Even if it's true, it doesn't change anything. We still don't know where Benjy is."

"Yes, we do," Jaida put in. Her words had captured everyone's attention. "The motel they're at is called Glenview." She recalled the flickering neon light that had shone in the window the woman had stood at. "The 'V' in the vacancy sign is burned out. The road sign out front reads Highway 128."

Chapter 3

"This is wonderful!" Raine enthused. Her gaze sought her husband's. "Honey, can't we do something now?"

Mac was rubbing the back of his neck in consternation. "Do you want me to check this out?" he asked Trey quietly.

Trey didn't even spare him a glance. His gaze speared through Jaida. "Lady, don't mess with me. You'll be very sorry if you do."

"For heaven's sake, Trey, she's trying to help," Raine admonished him. "Quit threatening her!"

The pounding in Jaida's skull had lessened slightly from the effects of the medication, but the resulting drowsiness made it just as difficult to concentrate. "I can't tell you exactly where the motel is, but..."

"We can get that information ourselves. If—" Trey's voice was loaded with meaning "—it actually exists."

"I've got Steward manning the office," Mac said, interrupting the silent battle of wills. "Let's call him and get this settled."

After one last steely look in Jaida's direction, Trey followed his partner out of the room.

Raine turned to Jaida and let out a sigh. "Sometimes it's hard to tell which of those two men is the most stubborn."

"They do seem to have a lot in common," Jaida observed wanly.

Raine's gaze narrowed in concern. "You look ready to pass out. I'm going to make you something to eat and then you may as well get some rest. I'll bring in your luggage and get the guest room ready for you." Not waiting for an answer, she rose and joined the men in the kitchen.

Jaida sighed, and gave in to the temptation to close her eyes for a minute. Unbeckoned, a picture of Trey formed behind her eyelids. She'd never met a man like him before, one who wielded such tight control over his emotions. The only time that careful mask slipped was when he was talking to his sister. Then one could catch glimpses of the same frustration and anguish that ate at Lauren. He was a hard man, but not a completely unfeeling one. She wondered fuzzily what it would take for the man to show that kind of devotion to someone other than his family.

Four hours later, Trey rubbed a hand across his burning eyes. His system was feeling the effects of an overdose of coffee and too little sleep. "If that damned Steward doesn't call pretty soon, I'm going to the office myself," he muttered bad-temperedly.

Mac was slouched in a kitchen chair, his booted feet propped on another. He opened one eye at his friend's remark. "He'll phone as soon as he finds something," he said quietly. The house was silent except for the two of them. He'd sent Raine home to bed long ago. Since they'd called the office to give Steward his orders, the phone had remained stubbornly quiet.

Their company, Security Associates, had expanded greatly in the past few years and, at Trey's insistence, had acquired some of the most sophisticated computer equipment on the market. There was an amazing amount of information to be had by accessing various data banks if the computer operator knew where to look.

And if, in fact, the information even existed.

When it finally sounded, the phone didn't even complete its first ring before Trey had it to his ear. After a few crisp questions, Trey hung up. His gaze met Mac's. "Steward found one motel on Highway 128 called Glenview." His tone was grim, his jaw tight. "It's located outside of Boston."

Mac's face went still. "Boston. Where Lauren's husband lives."

"If I believed in even a word that came out of Jaida's mouth, I'd be real worried right now," Trey said tersely.

"If Jaida's on the level—" Mac started.

"She's not," Trey interrupted.

"But if she is," Mac continued doggedly, "we'd be almost certain that Penning has finally tracked Lauren down."

"We still can't be sure that he hasn't." Trey rubbed a hand over his face. "We always knew the jealous bastard wasn't going to just let her disappear without a trace. I've been aware of his efforts to trail her ever since I rescued her from his estate." Although Lauren was using a new last name and Social Security number, those precautions wouldn't deter someone who had unlimited resources at his disposal. Penning had the money and connections needed to conduct a sustained search. And given his insane possessiveness, he was certainly determined enough.

Mac frowned. "So let's assume for the moment that Penning somehow discovered Lauren had a brother and tracked you both here. You said he was unaware of Lauren's pregnancy before you helped her escape him."

"Believe me, Benjy's existence would be an unwelcome surprise to him. He always insisted she use birth control. He was so damn jealous he couldn't even stand the thought of sharing her with children. She was terrified when she found out she was pregnant. She was certain he'd force her to have an abortion."

"She must have been just as scared of what would happen to the child if he was brought up with William Penning for a father," Mac said soberly.

Trey nodded. It hadn't take Lauren long after her marriage to discover that her husband was an abusive, controlling bully. In the years that followed, however, she'd become convinced that she'd married a monster. By the time her brother had reentered her life, she'd already begun taking steps to escape from Penning. With Trey's help she had done so, and he'd kept her hidden ever since.

It had been many long months before Lauren had stopped looking over her shoulder. Trey believed that his presence helped her make that transition. And Benjy's birth had given both of them the opportunity to revel in the simple pleasure of being a family again.

Mac frowned. "Something about this just doesn't add up. If Penning was so desperate to get Lauren back, why wasn't she the one snatched? If he hated the thought of kids so much, why would he have Benjy taken, instead?"

Trey didn't answer right away. That terrible rage was back, the one that threatened to encompass him each time he thought of the unknown persons responsible for snatching his young nephew away. If he focused on that emotion, however, he'd never be of any use in securing Benjy's return. He firmly slammed the mental door on that unproductive feeling and was left only with the now-familiar lingering sense of guilt.

His voice, when he replied, was clipped. "Who knows? He could be punishing Lauren, taunting her, putting her through a little agony before he uses Benjy to force her to come back to him."

"But the Feds have been keeping Penning under surveillance, right? And they've had nothing to report so far."

Trey shook his head. "That doesn't necessarily mean anything, though. Only that if Penning is involved, he hasn't been stupid enough to take Benjy to his own home." So far the Bureau had come up with no more than had the LAPD detective assigned to the case. Trey wondered cynically whether the Bureau would have been so interested in the kidnapping if it hadn't been for the identity of Benjy's father. The Feds must have jumped at the chance of catching Penning involved in something, anything they could manage to pin on him. William's law practice made millions a year defending men affiliated with one of the East Coast's most powerful mob families. Too many times he'd destroyed the cases of federal prosecutors, using highly questionable tactics to win acquittals for his clients. He'd been investigated himself on occasion, suspected of jury tampering.

Unconsciously, his fingers curled into fists. Trey had never intended to keep Lauren hidden away indefinitely. She deserved complete freedom, and only a divorce would accomplish that. But each time Trey had broached the subject with his sister, she'd become so overwrought that he'd always backed off. Her extreme fear of her husband was more than justified, he knew. People who crossed the man usually wound up missing or dead.

"If Penning *is* behind this," Mac said, "why haven't we heard from him? If his motive is to get Lauren back, he'd have to make a contact, right? The man has already waited almost ten days. That doesn't sound like someone with a bargaining chip to use."

One of Trey's fists came down on the tabletop, punctuating his words. "Hell, who can predict how that sick bastard's mind works? And why are we bothering to try? We still don't have any proof that he's the one behind this."

"Proof, no. But if you believe Jaida . . ."

"Believe a whacked-out hillbilly professing psychic powers?" Trey scoffed. "I'm growing desperate, buddy, but not that desperate. Oh, she's good, I'll grant her that. She's got Lauren dazzled with her lucky description of Benjy, but there's no way she's going to convince me she can hold on to a stuffed elephant and see across the country. No, she probably just described a motel she once stayed at, which just happens to be close to Boston. God." He raked his fingers impatiently through his hair. "If her 'help' has this effect on us, just think how it would affect Lauren."

Mac considered his words. "So what's our next move?"

"Next?" Trey pulled the phone toward him. Lifting the receiver, he started punching out a number. "Next we put the police to work. I'm calling Detective Reynolds and telling him of the 'anonymous tip' we received that Benjy was sighted at Glenview Motel, Highway 128, outside of Boston." He broke off when someone answered at the other end of the line. The detective didn't sound pleased to be awakened at that hour, nor did he put much stock in the "tip." Trey remained smooth and unruffled—and totally insistent. When he hung up, a slight smile of satisfaction curled his mouth.

"Success?" Mac asked.

Trey nodded. "The detective agreed to alert the Massachusetts State Police immediately."

"So we should know in a matter of hours whether Jaida can be of some real help to us."

Trey corrected him. "All we're doing is calling her bluff. In a matter of hours we'll prove that she's the phony I've always known she'd be. And then we'll still have a kidnapper to track."

The sedative that Trey had badgered his sister into taking had her sleeping well into the morning. Jaida seemed to be sleeping just as soundly. Trey sipped at what seemed to be his thousandth cup of coffee and contemplated the picture she made, curled up like a child under a blanket Raine must have provided. He'd never known another woman to wear her hair that color, so pale a blond that it looked like white gold. But it provided a sharp contrast to her dark lashes and brows, so perhaps that was why she'd chosen it, he thought cynically. Some women went to great lengths to draw attention to themselves.

Not that he had anything against women. When he had the time for it, his social life was as active and full as any man could hope for. He was able to don the mask of charming host at will, and there was never any shortage of women who were willing to accept what he could offer them. More were intrigued than put off by his candor when he informed them that he was not in the market for a lasting relationship. The women he chose either never realized how little of himself he was willing to share or they didn't care.

Had he met Jaida West at another time, he might have given her a second look, but he wouldn't have pursued her. He preferred his partners sophisticated, poised and as in control of their emotions as he was. From what he'd observed of her so far, this woman never had an unspoken thought. She'd also been alarmingly easy to rouse to emotion. She'd spit anger at him several times already in the past twenty hours or so.

He wondered what other emotions would be easy to rouse in her.

Frowning slightly, he banished the wayward thought. It was time to start planning for Jaida's return to Arkansas, but first he'd make her aware of the foolish mistake she'd made by attempting to hoax Trey's family. She'd committed a strategical error by concocting a story that could be so easily checked out.

He stared at the long hair that trailed like a ribbon of blond silk over her shoulders. He felt nothing but contempt for people like Jaida West, who would take advantage of a mother's grief to make a buck. He'd met his share of con artists before, some of them women, but he had to admit that he'd never before felt this compulsion to watch any of them as they slept.

Jaida's eyes flickered open; she woke as she always did, slowly and reluctantly. It didn't seem strange to her sleep-laden mind that her first sight was Trey. It was a logical continuation of her final mental image last night to see him standing there as unyielding as an oak, watching her with his impenetrable gaze. She wondered what he saw when he looked at her so steadily, his mysterious eyes giving nothing away. What had happened to the man to make him guard his emotions so closely, to build that wall of reserve that only a few were allowed to scale?

"You must have fallen asleep before you ate last night." He indicated a plate of sandwiches on the table before her. Raine had covered them neatly with clear plastic wrap so that Jaida could help herself if she awoke during the night.

For the first time Jaida realized exactly how she must look after sleeping in her clothes. She sat up, one hand attempting to smooth the hair away from her face. He appeared as unruffled as always, although she doubted he'd slept much, if at all. He'd already showered and changed. Although more casually dressed than yesterday, he looked crisp and polished. She was sure she appeared as though she'd spent the past few hours in a clothes dryer. Her mouth felt as if someone had driven a gravel truck through it, and she would have given her right arm for her toothbrush. Her suitcase had been deposited next to the couch, and she eyed it longingly.

"What have you found out about the motel?" she inquired tentatively.

Sheets of ice appeared in his eyes, and inwardly she sighed. Whatever he'd discovered hadn't improved his opinion of her; that was apparent. And though she felt much more capable of dealing with him today than she had last night, a shower and a change of clothes would go a long way in boosting her confidence still further.

She tensed as he unexpectedly approached the couch. And when he sat down next to her, all her senses sprang to attention. She damned the involuntary reaction, forcing herself to remain still, when her first inclination was to shrink into the corner of the sofa.

"The motel . . . um . . ." Her voice faltered as he lifted a section of her hair from where it lay across the back cushion. Thought momentarily deserted her as he rubbed the strand between his thumb and forefinger. Her voice was breathless when she finally found it again. "Have you uncovered anything yet?"

"We're working on it," he murmured. He didn't look at her, his attention seemingly snared by the rhythmic motion of his fingers. "Where did you say the motel was located?"

Her gaze followed his and she had trouble formulating an answer.

"Highway 128." The words sounded strangled to her own ears.

"You said that," he agreed, gazing at his hand fascinatedly as he slowly wrapped the blond strands around his index finger. "But what city is it near?"

"City?" she whispered blankly, her eyes never straying from his hand. With each movement, more of his finger disappeared under the blond wrapping. Each rhythmic twist sent a corresponding tingle to her scalp.

Swallowing hard, Jaida watched until his finger was covered from base to tip as if with a blond ribbon. Then his thumb rose to stroke the strands gently. Somewhere in the recesses of her mind she was dimly aware that she'd lost track of the conversation. With physical effort she forced her gaze to his face. His thick, dark lashes were lowered, his eyes still trained on the action of his hand. Concentrating fiercely, she picked up the direction of their earlier words. "I don't know. About the city, I mean. I couldn't tell . . ."

His lashes swept upward and suddenly she was staring directly into his eyes. She abruptly forgot what she'd been saying. She'd seen his eyes icy, skeptical and sardonic by turn, but right now they were devoid of those emotions. For the first time since she'd met him she didn't sense the familiar shield he used to keep the rest of the world at bay. That didn't mean, however, that he was any easier to read. She still wasn't able to recognize the light shining from those green orbs, but it filled the pit of her stomach with an undeniable heat.

"Surely you have an idea, though."

At those softly uttered words, her gaze fell to his mouth.

He continued in the same dulcet tone. "We need to know where to focus our search. If you could just give us a bit more information, we could use it to help Benjy."

The meaning of his words was lost for long moments as she watched his mouth form them. His well-shaped lips barely moved as he spoke, but each word uttered deepened the cleft in his chin. Those lips seemed much too close to her own.

"I'm sorry," she responded helplessly. "I don't know..."

The phone jangled then, breaking the spell that had shrouded them. Trey went still. A moment later Mac appeared in the doorway.

"State police," he said tersely. His eyes flicked over Trey and Jaida, taking in their proximity on the couch, then settling on the pale strands still trapped between his partner's thumb and forefinger.

Trey disentangled his finger from its silken bonds and rose with swift, sure grace. He reached for the receiver in Mac's outstretched hand and walked back into the kitchen.

Jaida took a deep breath and sank against the back cushions of the couch. She felt as though she'd just been released from a magnetically charged field. The force of Trey's presence was enough to keep her nerves jumping; his nearness had short-circuited her brain. At last, the meaning of Mac's words sank in, and she looked at him.

"Trey never got around to answering my question. Were you able to locate the motel from the information I gave you?"

He seemed to weigh her words before answering. Apparently deciding there was no harm in responding, he said, "One of our men traced the motel. At least," he corrected himself, "he found one by that name on Highway 128."

He turned and went back to the kitchen, leaving Jaida filled with relief. It wouldn't be long now. The fact that the state police were calling meant that they would already have something to report. Perhaps even now they were on their way to locating Lauren's son.

The state police were calling. The thought lingered in Jaida's mind, until her relief was pushed aside by something else. If Trey had known which state police to alert, he'd undoubtedly known where the motel was located. Which meant he hadn't needed that information from her.

Which meant he'd been *testing* her again.

Her fist slammed into the cushion next to her. She wished with all her might that it was Trey taking the blow. Damn that man, anyway! She couldn't let her guard down around him; she'd known that. But there was no denying that if she had been hiding anything from him, he would have gotten that information from her a few minutes ago. She gave a mirthless laugh at the polished act she'd fallen for. He'd been so smooth, so . . . so damn human for once. And he'd reeled her in as easily as a spotted bass on a spinning rod.

Her cheeks heated in remembrance of the scene. She was never at her best in the morning. Her mind didn't start functioning until her first two shots of caffeine, a shower and breakfast, in that order. She'd had none of those this morning. But she couldn't totally blame her gullibility on that lack. No, her real embarrassment stemmed from the fact that she'd *wanted* to believe him. She'd wanted to think he was coming to trust her and yes, dammit, that he was beginning to respond to her in some way.

The knowledge filled her with self-recrimination and she gave her suitcase a childish kick. Immediately she winced, and bent to rub her bare toes. So she'd been stupid and naive. It certainly wasn't the first time. But she'd do her best to make sure it was the last, at least where Trey Garrison was concerned. Using her sight to find Benjy was going to be traumatic enough. She didn't need the kind of emotional damage Trey could inflict with the blink of an eye.

She wished she knew what was going on in the kitchen as a result of that phone call, but darned if she was going to ask any more questions. Trey would have to come to her eventually. She knew that as certainly as she knew her name. And if needed, she'd help again, no matter what she thought of him and his tactics. Benjy Garrison was alone out there, snatched away from his mother and everyone who loved him. He was confused and scared and lonely, and she was going to help bring him home.

But, she thought, bending to pick up her suitcase, her nature wasn't so forgiving that she relished spending any more time in Trey's presence. She started toward the bathroom, then stopped and turned an appraising eye on the plate of sandwiches. From the dealings she'd had with Trey Garrison so far, she knew she was going to need her strength.

After her shower, Jaida took her time in the bathroom. She interspersed drying her long, pale hair with taking bites from the mound of peanut-butter sandwiches on the plate. As she dressed in loose-fitting silk pants and matching top, she mentally calculated how long it had been since she'd last eaten. Much too long, she concluded, reaching for another sandwich. Her body burned calories at a rate that would baffle modern science. Normally she took pleasure in restocking at regular intervals. Yesterday's fast had been out of the ordinary for her, another sin she could lay at Trey's door.

She looked in the mirror. She usually didn't bother with much makeup, finding the results garish with her unusual coloring. But today she'd used some concealer and a small amount of eye shadow. The concealer was to disguise the shadows beneath her eyes, attesting to the fact that she'd gotten much less than the twelve hours' sleep she preferred after one of her sessions. And the eye shadow was...well, because she needed every hint of fortitude she could muster to take on the man in the other room. To that end she'd put on her favorite outfit and a little highlighter. Somehow she knew her efforts would be woefully inadequate.

She returned to the living room, placing her bag near the couch and the plate on the table. A moment later a prickle ran down her spine. Even as she slowly straightened, she knew whom she would see when she turned around.

"Lauren is awake." Trey's voice was peremptory. "Do you want to join us in the kitchen?" She didn't even try to hide her irritation with him, he noted. She swept by him regally, leaving in her path the scent of perfume and shampoo. His nostrils flared in immediate masculine appreciation.

In the kitchen, Mac lounged against the counter, his arms crossed around the front of his wife's waist, holding her against him. Lauren already had a cup of coffee sitting in front of Jaida, and they sat next to each other at the table. Trey stood facing them, his countenance grim. "After you lay down last night," he told Lauren, "Jaida gave us some information that helped lead us to a motel she claims Benjy was at."

Jaida wondered if she was the only person in the room to hear the note of derision in Trey's voice as he imparted this information.

Lauren gave a little gasp, her hand rising to her lips. She spoke not a word, but the hope on her face was easy to read.

Trey's voice softened a little as he addressed his sister. "The state police were alerted, and they've searched the motel. There's no evidence he was there."

"Have they questioned everybody?" Lauren demanded desperately. "Surely someone saw him."

"The desk clerks have been questioned and they couldn't recall anyone traveling with a small child matching Benjy's description. Although," he added almost reluctantly, "they wouldn't necessarily have seen him. The rooms are accessed from doors that open onto the parking lot." That was as much of the conversation as he was willing to share with his sister. The night clerk had received a call complaining about a crying child, but he wasn't about to lay that one on Lauren.

"You have to go there, Trey," Lauren said firmly, meeting her brother's startled gaze. "I won't be convinced unless you check this out yourself. No one can get information from people the way you can."

His mouth flattened. "Honey, it's pointless. I told you, Benjy isn't there."

"But he might have been." Lauren's eyes were bright, determined. "And if he was you may be able to figure out where he was taken." Her gaze slipped to the woman beside her. "If you take Jaida with you."

Jaida's heart sank immediately at the words. Although she was committed to helping this family, the thought of additional travel with Trey was decidedly unappealing.

"You'll go, won't you, Jaida?" Lauren pleaded. "Maybe you'll know more when you actually see the spot where Benjy was."

Jaida could feel the force of Trey's gaze, and it was an effort to keep her eyes on Lauren. She was all too aware of what she would see in his eyes at any rate. "Yes," she responded quietly, surely. "I'll know more then."

Trey focused on the tremulous smile his sister aimed at Jaida and his face went still. Despite everything that had happened to Lauren in her life, she continued to be as trusting a person as he'd ever met. He'd wondered about that sometimes, how the events of their early lives could have had such opposite effects on the shaping of their personalities.

His gaze shifted to encompass both Jaida and Lauren. They were a picture of contrasts, his sister's dark hair providing a foil for the other woman's translucent blond shade. Doubtlessly, their differences went far deeper than the physical.

"Trey." Lauren's soft voice held an imploring note. "You'll take Jaida with you, won't you? You'll let her help?"

Trey studied his sister, remembering the promise she'd asked of him last night, the one he hadn't given. There was only one way to fully discredit Jaida to Lauren, and that was to play this scene out until Ms. West had enough rope to hang herself with. "I wouldn't even consider leaving here without Jaida," he said.

Despite his expressionless tone, Jaida felt a palpable chill settle over her at his words. She knew that he was far from trusting her yet. About as far as it was possible to be. That shouldn't have surprised her, and it certainly shouldn't have caused this forlorn feeling to spread inside. As she met his eyes, she wondered if it was even within her power to change his mind.

Their gazes clashed for several moments before Lauren's voice interrupted them.

"You never did say where the motel was. Where is it that you and Jaida will be going?"

Trey looked at his sister and smiled. He didn't miss a heartbeat delivering the lie. "Didn't I mention that?" he asked smoothly. "I could have sworn I did. We're going to Idaho, honey. Boise, Idaho."

Chapter 4

Finding herself airborne twice in two days was enough to severely dampen Jaida's normally sunny disposition. She forced her fingers to uncurl from the armrest she was clutching with white-knuckled desperation. Ignoring her queasy stomach, she exhaled a breath and snuck a glance at Trey, who was sitting silently beside her. He looked impatient, a little bored and lethally dangerous. The flight attendant didn't seem to interpret his dark good looks in quite the same way, however. She paused in her busy schedule several times to banter with him.

Jaida snorted delicately. She'd like to warn the other woman not to be taken in by Trey's handsome affability. It was a guise he seemed capable of donning at will.

She squirmed uncomfortably in her seat at the memory of how easily he had duped her this morning. She'd known from the beginning that he was a threat to her, although not in the physical sense. She supposed that if she really wanted to find out more about what made the man tick, what he was really thinking, she could manufacture a reason to touch him, could invite the unconscious bits of knowledge that would surely follow.

Just the thought had her shrinking deeper into her seat, away from him. She'd spent too many years trying to shield herself from human contact, avoiding the accompanying *knowing* that inevitably ensued. Few people took any pains to keep their thoughts and emotions hidden far beneath their surface, anyway. The most casual of touches could transmit them to Jaida, leaving her feeling buffeted and exhausted.

She sliced a glance at Trey from the corner of her eye. He'd circumvented her usual responses from the first. The few occasions when she'd been unable to avoid it, his touch had evoked powerful currents, the mere memory of which could still send her reeling. She hadn't received peeks into his emotional corridor at those touches, but the resulting sparks that had leaped between them were even more frightening for their unfamiliarity. There was no way she was going to invite that again. And there was really no reason to. The one thing that was easy to read about him was his complete disregard for *her*.

Trey glanced at the woman by his side. She hadn't said a word since they'd left the house, not on the way to the airport, not since they'd boarded the plane. He knew her well enough by now to be certain this silence was uncustomary for her. Noting her pale complexion and drawn expression, he gave an inward sigh. "You aren't going to toss your cookies, are you?" he asked abruptly.

She closed her eyes in embarrassment, then opened them again to glare at him. "Thank you so much for your delicately worded expression of concern. But I'm fine."

He grunted and turned back to his magazine. "Well, you don't look fine. You look ready to keel over at any moment."

"If I look nauseated, it's only in reaction to your performance with the flight attendant," she retorted. She leaned over and snatched a handful of magazines from his lap, taking care not to touch him.

That remark recaptured his attention. "My what?"

"Your performance," she enunciated. "You know. That little act of oh-so-charming civility. Why, with charm like that, you could make a killing selling Bibles at a Baptist revival."

His gaze narrowed at her gibing tone.

"I suppose that polished pretense goes a lot further in getting you what you want than, say, outward distrust. Although we both know that's really how you view the world." She stopped then, her wayward tongue as usual running ahead of her brain.

"You know so much about me?" he questioned *sotto voce.* "Your psychic abilities must be something indeed for you to have arrived at such an in-depth understanding." He made a gesture of invitation. "Go on. Let's hear this insight of yours."

She returned his stare with one of her own. Wiser women than she would hurriedly retreat from that silky tone. Unfortunately, she wasn't one to back down from a dare, and that was exactly what he'd issued. Added to the fact that she was at her absolute worst when she was hungry or sick, he had the makings of a human storm on his hands.

"You're an accomplished liar," she said simply. At the look of menace that crossed his features she raised her eyebrows. "Do you deny how easily you lied to your sister? Boise, Idaho, my granny's left foot. Don't you think Lauren deserves to know the truth about our destination? Especially since it concerns her son?"

"I have my reasons for not telling Lauren we're going to Boston. Reasons," he added meaningfully, "that have nothing to do with you."

"Of course they have nothing to do with me. I'm just the person you've dragged across the country and back to help you," Jaida agreed mockingly. "You couldn't trust me with your precious reasons, just as you couldn't share the information with your sister. Because there's only one person in the world you really trust, and that's Trey Garrison."

He surveyed her from beneath lowered lashes, battling, not for the first time, an urge to throttle her. "If that's the extent of your half-baked abilities, you wouldn't even make a decent living telling fortunes in the circus." After a pause he added deliberately, "But perhaps you've already found that out for yourself."

The plane hit an air pocket then, and Jaida's stomach did a nauseating roll. She swallowed hard and concentrated on his demeaning words. Circus fortune teller indeed. The big jerk. "You have a lot of nerve believing I'm a fake, when you're one of the biggest phonies I've ever met," she shot back.

"Lady, you'd better be damn careful," he warned softly. "You're really starting to annoy me."

"Great," she said smugly. "Because you've had that effect on me since yesterday. I'm used to people being skeptical about me, and that's okay, I can handle that." She even preferred healthy doubts to the macabre fascination some reserved for her abilities. "But just remember, *you* came to me. I didn't seek you out. I'll help in any way I can to find Benjy. But I'm getting darn sick and tired of being treated like some kind of fraud. And it wears a little thin, coming from you."

She halted abruptly as the flight attendant stopped beside them and spent an inordinate amount of time providing just the right snack for Trey. As an afterthought, she inquired about Jaida's preferences, turning quickly away when Jaida shook her head.

"That's exactly what I mean," she muttered, intercepting the easy smile he bestowed on the woman. "You've got hot-and-cold running charisma, and you use it so effortlessly when you want to. But it's nothing but a means to an end. If anyone is a fake around here, it's *you.*"

He tamped down his annoyance with conscious effort. The fact that her words had a grain of truth to them only fed his irritation. That certainly didn't mean he gave credence to any special powers she claimed, only that, as he'd suspected, frauds like her made a study of human nature. And he'd been admittedly lax about keeping his opinions of her and her abilities to himself.

"Do you have any other pearls of wisdom for me, or are you going to let me eat these—" he raised his food packages "—in peace?"

Her stomach roiled. "You should be aware—" she managed the words through suddenly dry lips "—that I'm a straightforward person, and I expect to be treated the same. I don't like games."

"And you should be aware that any games I play, I play to win."

It was clear that he considered the conversation at an end. Jaida wouldn't have been able to continue it at any rate. Oxygen suddenly seemed in short supply, and her stomach was doing gymnastics.

It was several minutes before Trey glanced at her again. He noted her pasty complexion and the dampness that had appeared on her forehead. Swearing silently, he took immediate action, placing one hand on the back of her head and forcing it between her knees. "Breathe," he ordered. "Deeply." He grasped her free hand in his and squeezed tightly. "That's it," he said encouragingly, ignoring the current that transferred from her palm to his, and her efforts to extricate herself. "Slow, deep breaths. It's mind over matter."

Jaida gasped at the jolt of raw electricity that sprang between them when he took her hand. Heat flowed from his hand to hers, with an accompanying charge of energy. When he didn't release her after a few seconds, the expected happened. The nausea, heat and electric charge faded and she felt as though she were being hurled at Mach-1 speed down a wind tunnel. Colors swirled wildly behind her eyelids, and then the colors receded, to be replaced with snippets of images, disconnected fragments that formed fleeting mental pictures.

Smoke and fire poured from the ruined building. Trey stumbled out of it, almost falling under the burden he carried. People were racing past him, and finally he fell to his knees, sliding the man he'd hauled out of the building to the ground. A pool of blood formed around them, and Trey's face was a mask of anguish and determination. She could feel his pain as sharply as if she were experiencing it herself, and something else, a combination of fury and fear. A litany pounded through his head. *Don't die, don't die, c'mon, Mac, don't die on me now!*

Jaida finally managed to wrest her hand free from Trey's at the same time that he let her raise her head. She pulled away from him and huddled deep in the corner of her seat. Her eyes were wide and her breath came in pants. Color had returned to her cheeks, a deep pink flush that didn't look any healthier than her former paleness.

"Are you sure you're okay?" Trey asked, his voice tinged with reluctant concern.

She raised a hand, as if by doing so she could keep him from reaching for her again. "Yes...I'm better. I'm fine. Just don't..." *Touch me.*

After piercing her with a long stare, Trey gave a shrug and turned away. Reopening his magazine, he turned his attention to an article on computers.

After several long minutes Jaida's breathing slowed, and she straightened in her seat. Noting that her hands still had a tendency to tremble, she clasped them tightly in her lap. Never had she experienced a vision as strong as the one she'd just had. Trey had touched her before, and the current that had run between them had shocked and, yes, frightened her. But it hadn't begun to match the vivid mental replay she'd just been a party to. She'd wondered several times in the past twenty-four hours whether Trey was capable of human emotion, at least toward anyone other than his family. She wouldn't wonder anymore. Now she knew there had been a time in his past when he'd been full of panic at the thought of losing . . .

His only friend.

The snippet of information flashed into her mind, unbidden. A chill pervaded her limbs, and she rubbed her arms frantically. She didn't like this at all. By some quirk of cosmic fate Trey seemed to have the power to heighten her uncommon powers, to magnify them. She managed a grim little smile. Fate did indeed, as Granny always said, have a warped sense of humor.

For a moment, she wished mightily for Granny's comforting arms and her uncommon wisdom. Maybe she could explain Jaida's uncustomary reactions to this man in a way that made sense of them, that relegated them to the ordinary.

But somehow she thought this strange pull that existed between her and Trey might even be beyond Granny's comprehension.

It seemed like déjà vu as they stood in line to rent a vehicle, a quick little Oldsmobile this time. Jaida waited off to the side, not even offering to help and let Trey retrieve their luggage. She got into the car while he stashed their bags in the trunk of the rental. Then he slid in behind the steering wheel and tossed her a map.

"Do you know how to read this?"

"I think I can manage," she answered dryly, shaking the map out and folding it neatly on her lap. She scanned the metropolitan map of Boston and its vicinity as Trey drove out of the Logan International Airport parking lot. After a few minutes, she gave him directions to Highway 128.

"So what's your plan once we reach the motel?" Jaida asked after long silent minutes had ticked by.

Trey took his time answering, as if weighing how much to tell her. "I called the state police and told them I was coming. Hopefully they will have left an officer for me to talk to. There's been plenty of time for them to have gone through the place pretty thoroughly. If proof exists that Benjy has been there, they will have found it." He spoke with more confidence than he felt. He hadn't been completely assured when he'd talked to the police that they were giving his nephew's disappearance top priority. And when they'd pressed him about the "tip" he'd received, placing his nephew at the Glenview, he'd been noncommittally vague. He didn't doubt that their questions would be more pointed when he arrived, and he felt a sense of distaste at the upcoming interview. He didn't believe any more than they did that Benjy had been there, was certain, in fact, that this whole thing was a lame hoax, perpetuated by the woman sitting next to him.

And yet . . . he couldn't deny the surge in his stomach as he drove toward the motel. He couldn't help remembering the complaint to the night clerk about the crying child. Not that he put any stock in psychic nonsense. Yet, in spite of his steady disbelief, there was a tiny seed of hope unfurling deep inside him. A bloom not nurtured by any faith in Jaida's ability, but born of his abiding love for his young nephew and his fervent desire to hold him safe in his arms again.

Jaida wanted to ask him more questions, but he was reticent at the best of times, and something told her now didn't number among those. Though no expression showed on his hard face, he was radiating energy, and maybe a hint of nerves. She slid a little closer to the passenger door. She was still shaken by their earlier encounter, and she desperately wanted to guard against a repeat occurrence.

Traffic snarled the freeways, even though it wasn't rush hour. It took well over an hour to drive to the motel. When they finally got to the parking lot, Jaida's stomach had tightened with nerves. She saw Trey's observant gaze go to the sign out front;

his face registered no emotion when he took in the flickering neon sign with the burned out *V*. She got out of the car and trailed behind him as he made his way quickly to the office. Reaching the area a few moments behind him, she found him already in a corner, deep in conversation with the state policeman who had been waiting for their arrival.

Jaida gave the employee behind the counter a tentative smile. The young woman, who looked no older than twenty-two or -three, wound a tendril of her frizzy red hair around one forefinger and popped her gum loudly. Then her gaze went back to the men.

Jaida didn't attempt to join in the dialogue between the policeman and Trey. She approached the desk, forcing the clerk's gaze back to her. "Could you tell me if the vacated rooms have been cleaned yet?"

The woman bristled visibly. "All our rooms are clean—cleaned every day. The owner would have my butt if that didn't get done."

"I'm sure they're cleaned thoroughly," Jaida soothed. "But there must be a lot of work around here. How long does it take your crew?"

"Hours," huffed the young woman. "Usually I help, but I've been held up today because he—" she jerked her head at the young officer Trey was talking to "—has been here since the others left. Too much going on for me to leave the office empty. So we might be a bit behind today," she allowed reluctantly. "On account of me having to answer a bunch of questions and all."

Jaida had the response she wanted. She gave the woman another smile and, turning, let herself quietly out of the office.

Once outside again, Jaida searched out the neon sign, the one that had figured so prominently in her vision yesterday. Slowly she walked past each of the motel doors. Her progress was halting but steady. Already the hair on the back of her neck was prickling; goose bumps appeared on her arms. Still she walked, past a door to a window, paused, then moved on. The chill skittering along her spine was increasing and owed nothing to the damp breeze. At the third door from the opposite end, she stopped. She didn't need the proximity of the sign from this particular window to know that this was the room that had housed Benjy last night. Her certainty lay in the waves that vibrated off the empty room to wrap around her. Sensations of confusion and tears shed by a child in a strange place. She closed her eyes, lost in the suffering and bewilderment that Benjy's brief sojourn had left in its wake.

A voice sounded in her ear. "What are you doing out here?"

Jaida opened her eyes to find Trey standing closer than she would have dared allow him had she been thinking clearly. "This is it," she said, her words barely loud enough to be heard. She lifted one hand with great effort and pointed toward the motel-room door. "That's where Benjy was last night."

Trey stared hard at her. "Give it up, Jaida," he ordered harshly. "The show is over. The officers searched all the vacant rooms, talked to all the guests who are still here. No one claims to have seen Benjy, not the clerks, not the guests. There's not a shred of evidence proving he was ever here, and there's a good reason for that, isn't there? Because you and I both know he wasn't."

She returned his hard stare. "Get a key," she said quietly.

He exhaled an exasperated sigh. "Look, there's no need to carry this farce out any longer. You've been caught. Surely it's not the first time for that. You may as well . . . where are you going?"

He was in midsentence when Jaida turned and walked back to the office. Trey stayed where he was, frustrated beyond belief. The woman was tenacious; he'd grant her that. She was determined to play this little melodramatic farce out to the end. He waved as the officer drove the state police cruiser by him and pulled out of the parking lot. The officer had been polite, but it was apparent that he'd considered this assignment today fruitless. He'd treated Trey as one would an overwrought, everhopeful relative of a crime victim. It had suited Trey's purposes to let the man believe that was true.

But it was finished now. He could pack up Jaida and shuttle her off on yet another plane, one that would take her back to Arkansas and away from him. She'd be out of his life for good, and he could forget all about her, forget her liquid drawl, moon-glow hair and the strange reaction he could create just by touching her. He could forget about the woman who'd used his

family's tragedy for her personal gain, so that she could...
what? What had Jaida hoped to gain by perpetuating this pa-
thetic little hoax? Was she hoping to cash in from her "help"
to a desperate family? Or did she just have a sick little side to
her that needed to feel important?

He shook his head impatiently as she approached him again.
It didn't matter to him what motivated Jaida West or others like
her. His time for her was at an end, and he was more than ready
to see the last of her.

She walked to the motel room near him and inserted a key in
the lock.

"What are you up to now?" he demanded.

"The woman in the office said we could look around for a
few minutes," she answered, not looking at him. Her palms
suddenly slippery, she pushed the door open and stepped over
the threshold. The barrage of sensation that bombarded her as
she walked farther into the room wasn't unexpected. She could
feel the confusion and hopelessness thick in the air, and in the
recesses of her mind a child cried. Benjy. He'd spent the night
sobbing intermittently, crying for the comfort of his mother.
She walked around the tiny, slightly seedy room, ignoring the
chill creeping over her skin, the familiar pounding starting at
her temples. Her gaze went to the window, with its view of the
neon sign outside, the one that had fascinated the young child.
Again her mind replayed Benjy slipping off the bed, toddling
toward the window. Again she saw a hand grasp him by the
back of his shirt and haul him back up on the bed. Closing her
eyes, she focused fiercely on the fragment of mental replay. A
man's arm, she decided, seeing the large bones and the dark
hair on the forearm. A thick gold watchband had encircled the
wrist.

"Jaida." Trey had followed her, unnoticed, into the room.
"Give it up. There's no point, and you're only making the situation worse."

"He slept over there." Her voice trembled a bit as she indicated the opposite side of the room, beyond the lone sagging
bed. She remained rooted where she was, victim to an intense
physical exhaustion. She wrapped her arms around limbs that
refused to warm.

Trey moved over the matted shag carpeting that had long ago given up any pretense of identifiable color. He rounded the unmade bed and stopped short. There on the floor was a drawer, pulled from the cheap dresser on the opposite wall. A pillow taken from the bed lined the bottom.

A muscle clenched in Trey's jaw, and for a moment, just for a moment, his heart leaped foolishly. His gaze swung to Jaida, who stood motionless by the window, not even looking in his direction. "How did you . . ."

Jaida released a sigh and, mobilized by his words, walked toward the door. She didn't want to wait and hear him finish the sentence. Even someone with his suspicious nature would have to realize that she hadn't had time to arrange that drawer before he'd followed her in here. She was too weary to provide him with explanations he was incapable of accepting. She needed to get out of this room, out of the swirling dervish of sensations that threatened to choke her with their intensity.

"Wait a minute," he commanded. "Where are you going?"

"To get something to eat." The incongruous words floated over her shoulder as she walked steadily away from him.

Trey frowned and then discarded his immediate inclination to detain her. She couldn't get far, not when he had the car keys. As determined as he was to send her packing, it would be on his terms, when he'd finished with her. She'd been acting oddly all day, but that wasn't important, either. Right now his mind was grappling with the startling coincidence she'd stumbled on in this room. The room was next door to the one from which the phone call had been made last night to complain of a child's crying.

His gaze swung back to the drawer and the pillow inside it. More than likely the room's previous occupants had used it to bed down a pet they were traveling with. It would make a snug pallet for a medium-sized dog.

But it would also be the perfect size for an eighteen-month-old boy.

"I'll have two double cheeseburgers with everything," Jaida said, snapping her menu shut. "And bring me an order of fries, a Coke and a chocolate shake."

The waitress scribbled down the order in her indecipherable shorthand. "Someone going to be joining you, hon?" she asked. The tag pinned to her pink uniform proclaimed her name as Elaine.

"Not if I'm lucky," Jaida answered obliquely. She refused to look out the window of the restaurant, to see if Trey had followed her from the motel across the street. She needed time alone to regroup after the emotional turmoil she'd experienced in the motel room. And it was much too soon for her to face Trey's contempt and mistrust again. First she needed time to shore up defenses that had crumbled badly in the past few minutes.

"Could I have the shake right away?" she asked the waitress.

The woman tucked her pad and pencil in the pocket of her apron, which was a snug fit around her ample middle. "Sure thing, hon," she agreed good-naturedly. "If I was a little bitty thing like you, I'd have myself two." She winked and headed around the counter.

The hammering in Jaida's temples showed no signs of abating, and she opened her purse and took out her pain medication. Swallowing a tablet, she placed the prescription bottle back in her bag just as the graying waitress returned with her shake.

"Here you go. Hope you enjoy." Elaine hovered until Jaida sipped from the glass and proclaimed it delicious. Beaming, the waitress said, "Old-fashioned malts and shakes are my specialty. Those young girls that work here," she snorted and jerked her head in the direction of a teenager who was wiping off the counter. "You just can't teach them a thing—they don't want to learn. Whichever way is easiest, that's the way they want to do things. But you just can't rush a good shake."

Jaida smiled at the woman's loquaciousness. "Do you own this place?"

Elaine's stomach shook with her laughter. "Heavens no, dear, but I guess you can say I spend a lot of time running it. Jake, he's the owner. Doesn't show up much these days, except to clean out the cash drawer. As long as he doesn't bother me, we get along just fine." The woman's eyes narrowed in concern as Jaida rubbed her temples. "Headache?" she asked sympathetically.

"I've taken something for it. It'll be gone soon." Even as she spoke the words, Jaida knew they were overly optimistic. Her limbs still felt heavy with a deep, pervading cold, and her shiver wasn't in response to the diner's air-conditioning.

The waitress clucked knowingly and bustled back to the kitchen to check on Jaida's order. A short time later she was back, bearing plates of steaming food. "There, now. You eat up. Nothing like a hot meal to chase a headache away." She watched approvingly as Jaida picked up one of the cheeseburgers and bit into it. Then her gaze went to the door, and her face went still.

Jaida didn't need Elaine's reaction to know who had just walked into the diner. The tingle at the base of her scalp was enough to tell her that Trey had come looking for her. The waitress scurried back behind the counter, and Trey slid his big body into the seat cross from Jaida.

He nodded toward the assortment of dishes in front of her. "You shouldn't have ordered for me."

"I didn't," she informed him shortly. She noted the expression of mild surprise that he allowed to show on his dark features as he watched her polish off the first cheeseburger with delicate efficiency. "I suppose I could spare you a few fries if you're feeling desperate," she offered grudgingly.

"No," he said in bemusement, "go ahead. I'll order something for myself." He turned his head and beckoned to Elaine, who was looking at him fixedly.

Jaida heaved a sigh. Even the amiable older lady seemed susceptible to the man's magnetism. He gave her his order and then turned his attention back to Jaida.

"Look," he said. "About what happened back there..."

"I'd rather not discuss it now," Jaida told him, reaching for her second cheeseburger. "I just got my appetite back as it is."

"Yours or a linebacker's?" he inquired. She made a face at him and didn't answer. He watched with a touch of awe as she made short work of the second cheeseburger and started on the French fries. By the time Elaine slid his sandwich in front of him, Jaida was neatly wiping her mouth.

"Can I get you any dessert, hon?" Elaine asked.

Trey's eyes widened as Jaida appeared to actually consider the offer. She finally shook her head.

"No, I don't think so."

"Wise choice," Trey commented. "I was beginning to think I was going to have to send you home in the plane's cargo compartment."

She ignored the dig. Her headache hadn't lessened appreciably, and even satisfying her returned appetite hadn't succeeded in driving away the chill in her blood. Stoically, she accepted the fact that the effects from the scene in the motel room were not going to be hastened away. "You won't be buying me another plane ticket, in the cargo compartment or otherwise."

Trey leveled a steely look at her. "Yes," he corrected her grimly, "I will. As soon as possible, as a matter of fact. This charade is over, and we both know it."

"The only thing I know," she said in exasperation, "is that you're as dense as an Arkansas mule and twice as stubborn. I am your best hope for finding Benjy. Why won't you accept that?"

"If you think that little scene in the motel room proved anything, you're dead wrong," he answered. He'd spent too many minutes staring down at that damn drawer, logic warring with involuntary, futile hope. He despised himself for having allowed himself to fall victim, even for a short time, to that immediate, desperate will to believe her. "The police found no evidence that Benjy had been there, and neither did we. I have some calls to make while I'm in Boston, but there's no reason for you to hang around until I'm finished, especially since we'll be heading in opposite directions when we fly out of here."

Jaida surveyed him impatiently. Never had she met a more obtuse man. "You can fly out—I'm not."

He closed his eyes briefly in frustration. "All right, we'll get you a train ticket. A bus," he said at her shake of negation. "Woman, what the hell do you want? Is it your fee?" A jeering note entered his voice on the final word. He pulled his wallet from his back pocket. Twenty-four hours ago he would never have believed that he would offer to pay off the little fraud, but right now it seemed well worth it to be rid of her.

Eyes narrowed dangerously, Jaida wished she'd ordered some of that cream pie Elaine had offered, for the sheer pleasure of shoving it in Trey's arrogant face. "Keep your money," she shot back, leaning across the table toward him. "I don't want it, and I'm growing tired of *you*. I'm staying, and I'll continue the search for Benjy by myself. I promised to help your sister, and I'm not going to be deterred by the fact that her brother is a cretin. You can go flying back to California and dabble in your precious proof and evidence. I, on the other hand, am going to bring that sweet nephew of yours home again."

"I don't know what you think you're going to prove by continuing this damn farce," he snarled, his face close to hers. "It's over, Jaida. You lost. He's not at that damn motel—he never was. So why don't you just give it up? And you *will* get on that plane, even if I have to forcibly carry you!"

With those words he shoved his plate out of the way and rose.

Elaine found his check and methodically rang it up on the register. "You know," she told Trey chattily as she leaned over to hand him his change, "you've got pretty unusual coloring. That dark hair and those eyes, whooee!" She winked broadly. "I'll just bet you have to fight women off with a stick."

Trey's voice was dry when he replied, "I usually try to be a bit more subtle than that."

She chuckled. "Yep, it's not too often a gal sees that combination in a male, and I've gone and got lucky enough to see it twice in two days."

Jaida froze at the woman's words. She knew what Elaine would say next, and the realization had nothing to do with her abilities. The physical reaction, which had only gotten stronger during her meal, began to make an ominous sense. Her headache picked up in intensity and her vision blurred.

"'Course, the specimen yesterday wasn't a man," Elaine went on, tabulating Jaida's bill. "And I just caught a glimpse of him as his mama carried him out the door. I don't usually take to kids, but that one, I'm telling you, he was a charmer." She looked at Trey consideringly, ignoring the stillness of his features. "He even had the same chin you do. Well, they say we all have a twin, and mister, yours is only pint-size." She shook her head over the coincidence, then waited expectantly.

Trey turned then and stared at Jaida. The look he gave her was so contemptuous, so filled with loathing, that she shuddered. Then he spun on his heel and walked out the door.

Jaida willed herself to action, reaching into her purse and extracting enough money for the bill.

"Gee, I'm sorry, hon," Elaine said with a frown. "I don't know what I said, but he seems real upset."

Forcing a smile, Jaida reassured her. "Don't worry, he's having . . . a bad day." She gazed in the direction Trey had disappeared, certain that for her the day was about to get worse.

Elaine leaned over and put her hand on Jaida's shoulder. "Well, you just hang in there. That one is worth putting up with a few moods."

Jaida started at the woman's touch, resisting the impulse to jerk away. This woman had been kind to her, a stranger. She picked through the sensations transmitting from the touch, and when Elaine dropped her hand, Jaida smiled wanly at her. "You've been very nice," she said simply. "Thanks for everything. And your bracelet, the one with the blue stones? It's under the sink in the kitchen. The clasp broke when you were fixing the pipes." She turned and walked toward the door.

Elaine looked puzzled and then her mouth made a perfect *O*. "Well, I'll be. Now that you mention it, that *was* the last time I saw the darn thing. In the kitchen here at the diner. . . ."

She frowned as the door closed behind Jaida. "But how in the heck did she know about that?"

Chapter 5

On the small balcony outside his hotel room, Trey stared broodingly at the lights blanketing the city of Boston. Despite the hour, the sounds of horns and sirens still sliced through the night. Most of the city would be asleep, and he wished wearily that he were, too. Jaida had retired hours ago, while it was still daylight.

Jaida. Just thinking of the woman in the adjoining room had his muscles tensing. The scene following their departure from the diner had not been pleasant. Though she had steadfastly denied it, it was apparent that she'd used her time alone with the waitress to feed her that description of Benjy. There was no other explanation for the woman's too-casual mention of a child who looked so much like Trey.

He closed his eyes in pain. The physical similarities that existed between him and Benjy mirrored their deeper emotional bond. A curious fluke of genetics had Benjy resembling his mother's family completely, with no hint of his father. Benjy would undoubtedly grow up to look like his uncle. Certainly he'd inherited the Garrison chin, which would later become a minor nuisance to shave. But Trey had always hoped the boy would take after his mother in all the ways that counted, with her sweet disposition and sense of wonder about the world. He didn't remember ever being that young and innocent, and had vowed from the first second he'd laid eyes on his nephew to do everything in his power to ensure Benjy retained that quality. He'd promised himself that he'd protect the boy, the same way he'd tried to protect Lauren when they were kids.

And he'd failed Benjy as completely as he had his mother almost thirty years ago.

Trey's eyes snapped open, and his fists clenched involuntarily. He'd been down that road of guilt often enough in the past, when the nights got too dark, and the solitude too oppressive. He'd been unable to take care of Lauren, but he'd been a boy himself at the time. Now was different; *he* was different. And nothing on this earth was going to keep him from finding his nephew and bringing him home.

He rubbed a hand over his face. It had been an incredibly long, frustrating two days, and his mind refused to relax. If he'd had his way he'd be halfway back to L.A. by now. But Jaida had thwarted those plans by her obstinate refusal to return to Arkansas. Maybe it was wounded pride—probably it was something more mercenary—but she'd been steadfast in her determination to continue the search. She hadn't backed down from his fury, and her temper had reflected his own. He'd finally brought her here and booked her a room, in an effort to avoid a charge of homicide. Justifiable, he added mentally, in light of some of the churlish adjectives she'd hurled at him.

He'd checked in with Lauren earlier. The disappointment in his sister's voice had left Trey with the desire to hit something. He'd soothed her as best he could, unwilling to give her any more false hope. Then he'd asked to talk to Mac. It was the memory of that conversation that kept him sitting out on the hotel balcony, too keyed up to sleep.

There had been no new developments in the investigation on that end, either. Mac had reported on the results of Lauren's doctor appointment that day. It would still be some time before Lauren would be able to travel.

"When her physician gives us the go-ahead," Trey had told him grimly, "we have to be prepared to move her immediately." If Penning had indeed traced Lauren to L.A. and ordered the kidnapping, every day she spent in her home left her in constant danger from her husband. Despite his faith in his partner, and the heavy security surrounding her home, Trey wouldn't rest easy until Lauren was in a new location.

"I'm way ahead of you," Mac had answered. "I already have a place in mind. Raine's folks have a cabin in Black Forest, Colorado. It's at the foot of the Rockies and pretty isolated. I think it has enough security to satisfy both of us."

"Sounds perfect," Trey had agreed. "Go on and make the arrangements, but don't mention anything to Lauren about it." Trey knew his sister would be reluctant to leave her home, which was filled with memories of her son. And if Penning did prove to be behind Benjy's disappearance, Trey doubted his ability to ever make her feel completely safe again.

He prowled the small balcony broodingly. He'd dialed his contact with the Bureau after he'd spoken to Mac, but had hung up frustrated. Despite around-the-clock surveillance, there was still no evidence that William Penning even knew of Benjy's existence, much less arranged his kidnapping. They had picked up one detail, however, which they were pursuing. Penning's parents were on an extended tour of Europe and were not expected back to the States for another two weeks. At that time Penning was planning to vacation with them at his family's beach home on the Cape.

He sighed deeply and rubbed at eyes burning from lack of sleep. His mind wouldn't quit until it came up with his next plan of action, but his options at this point were limited. That would explain the knot in his gut. His place right now was with Lauren, not chasing across the country after some psychic phony.

He needed to get rid of Jaida. The words were a litany running through his mind. He'd indulged his sister's whim, but as long as Jaida was involved, Lauren would cling to her false hopes and unrealistic expectations.

It was with that thought in mind that he headed determinedly for the door that led to the adjoining room. It opened easily. Jaida had obviously been in such a hurry to get some sleep she hadn't bothered to lock it. Not that a locked door would have kept him from this confrontation. He didn't feel any guilt at all about waking her in the middle of the night. She was partially responsible for his own sleeplessness, and if she had been true to her intentions, she'd been asleep a full eight hours already. Which was more than he was likely to get, at this rate.

He stalked silently to her bedside. She lay practically buried under the extra blankets she'd heaped on the bed, despite the rather warm temperature in the room. Her hair shone in the darkness. Unwillingly, he remembered the one time he'd given in to the urge to touch it, to wrap a strand around his finger and stroke its silkiness. He'd had an ulterior motive for weakening her defenses then—was it only yesterday? But he didn't deny to himself that he'd found pleasure in the action, as well. A man didn't have to like a woman, or trust her, to find her appealing on another, less discriminating level.

He'd always been an extremely light sleeper. He'd always needed to be. But Jaida slumbered peacefully, unaware of his presence. He sank gingerly to the edge of her bed, watching her. All that was visible beneath the cocoon of blankets was that mass of pale hair and her profile, as pure and delicate as a cameo. He knew well that nature had a way of masking even evil intentions with pleasant disguises. The most beautiful face could hide the soul of a harlot; the kindest demeanor could cover a terrorist. But there was something about sleep and moonlight that lent an air of innocence to this woman.

Deliberately, Trey clicked on the lamp on the bedside table. When Jaida still did not stir, he called her name and shook the bed urgently. "Wake up."

Frowning, Jaida snuggled down farther under the blankets, shielding her eyes from the lamp's light.

Trey paused for a moment, then in a louder voice he said, "Come on, Jaida, wake up. I want to talk to you."

The form under the mound of blankets remained motionless.

He stood abruptly, grasped the blankets and yanked them to the foot of the bed.

The sudden loss of her enveloping warmth roused Jaida as nothing else could. Grumbling sleepily, she rolled over in bed, searching for the blankets without opening her eyes.

If Trey's action had left Jaida feeling chilled, it had the opposite effect on him. Slow heat bloomed in his belly. She was decently covered in a sleeveless satin gown. But it had crawled up during the night, leaving an alluring portion of her slim legs bare. The gown's dark purple color glowed against her skin, and her hair streaming over it shone like a precious stone on a bed of velvet.

He wasn't even aware of moving. Sinking back down on the bed, he reached for her, filling his hand with streamers of her tresses. Then his hand moved, unbidden, as though charting its own journey. It smoothed a path up one silky shoulder and across to her graceful neck. The current that sparked immediately at his touch was becoming familiar. One finger lingered on the pulse beating beneath her jaw. The rhythm of her pulse accelerated sharply.

His gaze drifted to the vee of the gown's neckline, to the hint of shadowy cleavage. Feeling like a voyeur, he still made no move to retreat. He watched, fascinated, as her lips parted and her breathing became more ragged. Then her eyes slowly opened, and she looked at him fixedly.

The dark-blue stare was slightly unfocused, as if she were still not quite alert. "It wasn't your fault," she mumbled, her voice raspy. "You were only a boy—you couldn't help it. Too young." A shudder racked her then, as though she were overtaken with a chill. "Much too young... to take care of Lauren."

He froze for a second as her words washed over him, an instant replay of his earlier thoughts. Then he snatched his hand away and sprang up.

Their gazes clashed for long, charged seconds, before Jaida shuddered again and turned away. Seeing the blankets in a heap at the foot of the bed, she leaned over and caught the edge of one, hauling it up to wrap around herself.

He couldn't think, couldn't move. "Woman, who the hell are you?" he muttered finally, staring keenly at her. "*What* are you?"

Jaida refused to look at him. He'd awakened her from as sound a sleep as she'd ever known, and she was as shaken as he by the response he'd evoked. She'd never slept with someone beside her, had never been awakened by a touch. It was decidedly disconcerting to learn that her unconscious was as psychic as her alert mind. She was dazed and dismayed by the realization. And the fact that she'd found out now, with this man, was even more alarming.

"What do you want? It's still dark outside."

"It's only 3:00 a.m.," he affirmed. She was huddled in the center of the bed, shrouded in that blanket, her head lowered. He had the uncanny notion that she was hiding from him. "I wanted to talk to you."

She pushed her hair over one shoulder, still refusing to look at him. "It couldn't wait until morning?"

Her question hung in the air between them. Yes, he fervently wished he had waited until morning. He wished he hadn't seen her, half bare and erotically arousing in this bed. He wished he hadn't touched that pale tangle of hair again, or noticed the slim lines of her body. But most of all, he wished he hadn't awakened her, hadn't heard that strange husky rasp, so unlike her usual melodic drawl, repeat an echo from his mind.

There would come a time in the morning, after he'd slept, when a rational explanation for this scene would no doubt become apparent to him. But right now, arriving on the heels of his heightened awareness of her, it was downright spooky.

When he said nothing else, she raised her head and turned cautiously in his direction. "Trey?" she said, her voice tentative. "What's the real reason you didn't tell Lauren we were coming to Boston?"

He was silent for so long that she feared he wouldn't answer her at all. His voice was low, reluctant, when he finally spoke. "Lauren had married a wealthy lawyer, and they were living here when I found her. Her husband, a man by the name of William Penning, controlled her, abused her. He treated her the way he would a piece of property. His jealousy ruined their marriage. I arranged for her to get away from him, and I believed he didn't know where she was."

"Or of Benjy's existence," Jaida murmured.

He looked sharply at her. "Or of Benjy's existence," he agreed.

"Do you think he found her? Did he arrange the kidnapping?"

"I don't have any reason to believe that," he said deliberately.

She didn't need his words to tell her that he'd never trusted her, not when he'd asked for her help, and most certainly not now, despite what had passed between them. Something had happened to Trey Garrison, made him close out the world, eyeing it with suspicion. Only a very select few were allowed inside that barricade he'd erected around his emotions. She'd sensed that since she'd met him. But instead of finding it maddening now, she was curiously empathetic to the events that must have built those inner walls, brick by brick.

The feeling was frightening. She didn't want to know Trey any better, didn't want to like him or to understand him. He was getting too close to her, having too strong an effect on her to be ignored. If she had any choice in the matter he wouldn't have to urge her to return home—she'd hightail it back to her safe Arkansas Valley in no time.

She'd run home and hide, just as she had before.

The voice inside jeered at her. That was what she'd done when life had become too complicated to handle. But that time had been nothing like this. She hadn't run from one man then; she'd fled the crowds under the bright lights, the people who'd come to hear her sing and who thought they owned a part of her because they'd paid the price of the ticket.

But she wasn't running this time. She had to bring that baby home to his mother. She raised a fatalistic gaze to the man staring at her unrelentingly from across the room. He looked no more eager than she to continue this odd relationship of theirs.

A sudden thought struck her. "When you found out that the Glenview Motel was close to Boston you must have suspected Penning right away."

"He's always been a suspect," Trey acknowledged. "He's being watched."

"We need to know whether he masterminded this whole plot," Jaida said, frowning. "If he's as obsessed as you say he's capable of anything. We have to be certain—"

"*We* don't have to be certain of anything," he corrected her. "Penning is being taken care of. There's no need for you to concern yourself about him." He stopped then, having said more than he wanted. The events here had circumvented his normal caution. "We'll talk tomorrow. I'm sorry I woke you up."

"We'll talk tomorrow," she repeated softly to his retreating back. The door closed behind him quietly. Reaching down to the foot of the bed, she retrieved the rest of her covers. No doubt by morning Trey would regret his uncustomary candor. But his disclosure about William Penning had been valuable indeed. It was apparent that no one knew for sure whether Penning was involved.

And she was the only one who could find out.

Sunlight flooded the room, filling it with an uncomfortable amount of warmth. Trey woke up perspiring, squinting into the bright room. He hadn't bothered to pull the shades after he'd come in off the balcony, wouldn't have seen a need to if he had thought of it. He rarely slept much past dawn. But it had been late when he'd returned from Jaida's room, later still before he'd finally slept. Even then his slumber hadn't been restful. It had been filled with a mysterious specter with moon-glow hair, who gave voice to the thoughts in the recesses of his mind.

He got out of bed and padded to the bathroom. While he showered he went over the conversation he'd had with Jaida the night before, and discovered her insight still had the power to make him uncomfortable. He searched his memory for something he might have said that would have led to her remarks.

By the time he'd finished shaving and gotten dressed he was no closer to figuring out the source of her knowledge. Having learned from his mistake of the night before, he knocked on the adjoining door this time. On the day of Jaida's certain departure from his life he was feeling somewhat magnanimous. He'd be willing to take her to breakfast, to see if her appetite of yesterday was only a fluke. He knocked again, and still there was no answer. Letting himself into the room, he strode to her bed. On the table next to it was a note addressed to him. Reading the brief message, he cursed, then crumpled it in his palm. What "matter" could possibly have needed her attention today?

And why did her disappearance make him so damn nervous?

It was shortly after one o'clock when Jaida walked into the law office of Penning and Associates. After inquiring for directions, she made her way down the hallway to the corner suite of rooms. She paused for a moment to appreciate the beauty in the etched glass panel of the door, then pushed it open to find herself in an elegantly furnished waiting room. The man at the desk was probably close to her age, she estimated. His dark hair was thinning on top, and he looked up from his computer and surveyed her disapprovingly through gold-framed glasses.

"I believe you have the wrong office," he informed her dismissively.

She tried a tentative smile, one that had no visible effect on him. "I don't think so. I'm here to see Mr. William Penning."

"You don't have an appointment," the man stated surely, not even consulting the book on his desk.

"No, I..."

"Mr. Penning sees no one without an appointment." He went back to his typing.

"Perhaps I can make an appointment," Jaida offered.

The typing never ceased. "He's booked through the rest of the month. If you have a legal matter to take care of, I suggest you find someone else."

"It has to be Mr. Penning."

The man sighed heavily and stopped typing. "He will be in conference for the rest of the afternoon. Perhaps you'd like to leave a message with me."

Jaida smiled serenely. "No, thank you. I'll wait."

The man tried, with diminishing degrees of diplomacy, to dissuade her. Finally, he turned back to his typing, his fingers flying over the keys more furiously than ever, as if by ignoring her he could make her go away.

Three hours later Jaida had decided that the disagreeable man had the makings of a sadist. He'd poured himself several cups of coffee and even nibbled at a sandwich at his desk. He never addressed another word to her, didn't even look in her direction. She spent her time dismally counting the meals she'd missed recently and spinning fantasies about ways she'd like to see Penning's secretary spend the rest of his days. Choking on his keyboard.

When the desk phone rang, Jaida straightened. The man listened and then said, "Very well, sir, I'll see to it." Hanging up the receiver, he shot a superior smile in Jaida's direction. "Mr. Penning will be leaving for the day now. I'm afraid you've wasted your time." His tone was smug.

The inner door to the office opened then, and two men dressed in suits came out. One walked by Jaida and left the area, and the other stopped at the secretary's desk. Jaida stood up, nervously smoothing the wrinkles from the royal-blue dress she'd bought that morning. She'd purchased it, along with the matching shoes, with total confidence in her ability to pull this charade off. But now that the moment had come, her stomach was fluttering wildly.

The man in the suit turned away from the secretary's desk and saw Jaida for the first time. "Roland," he said. "You didn't tell me I had a client."

"You don't, Mr. Penning." Roland's voice held a hint of peevishness. "This young...woman does not have an appointment, but she refused to leave, even when I told her how full your calendar is."

"I had to see you, Mr. Penning," Jaida said quickly. "I'm terribly sorry to bother you like this—I know you're a busy man—but this was the only opportunity I had." Her breathlessness wasn't completely contrived. "Please, I only want a minute of your time."

"As I tried to tell you repeatedly, Miss—" Roland began.

"Never mind, Roland," Penning said, without taking his eyes from Jaida. "I think I can spare this young lady a few minutes." He held out a hand for her to precede him into his office.

Jaida hoped her inner reluctance didn't show as she walked into the office. Penning closed the door behind her and stepped around his desk to his chair. He indicated a chair in front of his desk, and Jaida sank into it. If the outer office seemed lavish, this room was opulent. Rows of windows were at Penning's back, offering a magnificent view of the skyline. But it was the man, not the room, that commanded attention.

Lauren's husband was arrestingly handsome, with dark hair combed straight back from an aristocratic forehead. His nose was slightly long and aquiline. His eyes were dark and fathomless. Jaida didn't have to fake speechlessness for the first few moments. She couldn't imagine Lauren married to this man. He exuded money and power. And something else, something infinitely more disturbing.

It wasn't until he glanced at the gold watch on his wrist that Jaida was propelled to speech. "I apologize again for dropping in like this, Mr. Penning. Now that I'm actually here, I can't believe I had the nerve." That was certainly true enough, she thought a little frantically. "The truth is..." She took a deep breath. "I'm a law student. Or at least," she corrected herself, "I *will* be a law student. Actually, I've been working a few years, trying to earn enough money for college, where I'll major in prelaw. But I've been doing some studying on my own, and your cases intrigued me." She turned wide eyes on him. "I just had to meet you while I was here."

"And your name..." He cocked his head slightly.

"Oh!" She raised her hand to her cheek in feigned embarrassment. "I'm so sorry! It's Rhodes. Gwen Rhodes."

"Rhodes." He leaned back in his chair, surveying her over a steeple he'd made with his fingers. "Are you by any chance related to Arthur Rhodes of Boston?"

Jaida let her expression go blank. "No, sir. Not that I know of. I'm not from around here."

A small smile played across his mouth. "Of course not, not with that delightful accent. I'd place you in ... South Carolina? Or is it Georgia?"

She smiled in return. "I am from Georgia, although I've lived with my sister and her husband in Maine for the past four years. But I plan to—"

"Go into law," Penning finished for her, his opaque eyes intent on her. "So you've said. With those looks, you'll go far."

She couldn't prevent herself from stiffening slightly at the blatantly sexist remark. Her reaction didn't escape his observant eyes.

"I hope I haven't offended you—" he paused inquiringly over her title "—Miss Rhodes?" At her nod, he continued smoothly. "That certainly wasn't my intent. My meaning is that a good lawyer must be a powerful lawyer. And a powerful lawyer has presence. Do you understand me?"

Jaida shook her head.

"A lawyer has to put everything he or—" he nodded toward her "—she has into a case. All your knowledge, all your skill will not necessarily be enough to win. You, the lawyer, are also a tool in trying a case. And you need to use every accessory you have when you're in front of a jury."

"You mean the lawyer is an influencer in his or her own right."

Penning nodded approvingly. "Exactly. Some lawyers are gifted with marvelously modulated voices, the mere sound of which has the jury following every word they utter. Others command by their stature, and still others by—"

"Their presence," she said softly, and he inclined his head in agreement. "I think I understand." And she did. She could only imagine the effect this man would have on a jury. The aura of power about him made him a commanding individual.

"What brings you to Boston, Miss Rhodes?"

"I've been living with my sister and her family, and they summer at the Cape," Jaida lied. "I enjoy following your cases in the newspapers." She thought she saw a glint appear in his eye for a moment, and then it was gone. She affected an ingenuous shrug. "It took me all summer to gather up the courage to approach you like this."

"I'm very glad you did," he murmured, his dark eyes revealing nothing. "Tell me, Miss Rhodes, which of my cases intrigued you the most?"

His question made her palms dampen, and she had to fight the urge to wipe them on her dress. She thanked God she'd thought to do a little homework before coming here. "I think I was most curious about the *State of Massachusetts v. Marcus Temple.*"

His eyebrows raised. "That case attracted much media attention. It was very complex." He leaned forward and placed his folded hands on his desk. "Earlier you mentioned being intrigued by my cases. Now you admit to being curious." At her silence, he chided, "Come, now, Gwen, don't be shy. I'm very interested in hearing what arouses your curiosity."

Jaida bit her lip, feigning consternation. "I feel silly questioning you, Mr. Penning. But it seemed as if you were more a focus of the case than was your client. All those motions and countermotions, claiming bias on the part of the judge. It seemed to draw attention away from the facts you were presenting."

He leaned back in his chair again, rocking a little. "Ah, but Miss Rhodes, it did set the stage for an appeal, should the jury have found my client guilty. Given the judge's bias, of course. I'm sure you'll be wonderfully inventive on behalf of your own clients, once you've had the proper training. Where do you intend to go to school?"

"Mississippi University." She nodded toward the diploma hanging on the wall next to his desk. "Harvard doesn't fit my budget, I'm afraid."

"Don't sell yourself short," he murmured, his eyes trailing over her face and wandering down her figure. "You may go much further than you think."

Jaida barely managed to contain a shudder. She suddenly wondered how much longer she could stand to be in the man's presence. He made her flesh crawl.

When he checked his watch again, Jaida stood up, eager to have a reason to leave. "I'm sorry—I've kept you late enough. And I need to get back to work."

"What is it you do?" he inquired, rising to round the desk toward her.

"Oh," she said, managing a little laugh. "I've been a nanny for my sister's two children for the past four years. They're precious, but wearing. Still, I will miss them when I leave to start school." He came to stand near her and she glanced up at him artlessly. "Do you have children, Mr. Penning?"

His smile never faltered. "Unfortunately, no. I'm not married."

He put his hand possessively on the small of her back to usher her to the door, and Jaida trembled in reaction. She'd spent a great deal of time over the years avoiding human touch and the bombardment of sensation it could elicit. It was a curious turn of events to try to direct her ability, to use it for her own purposes. But this man's presence was too strong to be denied. The sense of evil that surrounded him was like a noxious gas, and she almost wavered in her resolve.

"I'd be glad to help you with any other questions you might have," Penning was saying. "It's been a long time since I had your kind of . . . passion . . . for the law."

He halted her before opening the door from his office, and she used the opportunity to step away from his touch, turning to face him.

"Perhaps over dinner some night?"

Everything inside her rebelled at the idea. There was no need for further pretense; she had gotten all the answers she needed from this man. Now she just wanted to flee from his presence. "Maybe I can call you," she said. "My sister and I will be coming back to the city in two weeks. Although you may want to rescind your offer. My appetite is legendary in my family." He opened the door and Jaida forced herself not to run. The air in the outer office seemed fresher somehow, and she took a deep breath.

She lost it in the next instant. "Please do call," Penning said, his bottomless eyes searching hers. He grasped one of her hands in both of his in an action that should have seemed debonair. Instead, it was like being encased in ice. And then a roaring ensued in her ears, and she heard him say, as if from a great distance, "And don't you worry. I'm a man of rather... intense... appetites myself."

Chapter 6

Jaida's fingers were still shaking as she attempted to fit her card into her motel door. Frustrated, she tried again, but before she could turn the knob, the door opened inward, and she nearly fell into the room.

Trey grasped her by one wrist, drew her ungently over the threshold and slammed the door behind her.

"Don't!" She wrested her arm away and backed into the room, eyeing him warily. "Don't touch me." Her skin had flamed immediately under his touch. Coming so quickly upon the heels of her encounter with Penning, it was sensory overload, and she was incapable of taking much more.

"Would you mind telling me," he said through clenched teeth, "where the hell you've been?"

Jaida dropped her bag and sat down on the edge of her bed. Despite the time it had taken her to change and get back to the motel, she was still undeniably shaky. Drawing a deep breath, she said, "I went to see William Penning." She should have been terrified by the look of savagery that came over Trey's face at her words. But after her ordeal today, he could no longer elicit fear from her. She'd just found out about real terror, from a man who possessed no soul.

His voice was a measured whisper. "You . . . did . . . what?"

She met his gaze squarely. "We needed to know for sure whether Penning was involved in Benjy's disappearance. There was only one way to be certain. So I pretended to be a prelaw student interested in some of his cases . . ."

"Who just decided to jog over there?" he finished incredulously.

She blinked for a moment, then looked down at her brief black shorts, pink tank top and sneakers. "No, I rented a locker at the fitness center on the corner. That's where I changed. I thought if someone followed me, it would be easier to lose him if I was wearing something else and then slipped out the back. . . ." She summoned up a shaky half smile. "Your paranoia must be catching."

"Let me tell you about paranoia, lady," he rasped. "Paranoia would suggest to me that you had your own reasons for meeting with Penning. Like maybe you got some juicy information last night and you were too opportunistic to pass it up. Maybe you decided to cash it in by telling Penning where his wife is and that eighteen months ago he became a father."

"You can go straight to hell, Garrison!" Jaida said, her voice unsteady. She should have known that he would put his own spin on this, that he would credit her with the most malicious of motives. To have Trey continue to spout his suspicions of her was more than infuriating; it was downright hurtful. "I didn't go to see Penning because I get a kick out of sadistic, twisted men. I went to find out exactly what he knew about Benjy, and only I could find that out. Not you, not anyone else you have working on this case. Me."

"And exactly how did you do that, Swami?" he asked sarcastically. "Did Penning have a toy for you to handle so you could be visited by one of your brilliant insights?"

She was shaking with anger and with something else—residual fear and disgust from Penning's touch. "I don't need an object to handle when I have the person himself. All I have to do is touch someone. The way I did with you," she reminded him recklessly. "How else would I know that you've been Lauren's protector since the day she was born, and that you feel guilty because you were unable to provide for her, even though you were just a kid yourself? That you feel the same kind of guilt for Benjy's kidnapping. Or that your friend Mac owes you his life, and there was a time when he was the only person in the whole world you thought gave a damn about you.''

He didn't back away from her then, but his withdrawal was just as complete. He retreated into himself, shutting her out effectively, but not before she'd read his reaction to her words. She'd shocked him—that was certain—and Trey Garrison was a hard man to shock. It wasn't an emotion she'd wanted him to regard her with, although his carefully guarded expression was a sure sight better than the fascinated horror with which some people regarded her talents.

She turned away then, suddenly on the verge of tears. The effects of the day—and of each day since she'd met him—were hurtling her to the brink of hysteria, and she had to get her equilibrium back if she wanted to be of any use in the search for Benjy. She had never been one for parlor tricks, had never used her gift to amuse friends and impress others, but she would have given anything to be able to convince him, finally.

"Penning doesn't know," she said dully. "He has no idea where Lauren is. He hasn't a clue that Benjy even exists. And he wouldn't care about him if he did know," she continued in a haunted whisper. Tears filled her eyes. "He wouldn't care about his own son."

Trey surveyed her through narrowed eyes. She'd hit the nail square on the head with that statement. And how could she have known Penning's feelings about children? Either she had to be the best damn actress he'd seen outside of the movies, or she was telling the truth.

The truth. If he believed her, he'd have to believe in her... ability, for lack of a better word. And he was too much a pragmatist for that. Life had taught him not to put his faith in others, to depend solely on himself. There was very little he did believe in in this world, and the things he put his faith in tended to be things he could see and feel and touch. Not some hookie-pookie nonsense about ESP and reading minds and such.

And yet... how did he explain those pieces of his personal information that she kept coming up with? If he let himself believe that they came from some inexplicable psychic ability, she suddenly posed a far greater threat to him than he'd ever before faced. He'd started building a wall of defenses when he was a child. As an adult, it was damn near impenetrable. Imagining for even a moment that she could scale that wall with only a touch was more than eerie; it was damn near frightening.

That stuff about him and Mac—only a few knew about it. Just he, Lauren, Raine and Mac himself. His mind flashed back to the moment when she'd delivered those words about Lauren and him last night. Her eyes had been covered with a metallic sheen, the deep blue dimmed. And her voice had sounded as if it were coming from someone else.

He felt the hair on the back of his neck rise. "You'd better tell me the whole story," he said hoarsely.

"Later," she said, rubbing her arms. "After dinner." She was only barely hanging on to what remained of her control. She couldn't relive it now—not yet, at any rate. Not until she'd had a bit of time to recover from the psychic battering she'd taken that day.

At his frown she summoned up enough energy to glare back at him. "I haven't eaten all day, Attila, and I'm not exactly steady on my feet here. I'm going to take a shower and get dressed. You can take me to that restaurant downstairs." Not waiting for an answer, she turned and headed toward her bathroom. The sooner she could wash the feel of William Penning from her skin, the sooner she'd feel clean again.

Trey bent down and retrieved the bag she'd left lying on the floor. He pulled the blue dress out and held it up, surveying it. She'd obviously found time to go shopping. When he shook the bag upside down, matching blue shoes hit the carpet with muffled thumps. He thought about what she would look like in the dress, the color showcasing her pale hair and sapphire eyes. "You can wear this," he called after her, as she was about to close the door.

She turned her head to look over her shoulder. Just the sight of the dress in his hands sent an icy prickle down her spine. "Get rid of it," she ordered flatly. "I don't care what you do with it. I never want to see that dress again."

"Pardon me?" The waiter halted in the midst of Jaida's order and stared dumbly at her.

"The surf-and-turf," Jaida repeated patiently. "The largest order you have, please. A Chef's salad with both Ranch and Italian dressing, a baked potato, and...will there be fresh bread served with the meal?"

"Yes—yes, ma'am," the waiter stuttered, writing furiously. "There will be rolls."

She nodded in satisfaction and handed back the menu. "Excellent."

Trey watched the scene with a gleam in his eye. "You're going to eat every bite of that," he stated.

"Of course I am. Which means there won't be any for you, so be sure you order enough for yourself."

Raising one eyebrow, he did as he was told, and the waiter left them alone. Then he looked across the table at her. He would have much preferred seeing her in that bright-blue dress, but he'd done as she'd said and stuffed it, with the shoes, in the trash container. She'd changed into a maroon one-piece jumpsuit, made out of some soft, shiny material. In ordinary circumstances he would be prepared to fully enjoy himself. He was used to dating beautiful women, but Jaida was totally unlike any of those in his acquaintance. One couldn't call her beautiful, but she was striking, with that sheaf of startlingly blond hair and those dark-blue eyes with their intriguing gold flecks. "Do you wear contacts?" he asked abruptly.

She looked up, startled. "No. I have perfect vision."

Her words struck him oddly, and he was reminded again of the other "vision" she was expecting him to believe in. "How about your family? Your parents? Did you inherit your sight from them?"

She caught the nuance in his voice, the tinge of taunting, and stifled a sigh. "No, my mother doesn't share my gift." She gave him a brittle smile. "She thinks I'm a freak. Just as you do. As for my father, I never knew him. But something tells me that Bobby Earl West was a pretty simple country boy. His talents, I'm told, lay in other directions."

Her candid response had him feeling vaguely ashamed for the remark he'd made earlier. But not ashamed enough to change the subject. He wanted to know more about her, and he wanted to hear it from her. All at once he was interested in just what it was that made Jaida West tick. "You don't get along with your mother?" he asked carefully.

She considered the question. "We don't have anything in common," she corrected. "We don't think the same way, and we don't consider the same things important." Mary Lee—or Marilee, as she'd called herself for years—had shown interest in her daughter only sporadically. The one thing Jaida had ever done that had earned her approval was embarking on her concert tours. But once she'd decided to return to Granny's home and focus on songwriting, her mother's short-term attention had faded.

"It must have been difficult being a teenager with a mother who didn't understand you," he prodded.

"I lived with Granny for most of my life. We're kindred spirits," she said with a secret smile. She saw no reason to tell him about Granny Logan's gift, the one that had had her aware of Trey's imminent arrival a week before he'd shown up at the cabin.

"So what is your fee for the—" He seemed to search for the appropriate word. "Help . . . you provide? We never discussed it, but it should be settled before long."

Before long. She considered the words dully. He was taking care to be more diplomatic than usual, treating her to some of the practiced charm he was capable of. In fact, it wasn't much of a stretch to imagine that they were on a date, that he was taking care to entertain her, to draw her out about herself. He would do so with an accomplished finesse, while sharing little of himself. She wondered if his women ever realized how little he gave back in return.

The waiter put her salad down in front of her, and she picked up her fork and stabbed fiercely at the lettuce. This wasn't a date, and she wasn't one of his women. He was just soothing her nerves, waiting until the perfect time to broach his favorite subject—that of her return home. She'd do well to remember his agenda and to stick to her own. Because no matter how thick he laid on the charm, she wasn't boarding a plane back to Arkansas.

She answered his question belatedly. "I don't charge a fee. Just expenses."

He frowned. "What do you mean you don't charge a fee? How do you live?"

By dressing up in red and hanging out on the street corners, she wanted to tell him. He so clearly wished to hear something that would be in keeping with the picture he'd already drawn of her character. "I don't need the money. I have a job." She took a moment to savor his surprise before adding, "I'm a song-writer."

He didn't have to ask how lucrative her job was. She didn't exactly live in the lap of luxury. She must live with her grand-mother because she couldn't afford to live elsewhere. But if she didn't have money, why didn't she charge people for using her "ability" to help them? Or was that just a line to throw him off?

"Have you written anything I might have heard?" he asked.

Jaida studied him. Something told her that her soft-rock ballads of heartache and simple pleasures wouldn't be to his taste. "I don't know. What do you like to listen to when you're relaxing?"

"Classical pieces, usually. Some opera."

Opera. That figured. "Then I think it's safe to say you've probably never heard any of my songs," she said dryly. She could see what it was costing him to keep from asking the questions he really wanted answered, the ones dealing with her encounter with William Penning. But he was respecting her wishes for once. In fact, he was treating her almost cautiously.

The waiter came back then and cleared away their dishes to make room for the steaming entrées he then set in front of them. Trey seemed amused by the sidelong looks he sent Jai-da's way. "Johns Hopkins is currently studying her metabo-lism," he said in an undertone to the waiter. With one more glance in her direction, the man scurried away.

"Very funny." She wrinkled her nose at him but didn't let his words bother her. The day the pounds started to show up she supposed she'd need to make drastic changes in her eating habits. But right now she appeared to burn calories by merely breathing.

He was slow to begin on his own steak as he paused to watch her. It wasn't often he saw a woman eat as if she were really enjoying a meal. Most of his dates ate sparingly, ordering only enough to make it seem as though they were merely keeping him company while he dined. Watching Jaida eat was an experience. She did it with delicate precision and obvious pleasure.

"Are you going to eat that roll?" she asked him later, after they'd both finished, indicating the remaining roll in the basket. Shaking his head in bemusement, he watched her take it out and butter it.

"You could have ordered dessert," he reminded her.

"I almost did," she confessed. "But I wasn't sure how much money you brought with you, and I left my purse in the room."

He looked at the pile of empty dishes the waiter was clearing away from the table and swallowed. "Very thoughtful of you," he commented, his voice sounding strangled. Then he leaned forward in his chair. "Now, why don't you tell me all about your little outing today?"

She startled at his words. "I didn't know until last night why you seemed so disturbed when you found out that the motel I'd mentioned was near Boston. It was because of the proximity to Penning."

Trey inclined his head.

She gave a small shrug. "There's no telling how long it would take you and the police to determine whether he was involved in the kidnapping. So I decided that I would approach Penning myself." She swallowed, as much from the resulting memories as from the grim mask that had descended over Trey's face. "But first I did my homework. I remembered the health club on the corner, and I got a pass from the front desk to use it. I went shopping for something appropriate to wear to his office. Then I stashed my shorts and top in a locker at the club and changed into the new clothes. I took a taxi to the library and spent a while going over microfiche for any mention of Penning." She shrugged again. "I read about all the cases he's tried in the past three years and then I called the *Boston Globe* and talked to a reporter who had covered a couple of Penning's cases. He's the one who gave me some background about them. A good thing, too," she said, grimacing. "I think Penning would have been able to trip me up if I hadn't had some information."

Trey was surveying her through narrowed eyes. "Quite the little detective, weren't you?"

She ignored his sarcasm. Although it had been glaringly absent for the past hour, its reappearance warned her that she had reached the end of his civility. "I didn't see any other way," she said simply.

"And I'm supposed to believe you when you say Penning isn't involved."

"He isn't."

"You ask for a lot to be taken on trust, Jaida," he said in a low voice.

She shivered a little, caught in the beam of his forest-colored eyes. That was the first time he'd addressed her by her name, and there hadn't been a trace of sarcasm in his voice.

"And you don't trust anyone," she whispered. She closed her eyes in frustration. "I don't know how to make you understand." She'd never been a person comfortable with labels, but others tended to be soothed by them, so she gave him some. "I'm psychometric and clairvoyant. I can determine information about a person by handling an object belonging to him. I can also...sense things sometimes through human touch."

His eyes hooded. He'd witnessed that so-called sense of hers. It was definitely startling. But his inability to explain those random bits of personal information that she'd come up with didn't mean he was yet convinced of her gift. He found he didn't want to believe her. Everything inside him violently rejected the possibility that this woman could read him as easily as a road map. "How does that work?"

"It depends. I never know who will set it off or when. But often the most casual touch is enough for me to pick up thoughts or emotions from other people. Sometimes I can try to shield myself from receiving their transmissions, but I can't always control it. The knowledge is just there." And walking around with that shield firmly in place was almost as exhausting as the emotional battering she took without it. Which was ironic, given the ability of the man sitting across from her. He seemed to carry such a guard effortlessly, without cost. She could envy him such an ability.

He frowned, but only said carefully, "And you claim...you sensed some information from Penning."

"I had to try," she whispered, her mind revisiting the brief horror show she'd experienced that afternoon. "I just wanted to find out whether he knew about Benjy, but then he put his hands on me and . . ." She shuddered wildly in remembrance.

"And what?" Trey asked urgently. "Jaida, what happened in there?" He leaned across the table, his voice harsh. "He didn't hurt you, did he?"

"I learned all I wanted to the first time he touched me, but then he took my hand in both of his . . . and it was like crawling into a vat of slick ooze. I felt like I was suffocating." She shivered. Just talking about it renewed the vile experience. "He's sick," she murmured brokenly, "and he's evil, and he isn't capable of emotion. The things he's done . . ." A deep, pervasive cold had crept back into her limbs, and deep shudders racked her. "I saw him standing in a pool of blood. A man lay at his feet, dying. His blood was on Penning's shoes." She raised her gaze to Trey's, and her voice was filled with revulsion and loathing. "And William Penning didn't feel a thing."

Jaida sat huddled in a chair in her motel room, a blanket around her shoulders. Trey crossed the room and squatted in front of her. "Are you okay?" She still hadn't regained the color in her cheeks, but at least she looked a little more composed than she had in the dining room. There had been a moment when he'd been certain that he would need to carry her back to her room. Then she had practically bolted from the table, leaving him to hurriedly pay the bill before he could go after her. He'd caught up with her at the elevators and accompanied her upstairs. Then she'd sunk weakly into the chair, where she remained. He'd brought her the blanket she'd requested with that flat, lifeless tone that he was growing to hate. And then he'd watched helplessly as she'd endeavored to control the shudders that once again racked her body.

"Yes," she answered, reaching a hand to push the hair back off her face. "I'll be fine."

He noted with relief that the familiar drawl was back in her words. He watched her for a minute more, before asking, "Are you up to talking?"

She hesitated, and then nodded jerkily.

Trey rose and pulled another chair up close to hers. He sat down and faced her again, his expression grim. "You said when Penning touched you, you 'saw' a dead man lying at his feet."

Jaida swallowed hard. "Yes."

"Did you see the victim's face?" She shook her head.

"Where did this take place? How long ago was it?"

"I don't know," she said huskily. "There's no way for me to tell. But it was so strong . . ." Her voice tapered off to a whisper. "So real."

"When I first found Lauren again, it was pretty easy to see that she was terrified. But it wasn't until much later, once she was safe in L.A., that she finally told me what had her so scared. She'd already concluded that her husband was involved in some . . . unsavory dealings. But then one morning she found a stain on their white bedroom carpet, in front of his closet. She opened the doors and discovered a pair of shoes with matching stains. She said," he went on, gazing steadily into her eyes, "that she thought the stains looked like blood."

Jaida gasped and tried, unsuccessfully, to still the trembling of her lips. "When was that?"

Trey shrugged. "I don't know. Two and a half years ago, I guess. The pants he'd worn the night before, when he'd supposedly gone out on business, had matching marks on the cuffs."

"He killed a man," Jaida said shakily. "Or he had it done. And then he watched him die at his feet." She wrapped her arms closer around herself, trying vainly to get warm.

Trey continued softly, "That incident convinced Lauren she had to get away from her husband. She hid the clothing, determined to take it with her when she left. She hoped she would be able to use it later to put Penning away where he could never hurt anyone again."

Trey had the evidence Lauren had brought with her safely stored in a vault in his office. Tests had proven that Lauren's supposition was correct—the marks were bloodstains. So far, however, neither he nor Mac had been able to devise a way to use it to put Penning away. Lauren had had no idea who the victim might have been, and the bloodstained clothing, though damning, didn't prove her husband had been a party to murder.

Now Jaida West professed to have witnessed the murder scene through her psychic senses.

"Oh, God," she whispered, "Lauren is so lucky you found her. William Penning is capable of anything. Anything."

"Except having his own son kidnapped?" he prodded, watching her reaction.

"He didn't order that," she said with quiet certainty. "He doesn't know about him, and he has no idea where Lauren is." The events of the day had drained her, and exhaustion was threatening. She looked up at Trey. "I'm not getting on a plane for Arkansas tomorrow," she said with quiet determination. "You can fly back to L.A. or continue here on your own. I don't care. But I'm leaving in the morning, with or without you."

He was silent for a long time before asking, "What are you planning to do?"

"I'm going to do whatever it takes. The question is, what are *you* going to do?"

Her words hung in the air, taunting him. Yeah, that was the sixty-four-thousand-dollar question. What the hell was he going to do next? He'd spent a lifetime cultivating his iron control, learning patience. His rational mind demanded he return to L.A. There he could at least see to Lauren's safety while he waited for the authorities to solve Benjy's kidnapping.

But he found he was no longer able to dismiss the inexplicable accuracy of Jaida's words. He couldn't deny the pressing need to explore the extent of her ability if there was even the slimmest possibility she could lead him to his nephew.

"What am I going to do?" he repeated. "Well, that's real easy, honey. I'm going with you."

Chapter 7

Jaida sat on the edge of the bed. She could hear Trey moving about in his room. She didn't have much time before he'd be knocking impatiently at her door. She got up and walked to her suitcase. Reaching down, she withdrew a small canvas bag and carried it back to the bed with her.

She shook out the bag's single content. Benjy's stuffed elephant looked incongruous against the elegant bedspread, which had been carefully selected to match the wallpaper and draperies. Her hand reached for the toy, hovered for a moment, before she pulled it back.

It was always difficult to drop her defenses and voluntarily undergo such an experience. She was never sure exactly what she was opening herself up for.

The stuffed animal seemed to grin up at her, inviting her touch. Nervously she pushed her hair back over her shoulder, chewing her lip, trying to screw up her courage. She was already far too caught up in this case, too close to the parties involved. What would she do if she saw Benjy hurt, suffering? Or worse?

With a little gasp, she bounced off the bed and paced halfway across the room, wrapping her arms around her waist.

There had been other times when the scenes she saw in her mind were full of heartache, horror and death. She didn't think she could stand it if this was one of those times. What could be more horrible than knowing a young child was a victim to some terrible suffering?

She closed her eyes in anguish. What could be more horrible than *not* knowing?

Taking a deep breath, she turned to approach the bed with leaden limbs. Sinking down next to the toy, she forced herself to pick it up.

She cradled it in her hands, her thumbs moving over the frivolous corduroy material of its overalls. The texture abraded her skin lightly, pleasantly. She waited for the visions to come of the little boy who had loved it, who might even now be missing it, feeling lost, feeling . . .

Cold. It crawled over her skin and down her spine, encasing her with icy fingers. It sank into her bones and turned her blood to glacier-fed streams. She started to shake, so violently it seemed as though something inside her should crack and splinter. The vision swept into her mind with a rush, then ebbed to part like a giant filmy curtain.

Benjy sat on the beach, both chubby fists full of sand, throwing his hands up and releasing it. The sand felt hot and gritty as he filled his hands again and threw it wildly. The sound of the ocean pounding the shore was nearby, and miles of beach stretched in all directions. A man's voice sliced through the scene, startling the boy as he bent to scoop up more sand. "I said stop it!" He delivered a stinging slap to Benjy's cheek, and tears welled up in the boy's dark-green eyes, and his poignant yearning, momentarily waylaid, came flooding back . . .

Giving a strangled gasp, Jaida bent over at the waist and opened her eyes, putting an end to the vision. Tiny hammers inside her temples kept the throbbing climbing in intensity with each passing second. She dropped weakly, full-length on the bed, grasping the elegant bedspread and rolling up in it. She curled up as best she could, a cocoon of pain, trying, without too much success, to bring her body under control again.

That was how Trey found her seconds, or minutes, later. When she reluctantly opened her eyes again, his face was swimming above hers.

"What can I do?"

"A pill." Her teeth were chattering, her whole body still quaking. "In my purse."

He was a man used to dealing with emergencies, she thought fuzzily. He obeyed her immediately, not asking unnecessary questions. Then a tablet and a glass of water were in front of her.

Her fingers were thick and clumsy as she endeavored to pick up the tablet without touching him. His body heat seared up from his palm and she thought wildly that if he wrapped his arms around her right now, he'd melt the glacier encasing her, turning the ice into clouds of hissing steam. She swallowed the pill and fell back to the bed, edging way from him.

She shouldn't be surprised that it was in his nature to be patient. He was totally still now, waiting for a sign from her. As the time stretched between them, the medication worked its magic, sending the pain to a distant chamber, where it would remain, steady but tolerable. Two tablets would have been better. They would have pulled her deeper and deeper into a vortex where blissful unconsciousness beckoned. But she couldn't afford the luxury of sleep now—time was growing too short.

Jaida wasn't sure how long she lay there, waiting out the physical reaction that had accompanied the vision. Trey sat next to the bed, watching her, his green eyes shadowed. He was holding Benjy's stuffed elephant in his big hands.

But then he spoke, reminding her his patience was finite. "You tried it again, didn't you? Using this." He indicated the toy he held. At her jerky nod he asked reluctantly, "What did you . . . see?"

She sat up, and her voice was rusty when she answered. "He's on the beach. Somewhere near the ocean."

He waited, but when she didn't go on, he prodded, "That's all? He's by *some* ocean, on *some* beach? That's the lead you want us to follow?"

She fought her arms free of her self-made cocoon and sat up to face him. She needed to be at her best when she did battle with Trey. "That's the lead I'm following. You can do whatever you wish." She unrolled herself from the blanket and looked at the toy he still held. "You'd better put that back in the bag." She nodded toward the canvas tote she'd taken it from. "We'll probably need it."

"Why?" he asked, his sarcasm biting. "Are you planning to go into one of your trances every hundred miles or so?"

"No," she replied, the word reverberating in her pounding head. "I'm planning to put it into Benjy's arms when we find him again."

The cool breeze kissed her face and the sun sent dancing rays of light across Jaida's tinted sunglasses. She leaned her head back and smiled, smug at winning this latest skirmish with Trey. He'd been opposed to renting a convertible, but, she'd argued, if they were going to investigate the coastal areas with beaches, they might as well enjoy the view. He'd given in gracelessly, but at least his ill-temper was a genuine emotion. She'd take that over his phony charm any day.

"So, let me get this straight." His voice was a frustrated rasp. "We're just going to hunt beaches? Any particular direction in mind, or should I just circle aimlessly?"

"South," Jaida answered. "They've left the immediate area." She was unable to explain to him how she knew that for a certainty, but the feeling was too strong to ignore. "We'll need to focus on the public beaches."

"Why?" he challenged her. "What makes you think Benjy isn't at some posh resort on the Cape? Or on a beach at any one of hundreds of private homes? For that matter, what makes you think he's still in the state?"

"From their last selection of a motel, it didn't exactly look like the kidnappers were spending money lavishly. So that rules out resorts and expensive beachfront property. And I don't know whether they've left the state."

He waited, but when she said nothing else, he snapped, "Massachusetts alone has almost two hundred miles of coastline. You couldn't narrow it down a little, could you?"

"No," she replied honestly, "I can't. All I can do is follow my instincts, and my instincts say to head south."

"And will your *instincts*—" he gave the word a sardonic inflection "—also tell us where to stop, or will we drive right by my nephew on our scenic tour?"

"I'll know the place when we get there," Jaida said. "I'll be able to feel it."

He muttered something that sounded suspiciously like a curse. "Well, I'm feeling something already, and we've just started driving."

"At least you're *feeling*, Trey." Jaida smiled serenely and looked at the scenery whizzing by. "Somehow I think that's rather new for you."

He glanced at her sharply, but her attention remained on the sights they were passing. Her pithy remarks were starting to make him edgy. *She* was starting to make him edgy. There was a distinct disadvantage in the feeling that she was somehow able to guess more about him than he knew about her.

"Were you born and raised in Arkansas?" he asked abruptly.

"I was born in New York City," came her surprising answer.

He waited, but she didn't elaborate. That was new for her. Usually she was full of conversation. But now, when he wanted information, she wasn't offering any. He decided the woman had a patent on obstinance.

"How long did you live there?" he prodded.

She yawned. The sunshine and fresh air were not as invigorating as the twelve-hour nap her body craved after summoning another vision. She wondered how long they would have to travel before he'd stop so she could eat. "Long enough for my parents to split up and for my mother to dump me on Granny for the first time. About three months."

"You've lived with your grandmother since you were three months old?"

He sounded interested, and a little appalled. She cast him a sidelong glance. It was unusual for him to make idle conversation. Which meant he was after something, although she couldn't imagine why he'd be seeking information on her. An idea occurred to her then, and she deliberately turned away without answering.

She waited several moments, then heard him say impatiently, "Well?"

Grinning to herself, she replied, "I'll make you a deal, Trey." She paused a heartbeat. "For every question I answer of yours, you'll answer one of mine."

He didn't like the suggestion. She could read that, despite the dark-framed sunglasses he was wearing.

"What kind of questions?" His voice was filled with reluctance.

She lifted a shoulder lazily. "No conditions. And no lying," she added swiftly. "You . . . we . . . have to answer truthfully."

He was silent for so long she thought he'd reverted to his earlier taciturn manner.

Then he said, "Why didn't your mother raise you?"

Jaida gave a sigh and settled back into her seat. He had a lot to learn about following rules. But they had miles ahead of them in which she could teach him the rudiments.

"You're not going to answer?"

"It's my turn to ask you a question," she responded patiently. "Remember?"

"But I asked you before . . . Ah, damn," he sputtered out frustratedly. "What do you want to ask?"

Better start out with something easy, she thought. He really wasn't much for reciprocal arrangements. Smooth coercion was much more his style, or outright demands. And finding himself thwarted hadn't done much for his mood.

"Where did you and Lauren grow up?"

"Kansas City. Now tell me why your mother let your grandmother raise you."

It was easy to see that his capitulation was merely to further his own end. He was as tenacious as a pit bull when it came to getting what he wanted. "She was only eighteen, and her husband had deserted her. She had nowhere to go, no money and no way to get a job and care for me at the same time. Not," she added wryly, "that caring for me was high on her list. Anyway, she called Granny, who wired her money, and she went back home. But it wasn't long before she started looking for a way out again. She'd spent her whole life dreaming of leaving Dixon Falls. She wasn't about to let a baby put an end to her aspirations."

"So she dumped you and took off again?"

"Ah-ah-ah, Garrison. That's two questions. It's my turn again. Do you have any other family?"

"No. What happened to you when your mother took off again?"

Jaida paused to consider the inequities in their answers. His were unsatisfyingly brief, to the point of rudeness. The trick seemed to be in the way their questions were worded, but she was annoyed nonetheless.

"I was left with my grandmother while my mother went to Savannah to find work. I joined her occasionally over the years, in Savannah, Mobile, wherever she was calling home at the time. Things never worked out." That was the understatement of the world, Jaida thought. She'd spent her first few years wishing fiercely for her mother to send for her, not for a visit, but to live with her for good. And then later, when it became clear just how Marilee felt about her, Jaida had wished just as fiercely to stay with Granny forever.

"What were your parents like?" She asked the question after a great deal of thought, attempting to word it in a way that would prevent a monosyllabic answer. But the silence that followed was filled with tension. She turned to look at him, puzzled.

A grim smile played across his lips. It hadn't taken her long to catch on to the little game, and somehow she'd managed to stumble onto his least favorite subject. "My mother was...fragile," he answered with irony.

Weak. That was the word to describe Patricia Garrison. Too weak to stand up to her husband, to protect herself or her children. Trey had taken many a beating trying to intervene on her behalf. She'd been too weak to stay alive long enough to be any kind of mother. The only thing she'd ever done for Trey was give him Lauren. And when Patricia Garrison died, he'd eventually even lost his sister. "My father...used his hands a lot." He turned off the old memories. "Hand me the map, will you?"

Jaida obeyed, and he folded it so he could hold it before him on the steering wheel to study it. "We're getting close to Scusset State Beach. Does that sound familiar at all to you?"

"It doesn't matter if it *sounds* familiar," she retorted. "It will have to *feel* familiar. And I won't know until we get there. I've told you that before."

He started to hand the map back to her and almost lost it in the wind. Involuntarily Jaida leaned over to catch it, and found her fingers touching his. The now-familiar current sparked to life at the inadvertent touch and then a scene flashed into her mind, so quick and ugly that she caught her breath. It vanished as suddenly as it had come, swirling away like mists of fog.

She refolded the map with trembling fingers. She had to be more careful. She couldn't afford to touch him, even by accident. Each time set off too many disturbing reactions, on too many levels.

My father used his hands a lot. She shivered, still responding to the short violent scene she'd experienced at their brief brushing of hands. An interesting way to describe a man who had used his fists on his family and drunk with indiscriminate fervor.

The inadvertent peek into his past left her with the need to reassure him. "Benjy is still okay," she told him softly. "He hasn't been ..." *Hurt,* she was going to say, and then stopped when she remembered the stinging slap to the toddler's cheek. She bit her lip. She would never relay that information to Trey, especially in light of what she'd just learned about him.

"He's safe. They have plans for him, though. This wasn't a random snatching."

Her words snared his attention. "Why do you say that?"

"You said Lauren was drugged so that the kidnappers could grab Benjy. People don't normally just walk around armed with drug-filled syringes in their pockets. The kidnappers were prepared to snatch him that day."

"Yes, but that still doesn't mean that Benjy had been singled out. A sicko could have gone to the park that day with the intention of picking out a child, any child. There's no way to be certain whether he'd been specifically targeted."

"Oh, he was specifically targeted," she said. "I don't know how, but I *know* it."

"But if you're right, and Penning isn't involved ..." he started, dubiously.

"He isn't," she said surely. She shivered suddenly. "I'm certain he isn't."

"Then we're still no closer to the answer than we were before. Benjy could have become the target once the kidnapper saw him. He's a cute little guy..." There was a pause, and when he continued, Trey's voice was gruff. "There are any number of reasons someone would pick him out of a crowd if he was looking for a kid."

Habit had him dodging the emotions that threatened to well up and choke him. He'd come a long way from the explosive teenager he'd been to the man he was today. In humid jungles and searing deserts he'd learned to practice patience, to be as still as his surroundings while waiting for his prey. His stint in the army had seemed peculiarly suited to his nature. A childhood spent growing up on the streets had taught him survival skills and cunning, natural tools for the work he'd done in covert operations. There had been a time when he'd wondered if he would be suited for anything else.

But something had irrevocably changed inside him the day he'd dragged Mac from that bombed hotel, sure that his friend was dying at his feet. He'd started to envision himself suffering such a fate, half a world away from the only family he had in the world. He'd kept his past tightly sealed away, rarely allowing himself to think about it. But once he allowed the vault door of those memories to crack open, their power was impossible to deny.

Once Mac had left the military, it really hadn't taken much to coax Trey into joining him in his security company. It had presented Trey with the opportunity to search for the only family he had left.

It had taken him better than two years, but when he'd found Lauren again, a part deep inside him, a part he would have thought was dead, had come back to life. And Benjy's birth had nurtured that element. He couldn't bear to think that Benjy had entered their lives, only to be snatched away so quickly, so completely.

He glanced at the woman next to him, who was quietly humming along with the radio. Anyone seeing the two of them would think they were just another vacationing couple. They'd never guess the desperation behind their search. Or the tenuous hold Jaida was exerting over him, despite every effort he made to fight it.

The fragile bond of hope.

* * *

"I trust I didn't rush you." Trey's voice was a little too po-lite when Jaida finally strolled out of the truck stop, carrying a grocery bag.

"Not at all," she answered airily. "While you were getting gas and checking the map again, I had time to grab a sandwich and a few things for us to munch on."

He eyed the stuffed bag before pulling out of the truck-stop parking lot. "A few things?"

Jaida rummaged through the sack. "I convinced them to make you a hot roast beef to go." She held it out to him.

He took it from her, peeling the wrapping back and eating with one hand while he drove with the other. He made short work of the sandwich, then reached for the soda she'd put in the container holder next to him. After a few minutes he glanced over at her. "What else do you have in that bag?"

Jaida peered inside it, drawing out one item after another. "Cheese popcorn, pretzels, red licorice and a couple packages of sandwich cookies."

"I see you're not concerned with the current low-fat craze."

"Not really," she replied, opening the bag of licorice and selecting some. She offered the bag to him, and he shook his head. "My mother thinks my appetite is quite unladylike. I guess she thinks I should hide in a corner to eat when I'm hun-gry."

"You'd have to spend most of your time there," Trey ob-served blandly. He held out his hand. "Give me a few cookies, will you?" He watched with sharp interest the way she opened the package and held it out to him, rather than take some cookies out to drop in his hand. It could have been fastidious-ness on her part, but he didn't think so. Jaida seemed to go to extreme lengths to avoid touching people, although he might not have noticed it if he hadn't been watching her so closely in the past few days.

As a matter of fact, he tried to recall whether he had ever seen her touch someone voluntarily, and couldn't recall that he had. He vividly remembered the times she'd been unable to avoid *his* touch, however. The shocking connection that had leaped to life each of those times was fascinating and hard to forget. An unbidden thought flashed across his mind then, and he wondered if the current would fade or intensify under a more intimate touch.

"Where does your mother live now?" he asked a few miles later.

"She lives in New Orleans with her fifth or is it sixth," she wondered aloud, "husband."

"Do you visit her frequently?"

She cast him an amused look. Was he resurrecting their "game" from this morning or merely bored? "As infrequently as possible, at her request. I'm a major source of embarrassment to Marilee, you see."

"Embarrassment?" His tone was sharp. He well knew that all mothers weren't blessed with a nurturing instinct, but the thought that Jaida had been as unwanted as he and Lauren had been was curiously disturbing.

"I did the unacceptable and grew up. It became very hard to explain to her high-society friends and potential husbands that she had a daughter only a few years younger than she was pretending to be." She shrugged. Her mother's shallowness had long ceased to be a source of pain for her. "The best thing she ever did was let Granny raise me. I had a normal childhood, as normal as possible. The worst times I remember are the experiences when I did live with Marilee, or went for a prolonged visit."

"Why, what happened then?"

Jaida paused to rip open the bag of cheese popcorn. "I wasn't the easiest child to have around. Even when she could keep me cleaned up long enough to introduce to her friends, I had an unfortunate penchant for blurting out personal remarks about them after shaking their hands." She smiled in vague amusement as she remembered a few of the choice tidbits that had transferred to her at a casual touch. She'd been too young to guard her tongue and too naive to realize the embarrassing nature of some of the information she'd blurted out— information that ranged from the price of a woman's dress to an indiscreet disclosure of a lover's name. She shook her head in silent sympathy for the young, confused girl she'd been. It had been a painful period in her life; she'd tried as hard as she could to fit in and be the kind of daughter that Marilee would be proud of, one she would finally love.

A fierce scowl came over Trey's face. A picture was forming in his mind of Jaida's childhood, and he didn't like what he was hearing. In a perfect world children should be protected, sheltered and loved. He knew better than most that the world some children lived in was far from perfect. He never would have dreamed that he had an idealistic side to him, but Benjy's birth had shown him otherwise. He'd vowed that his nephew would grow up never knowing what it meant to be hungry, afraid or unwanted. It should mean nothing to him that Jaida West had grown up with problems. Problems were, after all, what people were best at manufacturing. But the realization was troubling nonetheless.

He glanced at her then, but her revelations hadn't seemed to upset her. She was lounging next to him, with her feet up on the dash in front of her, her head tilted back to catch the breeze. She'd braided her long hair into a loose plait that reached below her shoulders, to keep it from becoming tangled in the wind. He decided swiftly that he didn't like the style. It might be practical, but he would much prefer her hair tumbling in disarray around her shoulders or whipping past her profile at the capricious mercy of the wind.

He returned his attention to the road, irritated at his mental wanderings. Jaida West was only a tool in the search for Benjy, and he'd do well to remember that. No useful purpose would be served by learning more about her or by beginning to understand her.

And there was no purpose at all in wanting her.

"Don't be such a grouch," Jaida snapped hours later as she struggled to get her luggage out of the trunk. "I was ready to stop hours ago. You're the one who insisted on driving farther."

Trey slammed down the trunk lid with barely restrained force. "I thought that the point of this little excursion was to drive until you *felt* something." His voice was mocking. "I'm beginning to believe that the only thing you're capable of feeling is constant hunger and the overwhelming urge to drive me crazy."

"Now, that would be a short trip," she muttered. She went only a few steps before she stumbled over the uneven pavement. "You refused to stop while it was still daylight. Is it too much to ask that you find a motel with a better lit parking lot?"

"You're lucky I found us a room at all," he grunted, his long legs striding past her. He was holding a flashlight, so he wasn't having trouble finding his way. "You never thought of the fact that we're traveling down the coast during the height of tourist season. Maybe the next time you go into one of your trances, you can make us some reservations."

She made a face at his back, her childish reaction lost in the darkness. She followed almost blindly in his path as he led her past the string of motel rooms and down a hill. Something furry ran in front of her, and she shrieked lightly.

"What?" Trey barked.

"You aren't by any chance planning a camping trip for us, are you? Because I'll tell you right now, I'm not real fond of sharing my bed with wildlife."

"Oh, you'll get a roof over your head," he promised. "Here we are. This must be it."

Trey played his light over the front of a rustic cabin that had obviously seen better days. She had a feeling that darkness did a small kindness to the cabin's appearance. "This is it?" she asked dubiously.

"This is all the motel had. Apparently there used to be a string of these, but the rest of them were torn down as they added rooms to the newer complex. This one was left because it was in the best shape." At least, that's what he'd been told by the motel clerk. He put the key in the lock and pushed the door open, reaching in to flip on the lights.

The room would be suitable. The dim lighting didn't reveal anything that crawled or flew, and that was always a bonus. He'd slept in far worse, of course, but in his time out of the military he'd quickly grown accustomed to more luxurious surroundings. He was tired enough right now, however, not to care overmuch about the amenities.

Jaida followed him to the doorway and peered into the room. It looked clean, although it was apparent no one had used it in a while. There was an old-fashioned dial telephone sitting on a small desk, but no television or radio. "It has running water, doesn't it?" she asked suspiciously.

Trey walked into the room and opened a door. "Right in here."

"Okay, this is fine, then," she said. A nice warm shower would be all she needed to fall asleep almost immediately. She had no doubt that they'd be back on the road at daybreak. "Where will you be staying?"

"Oh, I'll be close by," he drawled. "As a matter of fact, I'll be sleeping right beside you."

Chapter 8

Surely her ears had deceived her. Jaida looked at him, blinked, then swallowed hard. Her heart responded by accelerating its rhythm. "You mean ... you have a room in the motel?" she asked hopefully.

Trey crossed over to the suitcase he'd dropped by the door, and slung it onto a bed. Clicking open the locks, he replied, "No, I mean here. In this bed."

It was impossible to miss the taunting gleam in his eyes. "Is that going to be a problem?"

Spending the night with Trey Garrison? It didn't qualify as a problem, exactly. Calamity came closer to describing it. Disaster. Or plain, old-fashioned catastrophe. "No." Her voice squeaked, and she cleared her throat, hastening to add, "No problem."

A faint smile crossed his lips and he turned back to his suitcase. "Good. Because there's not another place within thirty miles and I'm not in the mood for arguing. I haven't had a lot of sleep in the past few nights, and I'm beat."

"Yes. Well ..." Her voice tapered off, and she just stared at him. He was making himself at home already, taking his shaving kit out of his suitcase and pulling his shirt free from his pants. What was the protocol in a situation like this? Her experience was depressingly limited. "Would you...do you want to use the bathroom first?"

He shook his head. "Go ahead. I have some phone calls to make." He walked over to the phone, his back to her, and started dialing.

Jaida stared hard at him. Already he seemed to have forgotten her. She had a feeling it was going to be a bit harder for her to forget *his* presence, however. He seemed to fill the room, to command it. Her imagination had the walls shrinking in even further on the two of them, until she found it difficult to breathe. She forced herself to turn away and moved jerkily to her own suitcase, giving him a wide berth. He didn't even glance up from his conversation. His call had gone through, and it sounded as if he had Mac on the line.

Why, oh why, did this have to happen to her? The first time she shared a room with a man, it was forced by circumstances and the man had to be Trey Garrison? Did she live under some kind of bad karma, or what? She grabbed her nightgown and overnight bag and almost ran to the bathroom. She shut the door and found that it didn't have a lock. She leaned against it weakly. What possible difference would a lock make, after all? Trey wasn't about to come in here and join her; the man thought she was half nuts at best. Maybe, she thought, moving to the sink and looking at her reflection with wide eyes, maybe it wasn't Trey she was so nervous about. Maybe it was herself.

She reacted to his touch in more than the usual way. That in itself was enough to keep her wary of him, at the same time causing some very forbidden thoughts to arise. What would it be like to be touched by him in more than a casual manner? Would she respond each time with involuntary peeks at old wounds from his past, or would that unfamiliar current between them strengthen in voltage?

She watched a flush crawl up her cheeks and turned away from the mirror, stripping with jerky movements. She was unaccustomed to such erotic thoughts about a man, but she'd been off kilter since Trey Garrison had stalked into her life. She adjusted the temperature of the water and stepped into the shower. It didn't provide the relaxation she'd hoped for. The thought of sharing the bedroom with Trey kept her muscles tight, her nerves jumping.

Jaida took as long in the bathroom as she dared, spending so long that her hair was half dry. She was hoping that Trey would have his phone calls completed and be ready to take his place in the shower. Unfortunately, she hadn't brought a robe with her, but her nightgown was hardly daring, and he'd seen her in it before. It hadn't, she thought dryly, enflamed him to passion then, and there was no reason for her to feel so uneasy about wearing it before him now.

When she opened the door, she took two steps into the other room before stopping cold. Trey was just hanging up the phone, and in the next moment he unbuttoned his shirt, stripped it off and tossed it casually over to his bed. Jaida swallowed hard as her gaze took in the way his muscles played across his back. Then he turned his head, catching her staring at him.

"Did you use up all the warm water?" he asked.

She tore her gaze away from him and shook her head. Going toward her bed, she busied herself with putting her things back into her suitcase. "Did you finish your phone calls?" she asked, trying for a disinterested tone. At his silence she looked up, which was a mistake. A very serious mistake. Her eyes went immediately to his bare chest. She stopped breathing.

His torso was lightly padded with muscles and bisected with neat patches of dark hair. His arms were roped with strength, a strength that was belied by the fluid, stalking way he had of moving. She watched in fascination as his muscles flexed and released as he walked toward her.

"I was talking to Mac. He's wondering just how long this chase down the seaboard is going to take. I had to tell him that I've been wondering the same thing."

She strove to concentrate on his words. "I've told you . . ." Her voice was husky. "I won't know the place until we get there. I don't know what you want from me."

One corner of his mouth tilted. What he wanted from her. The answer to that was becoming more and more complex. "What I want is what I've always wanted," he murmured. He smelled the fragrant shampoo she'd used on her hair, and his nostrils flared in immediate masculine appreciation. "I want to know where this will end. I want to know whether you can help find Benjy."

She realized that she'd reached a milestone with him. He was gradually, grudgingly, beginning to trust her ability, at least on some level. But her logic seemed relegated to a distant corner of her mind. He was much too close. She continued to edge away from him, as carefully as she would having encountered a panther. That was what he most resembled, she thought a little wildly. All sleek muscles and tensile strength, luring its prey to complacency by its stillness.

She felt the wall against her shoulders. He appeared just as close to her as before, although she couldn't recall him having moved. And there was no room for retreat. "You'll just have to wait," she said, attempting to pick up the thread of their conversation. "We both will." Her voice tapered off as her attention wandered to the hollows of his shoulders. The skin stretched across them tautly, a silent invitation to explore.

His eyelids drooped. The shower had washed away her light makeup, and her skin appeared translucent. The neckline of the gown was demure, but the satiny material made it impossible to hide the fact that she wasn't wearing a bra. Her wet hair had left moist paths on the gown, and one arrowed across her breast, over the nipple, and disappeared. He was dimly aware that he was about to make a mistake. A huge one. And Trey Garrison prided himself on not making mistakes.

"Do you know what else I want?" he asked in a low voice. Her startled gaze flew to meet his, and he noted with satisfaction that her emotions were remarkably easy to read. He leaned toward her, and she jerked wildly, but his face moved past hers to the pale hair streaming over her shoulders. He inhaled and drew back a little. "I want you to tell me something, Jaida." He paused, sidetracked, watching as her lips parted and she moistened them with the tip of her tongue. Her scent was fresh, sweet and intriguing. Just like her. "Tell me what happens to you when you touch me."

She shook her head, not able to answer.

A slow smile crossed his lips. He already knew, even without her words. Hadn't he experienced the same thing since he'd met her? "I'll tell you what happens to me," he offered huskily. "Little currents of electricity jump under my skin every time we touch. You feel it, too, don't you?"

His words sent a flutter of excitement through her. He felt it, too. She'd thought he did, but he was so difficult to read she hadn't been sure. The knowledge was heady and terrifying at the same time. It was gratifying to know the unusual response wasn't one-sided. It was the implications of that certainty that had her pulse pounding, her stomach jumping.

She was very still, staring at him. He found himself hypnotized by the delicate gold flecks in her blue orbs. "I think you do," he murmured. "I think you felt it the first time I touched you, in the meadow. And you know what else?" He raised his hands to rest them against the wall on either side of her face, caging her effectively. "I think it frightens you."

"I wasn't frightened," she lied weakly. A show of fear would be a mistake with this man; she knew it intuitively. And how many times had other men taken her carefully acquired caution as an invitation? Some just couldn't seem to resist the chase.

That husky voice came again. "I think you were. Still are. Startled and afraid. Why is that, Jaida? Because it's the reaction you're used to avoiding? Or because you've never felt it before?"

His lips brushed her bare shoulder and she began to tremble, as much in response to the accuracy of his guess as at the intimate gesture.

"Tell me, Jaida," he whispered.

His mouth moved until it was a fraction from hers, and all her attention focused on his lips. She watched fatalistically as they drew closer to hers.

She couldn't deny having wondered what would happen if she got this close to Trey Garrison. But she was afraid she already knew. She longed for the same things from life that most people did—someone to love, someone to love her back. The nature of her ability had always precluded physical intimacy. The most innocent of touches could bring flashes of visions, but if she concentrated, she could often block those. An embrace was different. Too many emotions were emanated, buffeting and overwhelming her. She'd never felt real desire; she'd never been allowed to. Her senses were overtaken by the man's thoughts and responses, and those hadn't always been particularly flattering. Intimacy seemed to intensify her ability to an unbearable pitch. In her frantic haste to escape the psychic onslaught, she'd never failed to embarrass herself.

But this time might be different, a tiny voice inside cried. *He might be different.*

"I want to hear you admit it," he said in a low, rough whisper. "You don't react that way when anybody else touches you, do you?"

He was so close his words caressed her cheek. Her eyes fluttered shut as he dropped a kiss, feather light, on her mouth. She tensed, waiting for the familiar, inevitable response. It didn't appear, and her breath came out in a little sigh, mingling with his. When nothing else happened, she opened weighted eyelids to see him watching her. The message in those dark-green eyes was impossible to misconstrue.

Her answer came softly, hesitantly, without conscious volition. "No."

He was amazingly easy to read now, for once. Satisfaction was stamped on his hard features. "Touch me now," he demanded in a low, rough whisper. It was a dare, intimately appealing and so very tempting. "Do it, Jaida."

She shook her head fiercely, as much to clear away the fog that seemed to have settled into her brain as to refuse him. His lips went to her throat, and searing heat was pressed against the pulse that beat with rapid rhythm there. He was holding himself away from her by his arms braced on the walls, touching her only with his mouth. Yet her captivation was as total as if he held her in a complete embrace. A necklace of kisses was strewn lightly and deliberately across her throat, and then his mouth made its way back to hers, hovering above her lips.

"Jaida." His whisper was intense.

His lips came down on hers then and sent the ground careening away under her feet. There was an almost studied sensuality to his openmouthed kiss, one she recognized immediately. She'd known from the beginning that he was a master at coercion. Yet even as she sensed his practiced finesse, her knees weakened alarmingly. She'd spent her life eluding touch. It didn't make sense that she should, contrarily, crave it so much. The kiss of this man, above all others, was something she'd wondered about, dreamed of.

Even as she attempted to turn away from him, his lips followed hers, changing the angle of their kiss. Something else was different, too, something that sent flutters of desire humming through her veins. Closer. He was nearer than before. Only a whisper of space separated their bodies. His hands bracketed her face, creating a warm human cage. His body heat warmed hers. His lips pressed hers apart, and she tasted a measure of desperation. He wasn't teasing, wasn't pretending, and she detected the exact moment he lost his famed control. He made a sound low in his throat and the bottom dropped out of her stomach. His tongue pressed into her mouth, and all hints of finesse disappeared. Where he had coaxed before, now he demanded. His genuine desire was too enticing to ignore. She kissed him back, going on tiptoe to get closer, to make demands of her own.

The first taste of her response was heady, and his hands left the wall to cup her face, to hold her mouth steady under his. He savored the now-familiar sensation of electricity prickling between his skin and hers. She could try to hide her reactions to him, but she could never hide this. He drew her hands, hesitant and resistant, around his neck. And then he pressed closer, until her smaller, frailer body was trapped between the wall and the muscled planes of his chest.

Heat. His skin felt unbearably hot against hers, searing her sensitized skin. Her mouth twisted under his, and her shy, untutored response only seemed to feed his hunger. Her fingers clasped around his neck, before threading through his dark, crisp hair. She'd been afraid that to be this close to him would bring on sharper, more intense visions than ever before. But instead, the responses ran together in a brilliant kaleidoscope of sensation—the sweeping, dizzying hunger of his kiss, overwhelming in its complexity; the current that ran between them everywhere they touched; and the undeniably sweet reality of being wanted by this man.

She felt bereft when his lips left hers, and she opened her eyes, disoriented. His face was flushed, his breathing ragged. She looked away then, unable to meet his glittering gaze. She started to slide her hands down, away from him, but he caught her wrists and held her captive.

His fingers rubbed her skin with slow, sensual caresses. He seemed reluctant to let her go. And then it came to her with a blinding flash, the unbidden image she'd feared. But it, too, was different than expected. She gasped as the erotic scene unfolded in her mind and violently pulled away from him. He let her go, taking a step back so she could move away. As she stumbled to her bed, she heard his footsteps padding away from her and the bathroom door closing.

Jaida jerked back the covers and slipped into the narrow bed. Turning on her side, she deliberately faced away from the bed Trey would occupy. She was fiercely glad he'd seemed as shaken as she, as incapable of speech. Never would she have admitted to him the picture that had flashed into her mind before he'd let her go. An image of the two of them entwined on black silk sheets.

She felt her face grow hot. The vision had been brief and vivid. He'd been looming half over her, as bare as he'd been a moment ago and just as hungry. And she really couldn't tell if the short, erotic scene had come from her psychic response to his touch, or if it had been manufactured by the very physical reaction that still pulsed through her.

A half hour later Trey walked out of the bathroom. He allowed himself one quick glance at Jaida, and she seemed to be asleep. Or at least she was pretending to be. He locked the front door and flipped off the light, making his way to his bed. He attempted to settle his large frame on the narrow bed, cursing under his breath when it became apparent that his feet were going to hang over the edge of it. He grabbed the pillow from beneath his head and punched it fiercely, jamming it back into position.

His interest in warm water had lagged by the time he'd taken his shower. He'd run it as hard and as frigid as he could stand it. Unfortunately, the cold shower came a little late. He wasn't a man given to impulses, so it was impossible to explain to himself just what the hell had happened in here a while ago. And why he had let it.

Let it? a voice jeered inside him. He'd invited it, designed it. He'd wanted to force Jaida to respond to him again. He'd wanted to prove to her, and to himself, that he had that kind of power over her.

The joke, he thought grimly, was on him. Because he'd lost control very quickly, about the time she'd started kissing him back. And after that there had been very little thought at all. She was the one with the inexplicable rare gift, but it was he who was going to spend the night with a vision in his head, one that had sliced through his desire with rapier sharpness.

It had been so clear. He opened his eyes and stared at the ceiling, replaying the scene in his mind. He stifled a groan. That was exactly the line of thought a man shouldn't engage in when he needed to get some sleep. But his body told him that sleep was not going to be quick to visit.

Resigned to a restless night, Trey let the mental picture unfurl again. He could see Jaida on his bed at home in California. He could see himself leaning over her, his hand tangling in her hair. The hours passed sleeplessly while his imagination lingered over the image of Jaida's moon-glow hair spread out over his bed, spilling like white diamonds over his black, silk sheets.

Neither of them was talkative the next morning. Jaida avoided Trey's eyes as they swiftly packed and left the cabin. She put on her sunglasses when she reached the car, although the sun had just begun to splash color across the horizon. They rode in silence for a couple of hours before Trey pulled into a roadside cafe. The large breakfast they both ordered went a long way toward restoring Jaida's good humor, but had noticeably less effect on Trey.

He'd returned, she observed silently, to the taciturn man she'd met in the valley. She snuck a look at him. His too-perfect profile could have been carved from granite. The only time he'd spoken at all this morning was when he'd asked, in a brief clipped tone, which town she wanted him to drive through first.

Tourist towns dotted the eastern seaboard. She had been having him explore one, and then sometimes would ask him to backtrack to drive through another. He had been unabashedly verbal about his distaste for the practice yesterday. Today he followed her directions without comment.

She found that she would have preferred his sometimes sarcastic comments to his almost complete silence today. Jaida would have given a lot to know what he was thinking. Was he remembering last night and castigating himself for kissing her? She knew from experience that he was not above using such a distraction for his own reasons. It had been a very long time since she'd allowed a man close enough to touch her like that, to kiss her. She didn't like the idea of being vulnerable to him and having him know it. But he was much too observant not to be aware of it. Indeed, at first he'd been exploiting their mutual reaction last night, almost taunting her with it. But then something had changed; *he* had changed.

Jaida shivered and sank down farther in her seat. His very real desire had been impossible to ignore, especially once she'd sensed his control spiraling away. That was the memory that had invaded her mind last night and kept her spinning wistful, hopeless dreams about him. She knew without asking that it was his loss of control he would be brooding over, rather than the woman who had evoked it.

It was well past noon before Trey flicked a glance at Jaida. She was slouched low, her head against the cushioned seat, arms wrapped around her middle. She'd been unnaturally quiet for the last few hours. She presented a much different picture from the woman he'd ridden with yesterday, who had spent the day with her face tilted skyward, inviting the sun's kiss. Now she seemed withdrawn, despondent, and he mentally counted the hours since breakfast. He wasn't hungry yet, but it was possible she needed to replenish her limitless demand for calories. He pulled into a gas station advertising groceries and turned off the ignition.

"Could I have the keys for a minute?" she requested.

"What for?"

"I want to get a sweater out of my suitcase."

He handed her the keys. "If you're cold you should have said something. I'll put the top up."

Not bothering to comment, Jaida got out, unlocked the trunk and retrieved her sweater. She slid back into the empty car and put the keys back into the ignition. Donning the sweater, she settled down to wait for Trey to return. He did shortly, carrying a sack with him. Before they left, he put the top up on the convertible and latched it into place. Jaida watched without comment. She could have told him that his efforts were in vain, but lacked the will to do so.

Trey got into the car, and they headed back to the interstate. "I bought you something to eat." He nodded toward the sack. "There's string cheese, potato chips and some candy bars. I figured your appetite alarm is due to go off any minute."

Jaida smiled unwillingly. "Thanks."

She made no move toward the sack, and he gave her a concerned look. "You're not sick, are you?"

She almost smiled again at his suspicious tone. "No, I'm not sick."

He frowned at her answer, but she didn't embellish on it. They drove on in virtual silence again, and he used the time to try to figure out what was behind her unusual behavior. Had he offended her last night with that kiss? It hadn't seemed so then, and he had been as attuned to her reactions as he had to his own. It had been a stupid move on his part, enacted for the sheer pleasure of it and nothing else. It had been so long since he'd done something unplanned, uncalculated, that he was having trouble accepting it now. He'd *wanted* to elicit that exciting electrical current that jumped between them each time they'd touched. And he'd wanted more than that. He'd wanted to see if that current would transfer to her veins, if the response went any deeper than the surface. He'd gotten his answer and more.

He'd spent most of his adult life masking the wildness of his nature. As a youngster he'd struck out at the world in any way he could, to make it pay for the losses in his life. His mother, his sister, his home . . . all had been taken away by the time he was ten. Everyone he encountered owed him something for that, or so he'd believed. It wasn't until he'd met Colonel Lambert, and later started a career in the army, that he succeeded in developing an iron control, which he wielded most unbendingly on himself.

The first to lose control loses. The colonel's words, spoken to him as a surly fifteen-year-old, had stuck with him ever since. He'd learned that lesson well over the years. And he prided himself on never losing control.

But last night it had evaporated. Jaida West wasn't like the women he entered into relationships with. She wasn't sophisticated and polished, with artful conversation and attention-getting ploys. And he was betting that she didn't have a wealth of experience with men to draw from. That knowledge, accompanied by the intense physical response between them, had torched his own desires.

He knew too well that a man who wasn't in control of himself could scarcely hope to control his surroundings. And yet, for the few brief moments he'd been pressed close to Jaida, he hadn't been in control.

He hadn't recognized the strange compulsion he'd had to force her to admit the response she had to him, to demand she tell him it was experienced solely with him. And he wasn't comfortable with the deep satisfaction her admission had elicited and the compelling need to explore it further.

He should never have touched her. Not because it hadn't been planned and had served no useful purpose in the search for his nephew. And not because it had represented such a departure from a lifetime of careful habit. But because now it would be impossible to forget the feel of her or the taste. And he'd never get rid of the mental picture of her sprawled out over the slick, inky backdrop of his own sheets.

"Where to?" he fairly snapped when they came to the next town. He glanced sharply at Jaida. She hadn't said a word since he'd stopped to buy the food, nor had she touched the sack. Although with the top up he found it rather warm in the car, she had her legs drawn up and the sweater wrapped around her knees.

"South," she murmured, not bothering to look at him. Her head was relaxed against the seat again.

"You're sure you're okay?" he questioned gruffly. "You shouldn't be cold. It's eighty-four degrees outside, warmer than yesterday. Maybe you're getting the flu."

The chill permeating her bones had nothing to do with the temperature or illness, but she wondered how to explain that to him. "We're getting nearer," she replied quietly. "The colder I get, the closer I'll know we're getting."

He involuntarily lifted his foot from the accelerator, stunned at her words. "What do you mean, we're getting nearer?" he croaked.

Her eyes behind her glasses were shut. She was so tired. Normally she needed long hours of rest after being buffeted by psychic storms, but she'd gotten precious little of that since Trey had come into her life. "Just keep driving," she said. She didn't need to have her eyes open to recognize the place when she came to it. The recognition would seep into her bones with a deep, pervasive cold impossible to overlook. She just hoped that what they would find when they finally arrived wasn't going to tear the Garrison family apart with pain.

Trey pressed down on the accelerator more firmly, and the car spurted forward. Calling himself all kinds of fool, he couldn't discount the anticipation building in his gut. Logic still wanted to insist that Jaida West was a fraud. But logic couldn't explain her forays into his mind, her inexplicable knowledge of things he kept tightly locked away from others. That knowledge made her a threat, to his cautious defenses and his carefully managed life. He couldn't help hoping her ability would prove as accurate in this instance. Even as his rational mind jeered at him, the speedometer steadily climbed. And the car continued in the direction she'd indicated.

"We have to walk from here."

He turned to look at her, instantly uneasy at the picture she made. She was completely still, her cheeks ashen. He was about to question her again about the state of her health, but in the next moment she opened her car door and got out. Not waiting for him, she started swiftly toward the beach.

Trey easily caught up with her and they walked in silence down the picturesque boardwalk, until she came to a stone wall about three feet high that separated the street from the sandy beaches.

Jaida leaned forward slightly, her gaze sweeping the beach slowly, before coming to rest on a spot a hundred yards away. She stared for so long and so fixedly that Trey involuntarily followed the direction of her gaze, a chill prickling his spine. There was nothing of interest to see there, as far as he could observe. Children played noisily, couples sunned together and the odd brightly colored parasail dotted the sky overhead.

There was no toddler, large for his age, with a shock of dark hair and a babyishly charming grin.

Disappointment surged through him, strong and bitter. "Jaida." His voice was harsh. "Go back to the car."

She moved, but not in the direction he'd ordered. Instead, she turned away and started up another street.

"This is ridiculous. You can't expect me to believe that…dammit, come back here." He strode after her. "Where are you going now?"

"I'm walking around the town." The same streets that someone had strolled Benjy through, past the same stores, the same buildings. She never bothered to look at him. "You can go back to the car and wait if you wish." She neither noticed nor cared whether he followed.

It was a quaint town, one maintained primarily for the tourists it attracted during the summer months. They passed eateries, arcades and laundries. Jaida never hesitated before any of them. She trudged past the antique stores and souvenir stands. Finally she came to a stop.

Trey gave her a wary look. "What is it?"

"In there." Her breath left her with a visible shudder and she pulled her sweater closer around her. She was an oddity on the street, with most people milling around in swimsuits and tank tops.

He gazed past her and frowned. "An ice-cream shop? You want to stop for ice cream now?" His voice was disbelieving.

She pulled open the door and went inside. The air conditioner in the small shop hummed. A man with brown hair and a mustache wiped off the counter in front of him with a lazy purpose that spoke of a slow day. He looked up as the bell over the door signaled their arrival.

"What can I get you folks?"

Trey glanced at Jaida, but she said nothing, seemingly frozen in place. Her breathing was noticeably labored.

"We got over forty flavors," the man behind the counter offered. "They're all up on the sign. And we're running a special. If you want to sample the new trial flavor, you can suggest a name for it. Winner of the best name will get a gallon of ice cream each month for a year." He slung the rag he'd been cleaning with over his shoulder. Long moments stretched and he glanced, puzzled, from Trey to Jaida and back. "You guys want something, or what?"

"Your lost and found." Jaida's voice sounded hoarse and strained. "Do you have one?"

The man didn't answer, appearing to find her manner odd.

After a swift look at Jaida's white, set features and trembling lips, Trey stepped in. He gave the man a rueful smile. "Sorry. We're not here for ice cream, at least not this time. We were here—" his hesitation was barely noticeable "—a couple of days ago. My... wife lost something, and she's hoping she left it here that day. What do you do with lost items?"

The man seemed to accept Trey's explanation with alacrity. "We've got a box in the back room. We keep things for about a month. You wouldn't believe what we find in here. Craziest things..." His words were lost as he entered the back room. He returned moments later with a large box. "Go ahead and look through this stuff if you want. There's nothing real valuable in here, although there have been times we've found wallets, rings, ladies' purses, the works."

Jaida focused on the box he was holding out to Trey. She remained rooted in place. After a glance toward her, Trey took the box from the man and set it on the floor in front of him. Cursing silently, he started going through the items, unsure even what to pretend to be searching for. The man had been right; there was all manner of odds and ends in the box. Beach towels, sunglasses, hats and, inexplicably, a bikini top. Then his hand faltered in its search. Slowly, disbelievingly, he pushed aside the rest of the items and grasped what he'd at first thought was another towel. Freeing it from the rest of the junk, he drew out a small blanket.

It wasn't the sort of thing one would expect to take to the beach. It was small and quilted, printed with a selection of friendly animals, all smiling merrily. The colors had faded from their original state of primary brightness, and one end was looking rather ragged. It brought an immediate sense of recognition to his gut, and a hard knot formed in his throat.

It was the same blanket his nephew had clutched in his fist every day since he'd begun to crawl.

Trey's eyes slowly lifted to meet Jaida's.

It was the same blanket that had been in Benjy's stroller the day he'd vanished.

Chapter 9

"I've already told you, Detective, it doesn't just *look* like Benjy's blanket, it *is* his. I'm certain of it." Trey paused to listen to the man's response on the phone. His voice lost all semblance of civility. "Yes, it was purchased commercially, and no, I don't have any idea how many blankets just like that were sold. But one corner of Benjy's blanket was getting frayed, and this blanket has the same..." After a brief pause he said harshly, "What the hell do you mean, coincidence? What's it going to take to convince you?"

The one-sided conversation drifted clearly through the open French doors. Jaida sat outside the motel room on a small terrace overlooking a Tidy-Bowl blue pool. The sun was fading in glorious splendor, but the beauty of her surroundings was lost on her. She wanted to put her head down on the plastic white table in front of her and be sent off into immediate, oblivious slumber. She didn't move. Sleep, if it came at all, would be impossible for many more hours.

It took an enormous effort to turn her head enough to see Trey profiled in the room, his expression forbidding. "For a man who's come up with nothing so far on the disappearance of my nephew, you're damn casual about the first real lead we've got in this case." He listened for another moment, then snarled dangerously, "Fine. I'll Express Mail it to you tomorrow morning. And I want you to pass this information along to the Bureau. Maybe they'll take it more seriously than you do." He replaced the receiver with an audible bang.

Trey seemed to have forgotten her presence. He wheeled around agitatedly, and his gaze fell upon the crumpled child's quilt lying on the top of the bed. With footsteps slow and measured, he moved to the bed and reached down to pick it up. His fingers clenched on the soft, worn material, and the muscles in his jaw worked reflexively. He sank down on the edge of the bed and dropped his head, Benjy's quilt clutched in his big hand.

The poignancy of the scene brought Jaida out of her psychic-induced lethargy. Her heart ached for him. The sight of that dark head, so proud and confident, bent in sorrow stirred something in her she didn't dare name. But it was impossible to see Trey in pain and not wish to offer comfort.

She approached him silently and dropped to her knees in front of him. He didn't look at her. For a long time they were both quiet. His voice, when it came, sounded rusty.

"Lauren was three years old when our mother died. I was eight. She'd never been much of a mother, but she'd given me Lauren. I vowed then that nothing in this world was ever going to hurt my sister. She wasn't going to learn how ugly life could be, because I was going to do whatever it took to take care of her." The sigh he gave seemed ripped out of him. "I was cocky, big for my age and an accomplished thief. I could handle our drunk of a father, could steal enough food for the two of us, but I was no match for the great social system that supposedly rescues kids from unhealthy homes. We knocked about in foster homes for about a year and a half."

"Your father?" she whispered, remembering with clarity the startling image she'd had once through an accidental touch.

"Signed over his rights after he'd been charged with abuse and neglect. When I was ten Lauren was adopted by a couple who thought *incorrigible* was stamped on my forehead." One side of his mouth pulled up in a parody of amusement. "They were probably right. The last sight I had of Lauren was of the social worker pulling her away while she had her arms stretched out to me, crying." It had taken three adults to hold him back, to keep him from chasing after his sister. And after that, no adults, no foster home, could keep him when he chose to run. And he'd chosen to run often.

The expression in his eyes was terrible to see. Jaida had often wished she could tear through his guarded defenses, read the emotions she knew he must feel. But being faced now with his agony was heartbreaking.

"I failed her," he said in a low tone. "I promised to protect her, but I couldn't. I thought I had a second chance when I found her again and Benjy was born. And then Benjy was kidnapped."

Her eyes filled with tears, blurring her vision. She blinked rapidly, determined not to let them fall. "I heard you on the phone with that detective," she murmured, her voice trembling. "Trey, it doesn't matter what he thinks. I know this blanket belongs to Benjy. I know he was on that beach, in that ice-cream store." She shook her head helplessly. "I realize you didn't believe me at first—"

"I believe you," he interrupted her, his voice almost soundless. He could read the confusion and the hope in her eyes. And something else, something much more intriguing. "God knows, I don't want to. I don't pretend to understand this, but I have to believe what I can see, what I can touch." He raised his hand, indicating the soft quilt. "I don't need fancy tests and lab work to tell me what I'm holding in my hand. And all the lab work in the world won't explain how you knew where to go, how to find what we did."

She looked away. The yearning was obvious in her voice. "Some things have to be taken on faith."

"I'm not a man to whom faith comes easily."

She turned her head slowly to meet his gaze again. No, he wasn't a man given to putting his faith in people or things. Life had taught him to depend only on himself. It was easy to understand why after hearing some of the events that had shaped his childhood. And that made his professed belief in her all the sweeter.

"I can't fail again," he said hoarsely. "Not this time. Too much is at stake. Lauren's happiness . . ."

Benjy's life.

The rest of the sentence wasn't uttered, but they both heard it nonetheless. Their connection was beginning to seem so normal that it was hard to remember how unusual it was, how frightening. How... tempting.

"Benjy is alive," Jaida whispered, her lips trembling. She reached her hand out involuntarily, touching his knee lightly, for once failing to guard herself against a casual touch. Her instinct to comfort was far greater than her need to protect herself. "And we won't fail. We won't."

Trey stared at the delicate hand resting on his leg. He wanted to believe her words, but knew that he'd have to hold his young nephew again before the fear would be completely banished. He'd have to put Benjy in his mother's arms, and then he'd see to it that the people who'd torn their lives apart were punished. He wouldn't be satisfied until they were destroyed, as they had tried to destroy his family.

The feminine hand on his knee shook, and he was reminded with a rush that Jaida touched no one. Not willingly. His gaze traveled from that fragile white hand back to her face. He set the quilt on the bed next to him. Then his own hand covered hers.

Panic flared for a second in her eyes, before it was tempered by wariness. He guessed the exact moment she would pull away, both from him and from the touch that caused flickers of energy to prickle their skin. He tightened his hand over hers before she could move, then moved his other hand to her shoulder. He leaned toward her, urging her forward at the same time.

He was close enough to count the golden flecks in her mysterious blue eyes, and their mouths were only inches apart. "I don't pretend to understand this," he rasped. "I don't pretend to be comfortable with it. But if you're the only chance I have to find Benjy, then by God, that's a chance I'm going to take."

"We will find him," she promised tremulously, She wasn't sure whether her certainty stemmed from her visions or from a continued need to provide him solace. Providing him solace could be dangerous. It could encompass all sorts of things she could only guess at. The remembrance of her inexperience served as another reminder of the seductive danger she was courting, now, with this man.

"Let me go," she said softly.

His hand on her shoulders flexed and smoothed caressingly. He shook his head slightly.

"Please."

The word was a whimper in her throat, and he interpreted it as he wished. He slid off the bed to face her, kneeling just as she was. His stance was wide and he trailed his hands down to force her hips into the cradle of his.

Her gasp was buried against his chest. His mouth went immediately to her throat. She shuddered and reached up to anchor herself by clutching his biceps. More than anything else he wanted to lose himself in this woman. Emotion churned through him, aching for a release. He knew her skin burned where it met his, just as his did. Pinpoints of electricity danced between them everywhere they touched. The vision of black, silk sheets under their entwined bodies beckoned him further.

He captured the pulse that beat at the base of her neck with his mouth, teasing it with his tongue. It fluttered madly, signaling her distress, or her desire. He recognized the complexity of her emotions, because they mirrored his own.

Jaida shuddered. This time there was no conscious fear of visions that would intrude. Her response to his touch was too magnetic for that. Its nature was even more terrifying. She'd lived her life carefully, sure she'd never find a man she could trust enough to be vulnerable in this way. And she *was* vulnerable. His touch stripped her of all illusions, leaving her nowhere to hide, no way to pretend she could control her own responses.

Her lips parted naturally as his mouth covered hers, already knowing him, ready for his taste. Her fingers dug into his taut skin, and her head was driven back with the force of their passion. Their tongues mated, and a shiver of delight spiraled down to her stomach. When his hand rose to cover her breast, she felt scorched through her clothes. Still, she couldn't prevent herself from thrusting forward into his palm. He closed his hand around her, taunting her nipple with his thumb. The pleasure that careened through her was wildfire, leaving embers of desire in its wake.

She felt the carpet at her back, and her eyelids flickered dazedly; she was unaware she and Trey had moved. He was lean-

ing half over her. As he dropped a series of kisses at the corner
of her mouth, his knee parted her legs and pressed against her
warm center. His mouth came down on hers more fiercely then,
and he pulled her shirt from her waistband and slid his hand up
her smooth waist to cup her breast once more. The intimate
actions combined to jolt her from her desire-induced lethargy,
and she cried out in a mixture of surprise and fear.

He murmured something into her ear, low and soothing, but
she couldn't concentrate on his words. Last night had proven
that she couldn't predict her reaction to him. Far from being
assailed by his emotional sensations, she was swamped by her
own. They were exciting, enticing and totally unfamiliar.

They scared her to death.

"Let me go." Her words were more a plea than a demand,
and he went instantly still. A moment later he moved away
from her, using exaggerated care, and she rose, fleeing to the
terrace.

She sat down, hugging her knees against her chest. She
wished fiercely that Trey would leave without further words.
They'd been forced to travel almost forty minutes inland before they'd found a motel with rooms for each of them. She was
fervently grateful for that. She needed time away from him,
away from the flames that leaped so easily to life between them.

His approach was silent, but she sensed the moment he
stepped out onto the terrace.

"You have your own room," she informed him, her voice
shaking. "Use it."

"No."

"Leave me alone, Trey!"

"Not yet. Not until we talk this out."

"There's nothing to talk out. I want you to stay away from
me."

"That's going to be a little difficult, given the circumstances."

"You know what I mean," she said a little wildly. He was
being deliberately obtuse, and he wouldn't be denied. He was
as persistent as water wearing on a rock. She didn't have the
strength to argue with him.

"Why don't you tell me what has you running scared every
time I touch you?" he suggested. When she didn't reply, he

continued, "I know that the reaction you have to me is new for you. We've already established that. It's new to me, too." She refused to answer. He contented himself for the moment by examining her delicate profile in the approaching dusk. Her features were fine; her soft, pink mouth sulky. He was pushing her, and she didn't like to be pushed. He resisted the urge to cover that sulky mouth with his own.

"I don't have a lot of experience," she said in a low voice.

Her words, not totally unexpected, sent a curl of satisfaction through him. "That can't be from lack of opportunity."

She gave a little laugh that was devoid of amusement. "I'm a freak, remember?" She didn't look at him, didn't dare. She was afraid she'd see the agreement on his features. "I've dated, but I couldn't...I could never..." She stopped, chewed her bottom lip and wondered how to explain. "Being that close to someone, I couldn't block anything out. It's an enormous strain trying to shield myself from a person's thoughts and emotions any time I'm touched. I can't maintain that sort of defense indefinitely. And so I would pick up all his feelings, and they would just overwhelm my own. Or I'd get a glimpse of a vision and that..." Her voice trailed off for a moment. When it resumed, it was tinged with irony. "It sort of ruins the moment, if you know what I mean."

His voice was inflectionless. "Is that what happened in there? Are you saying it's the same with me, Jaida?"

She gave a bitter little smile in the falling darkness. She sensed the urgency behind that question. She wished she could lie to him. The one thing that Trey would be unable to tolerate was allowing someone close enough to sense what he was thinking.

"No." She shook her head uncomprehendingly. "And I don't understand that, either. Everything inside gets all jumbled up, and the feelings skyrocket through me. But they're not yours—they're mine. It's so different." She didn't mention the erotic image she'd had of both of them against black silk sheets. That had seemed more a fantasy than vision, at any rate.

A primordial surge of possessiveness arrowed through his gut. He doubted she recognized the significance of her confession, but he did. He suspected that she'd never felt real desire before. Once she had, with him, she found her emotions too engulfing to sense his. He was undeniably relieved at the realization. He was also completely, primitively, aroused. He'd have to be made of stone not to respond to her words.

He acknowledged the futility of the desire that still pulsed in him, and frustration ate at his patience. He rounded the table and put both hands down on its surface, leaning toward her. "I think you're beginning to understand what scares you so much, honey, but you can't run away from it forever. There's something between us, Jaida. And after we find Benjy, when we're sure he's safe . . ." He paused meaningfully until she raised her gaze to meet his.

"Then you and I will finish it."

He stared hard at her pale, still face before abruptly leaving. Moments later, she heard the door to the adjoining room close.

She took a deep breath and let it out in one long, shuddering gasp. His words had been rife with meaning, and her body couldn't decide whether to react with delight or fear. She hadn't replied to his words, hadn't needed to. She knew he spoke the truth. She should have realized long ago what it meant, this strange connection that leaped to life each time they touched. Certainly she'd understood enough to be wary.

But not wary enough. A wary woman wouldn't have gotten in over her head, wouldn't have cared so very much about making a man believe in her. A wary woman wouldn't have sought to comfort him at the risk of sending her own normally skittish reactions haywire.

A wary woman wouldn't have fallen in love with such a man to begin with.

She buried her face in her hands. How was it possible to be so certain of her feelings for a man she'd met less than a week ago, a man she hadn't been certain she even liked? Yet something inside her had known him the first moment they'd met, something that caused this purely electrical current when they touched.

She'd always been a sympathetic person, always become somewhat emotionally involved in a case. But never had she thought she might be in love as a result. She had picked a hopeless man to love. As sweet as it had been to hear him say he believed her, finally, she knew well what a long way that was from any deeper feeling. He'd said he was a man without faith.

She wondered if that meant faith in emotion . . . in love.

Yet she knew he was capable of emotion. At first she'd been convinced that he was incapable of feeling, but then she'd seen him with Lauren and known she was wrong. And her encounter with William Penning had taught her what a true lack of feeling felt like. Trey wasn't like Penning, although he guarded his emotions closely.

Granny had seen him so clearly the first time he'd come to the valley. She'd said there was a void inside him, and now that Jaida had a better understanding of what had caused it, she doubted even more her ability to fill it. Trey let only a chosen few into his heart, into his trust. What he had offered her— *promised* her, rather—was something else altogether.

She shivered at the tantalizing prospect of fulfilling that promise, before rising and returning to her room. She closed and locked the terrace doors behind her. Benjy's blanket still lay forlornly across her bed, reminding her that there was something even more important to finish than whatever existed between Trey and her.

With deliberate steps, she moved toward the brightly colored blanket. She knew even before she reached it that their desperate journey was near its end.

She awoke in stages, slowly and groggily. Her eyes stayed closed as she waited for awareness to completely set in.

Her sense of smell was the first of her senses to become alert, and after a moment one eye opened. She was unsurprised to see Trey sitting on a chair next to her bed. She was startled, however, to see the tray he'd set on the bedside table. The sight wakened her completely, and she sat up in bed.

Trey had learned a few things about Jaida West on this little trip. Waking her wasn't done easily and, for both their sakes, shouldn't be done by touching her. Still, short of an alarm clock in a cooking pot, he hadn't been sure how to get the job done. He'd hit on the idea of the breakfast tray, guessing that food would accomplish what he couldn't, or didn't dare to. He was amused to observe that his estimation had been correct.

"Breakfast in bed," she murmured delightedly, her voice sounding raspy with sleep.

The sound of that sleep-laden drawl had an immediate, predictable effect on his groin. He almost groaned out loud. Perhaps he shouldn't have been so hasty in congratulating himself for coming up with this plan. His eyes drooped as he watched her sit up, the covers falling to her waist as she reached for the tray. The nightgown this time was green, with tiny flowers strewn across it. It was as demure as her last one had been, but unable to hide her womanly shape for all that.

"You certainly know the way to a woman's heart," she noted happily. Spreading a napkin across her lap, she dug into the huge mound of scrambled eggs and fried ham. "You ate earlier?"

Amusement sparked again at her automatic assumption that the generous portions were for one. Which they were, of course. He'd observed her eating habits enough to realize the portions necessary to fill her up. "I ate earlier," he affirmed. "I figured this was the best way to get you out of bed before noon."

She shook her head at him, her mouth full. Swallowing, she inquired, "Did I sleep late? What time is it?"

"Barely nine."

"That's not bad," she replied. "The post office can't even be open yet, can it? Is that how you were going to mail the blanket back?"

He nodded.

"Did you speak to Lauren last night?" she asked after a moment.

"Yes." He'd called his sister after he'd left Jaida, and the tears he'd heard in Lauren's voice were just another reason he'd had difficulty sleeping last night. Although most of the credit was sitting in front of him, daintily downing a meal most truckers couldn't handle. "She was thrilled with what we found, but it's very difficult for her. The waiting."

"It's difficult for you, too," she said softly, watching him.

"I promised her it wasn't going to be much longer. I hope I didn't lie to her. Lauren can't take much more disappointment." Everyone knew the risks, had the same fears. The detective had told them that the chances for success in solving a crime declined significantly after the first three days. And Benjy had been gone nearly three weeks. It had been impossible for

Trey to keep from reassuring his sister. It went against everything inside him to put his trust in another, but Jaida was the
best chance they had for finding Benjy. Their future, Benjy's
future, was in her hands.

The knowledge should have made him feel helpless. He was
edgy in any situation until he'd decided the best way to manage it. This was a situation he was incapable of controlling.
And yet he felt energized, ready to act. Her presence did that
to him. He used to get the same feeling in the military when one
of his carefully mapped strategies was about to go down. He'd
been a civilian for years, but the edge hadn't dulled; the instincts were still there. They were getting closer to Benjy. He
could feel it.

Jaida finally pushed the tray away, her appetite satisfied. No,
it wouldn't be much longer. She had the same feeling, but was
helpless to tell him more. She could pinpoint Benjy's location,
but she didn't have the power to see what was in store for any
of them once they reached it. The sense of urgency was growing stronger. But she didn't know if that was because they were
on the verge of finding Benjy or because something else was
about to happen. She knew only that time was running out.

"After we drop off the blanket at the post office we need to
head to the nearest airport."

Trey's eyes widened. "You're suggesting an airport?" he
asked dubiously. Then swiftly comprehension dawned. "Do
you have a particular destination in mind?"

Her mind played back the surreal vision she'd had last night
when she'd clutched Benjy's blanket in her hands. It had been
too soon. The vision had been out of focus, difficult to interpret. And then it had rushed upon her, flinging her skyward,
and taken on a nightmarish quality. Looming medieval struc-
tures, huge lifelike figures from the Dark Ages that seemed
more monsterlike than friendly to an eighteen-month-old boy.
Being whisked away in a seat that whirled faster and faster,
awing Benjy, half frightening and half exhilarating him. A huge
place with a continuous mob of people, an endless vista of
characters in Renaissance dress and a carnivallike atmosphere.

"Have you ever heard of Kids' Kingdom?" she asked.

Trey leaned forward in his chair, his eyes alight with fierce interest. "Sure. It's a chain of amusement parks scattered across the country. Their theme is medieval times."

"I called the front desk. The closest one is eight hours away."

"Is that where you think Benjy is?"

"We need to hurry," she whispered. She couldn't explain the sense of urgency she'd felt in the last vision, but it had been too strong to ignore. She shivered in dismay at what lay ahead. "Somewhere, in the middle of all those people, is Benjy."

The customary sickness was almost welcome as the jet screamed down the runway. At least concentrating on that meant she didn't have to worry about where they were going. And how their destination would affect her.

Her hand was peeled back from the death grip she had on the seat and encompassed in a warm, tight clasp. She gasped and tugged at it, but she was held fast.

"Stop fighting me," Trey advised in an even voice. "At least when I'm touching you you're concentrating on something other than losing your breakfast. In comparison, I can't believe I'm that unacceptable an alternative."

She stared at him, wide-eyed. He was right, the nausea was fading, to be replaced with sensations much more powerful, much more alluring. The electrical impulses jumped and sparked madly between them, and she watched his eyes grow shuttered.

It was as if he were inviting it, daring the connection between them to prove itself again, and a satisfied smile curled his hard mouth when it did just that. Warm heat flowed between them, and Jaida slowly let her hand relax in his.

"Do you feel that?" he asked hoarsely. "A few days ago you jumped three feet if my fingers so much as brushed yours. But you don't anymore, do you, Jaida?" His voice was low, inexorable. "And it's not because the connection is any weaker, because that's still there, too. You're becoming accustomed to my touch." His thumb rubbed over the back of her hand, and she trembled in response.

She couldn't refute the truth of his words. She suspected that he enjoyed the reaction that leaped to awareness between them, that he savored it. And the thought of just why he'd want her accustomed to his touch made her heart beat madly and her mouth go dry. He wanted her. As badly as she wanted him. He wasn't going to let his desire interfere with his search for Benjy, but afterward, then she knew as well as he that there would be nothing else between them. How would she go back to her quiet life in the valley after he'd jetted home again to California, to his family and friends? Somehow she knew that if she gave in to the passion that simmered between them she would have a terrible time dispensing with the memories.

But then, the memories of him would linger, regardless. Would they hurt more or less if she just once followed her heart?

He was right; his constant touch steadied her. She closed her eyes fatalistically and awaited another type of reaction, the transient visions that would transmit from him to her. For they would surely come. Passion masked them, made it impossible to concentrate on any emotions but her own. But in a moment such as this one, there would be no such barrier. She made no attempt to shield herself from them. Part of the price of loving him would be understanding him far better than he would dare to let anyone else.

By far the highest price would be losing him when this was over.

They were the last ones off the plane. Trey had noticed before the way Jaida tended to hang back, making excuses to avoid the melee of passengers jostling one another as they retrieved luggage and jockeyed for position to disembark. When they were finally off there was only a short wait for their bags, and then they rented yet another car.

When Trey turned away from the rental window, she followed him wordlessly to the parking lot. He stopped at a pay phone and made a reservation at one of the many hotels near the park complex. They made the drive to the amusement park silently, energy smoldering between them. Unspoken was the knowledge that they were close to Benjy, closer than they had ever been. Trey pulled into the parking lot and stopped the car, addressing her for the first time.

"This is a huge complex. The sign says it covers more than four hundred acres."

She swallowed. "I know." There were several sections to the gigantic park, and she couldn't be completely certain which one the vision had entailed. Their only option was to go inside and wait for her to feel something, anything, that would lead them to Benjy.

Her eyes met Trey's. Neither of them voiced the question that was uppermost on their minds. They were at the area's largest tourist attraction at the height of the season. How were they going to find one small boy in the midst of thousands of people?

Chapter 10

"The day was a bust." Trey delivered the pronouncement in a tight, flat voice. Jaida sat slouched in one of the chairs in the motel room. He paced by her, as if unable to stop moving.

"It's going to take time," she answered quietly, exhaustion lacing her words. "It was impossible for us to cover the whole park in one day."

"How do we know they're still around here? The kidnappers might have gone to Kids' Kingdom for a day and taken off again. We could spend a week in that park and never run across Benjy, because he may no longer be there," he said frustratedly. "This whole thing is getting more and more bizarre. Why in hell would someone snatch a little boy in California, drag him to the other coast and then give him a trip to an amusement park? They could have stayed in California if the kidnappers had a yen to take someone else's child to a theme park."

Trey continued to prowl the large, comfortably furnished motel room. Jaida watched him from heavy-lidded eyes. Fatigue was rushing over her, and she would have liked nothing better than to give in to it. The park had been very close to sensory overload for her today. The skies had been bright and sunny, drawing record-number crowds. As skilled as she was, it was impossible to avoid being bumped into, brushed by. She couldn't afford to spend the hours at the park with her inner defenses constantly raised. She'd needed to remain open to any sensations that would lead them to Benjy. Unable to guard against the unwelcome, intrusive peeks into the lives of strangers, she'd been bombarded by their mental and emotional states.

"Perhaps there's a reason that the kidnappers need to be *here,* in this area." She sighed and leaned her head back against the chair. "All I can tell is they're feeling more...desperate. As though time is getting short."

Desperate. Trey reviewed the word grimly, acid churning in his gut. Desperate people were driven to extreme acts. What could happen to his nephew if the kidnappers felt threatened didn't even bear thinking about.

"All right, then, let's go with that." Trey nodded. "Someone kidnapped Benjy—"

"Two people," Jaida interjected. "A man and a woman."

"I think we can discount that he was snatched by a couple in search of a child of their own," he said. That had been one scenario espoused by the detective in Los Angeles. "Such a couple might take a child across the country to make a new home, where no one would know them. But this journey of theirs has seemed more random than anything else."

"Benjy wasn't kidnapped by a couple longing for a child," Jaida remarked distantly. She recalled the earlier visions in which a man's arm had yanked the child ungently and later delivered a stinging slap. No. She could tell very little about the man responsible for kidnapping Benjy, but she knew the boy was merely a means to an end for him.

"Okay, if we accept that, what do we have left?" Trey demanded, half to himself. "The adoption black market? Babies are their usual prey."

"Benjy is a beautiful child, though," Jaida said softly. She saw him clearly in her mind, his image branded into the visions. It seemed impossible for another human being to look so much like an adult, but he was a miniature of Trey, offering tantalizing clues to how Trey's own children would look.

The thought of Trey's future children made Jaida's heart ache. He would be a wonderful father; his devotion to his nephew proved that. Some men, unfortunately abused during their own childhood as Trey had been, were doomed to repeat the cycle of abuse. But whatever had formed Trey was more powerful than the blows his father had landed on him.

She blinked rapidly, banishing the tears that had inexplicably welled in her eyes. More than likely her imaginings were as mythical as Trey's children would be. She already knew how difficult it was for him to open his emotions. The idea that he would find a woman he could trust that much was unlikely. And the idea that the woman could be her was unlikelier still.

And yet…she very much wanted to be that woman in his life.

She watched him continue to pace, her vision blurring with exhaustion. She was miserably aware that whatever Trey felt for her would fall far short of what she would want from him.

"Are you all right?"

"Do you know how often you ask me that?" she replied, only half joking. She didn't need a mirror to guess what she looked like right now. The day had taken a lot out of her, and she felt like a wrung-out dishrag. She imagined she didn't look much better.

He surveyed her grimly. Her appearance was alarming. Her face was almost the color of her hair, and even her brilliant blue eyes appeared dulled. Castigating himself for not noticing sooner, he said, "You're white as a sheet. Are you hungry? We don't have to go out. I can order room service."

She shook her head. "You are learning. Most times food will cure just about anything ailing me. But brace yourself for the shock, I'm really not hungry at the moment."

Now he really was alarmed. When Jaida wasn't hungry it meant she was on the verge of being ill. Making a rapid decision, he strode to the phone. "I am ordering supper and you will eat. You're frail enough. No telling what will happen if you don't get your usual five thousand calories a day."

She opened her mouth to protest, then closed it. When Trey made a decision he was impossible to stop. She listened as he spoke on the phone, ordering enough food for five people. In spite of her recent protestations, she felt a spark of interest. Maybe he was right. She felt as weak as a newborn baby bird, and tomorrow promised to be a repeat of today. And perhaps the day after that. She was going to need all her strength to bring Benjy back home.

She'd helped numerous families over the years, provided them with information to help find a loved one or even a pet or valuable object. The cases rarely had taken more than a day or two. Never had she been involved in a case this prolonged or this complex. One complication was that the kidnappers weren't obliging them by staying put. No sooner did she pinpoint their location than they left again.

Another complication was standing across the room from her, hanging up the phone with a satisfied look on his face. Trey Garrison was the biggest complication in her previously simple existence. And before this case was over, he was going to irrevocably change her life, for better or worse.

When the food arrived in the next hour, she found she was glad he had ignored her wishes about ordering it. The aroma stirred her appetite. Jaida joined him without comment. They consciously avoided dining on the balcony, which gave a stunning view of the theme park. It would only have served to remind them of how close they might be to Benjy. And yet, so far away.

"You're looking a little better," he said after they'd finished eating. The color was gradually returning to her cheeks. But those beautiful eyes were still shadowed, and she continued to look more fragile than he would have liked.

"You seemed to know your way around today," he remarked. "You've obviously been here before. Did your mother bring you? I can't imagine your grandmother in a place like this."

Jaida smiled at the thought. "No, Kids' Kingdom wouldn't have appealed to Granny. As a matter of fact, she's only left the valley once to my recollection." The memory of that particular instance intruded, and she pushed it away firmly. "Actually, I was here about five years ago when my band was on tour."

His startled gaze met hers. "Band? What band? You said you were a songwriter."

"And so I am," she mocked him softly. "I've written songs since I was…oh, eight or so. But I've always loved to sing, and my biggest dream was to be part of a successful group, go on tour, record songs...." She smiled sadly at her naive hopes. She'd never allowed herself to consider just what it would all entail. And just how much it would demand from her.

"What happened?" he demanded, when it became clear that she wasn't going to say anything more. "Did the band break up?"

"On the contrary, *Pure Jade* is alive and well. Currently on yet another tour, I believe."

"I've heard of them," he said slowly. He regarded her with a fierce frown. "So why aren't you with them? Were you...replaced?" he asked, searching for a delicate wording.

"Your confidence is truly inspiring," she said, her drawl more pronounced. "But, in a manner of speaking, I guess you're right. I asked to be replaced, at least at most public appearances and on tour. I still record with the group, though, so that's my voice you hear on the radio." It annoyed her that it mattered in the slightest what he thought of her talent, but darn it, it *did* matter. "I still write most of the songs we record. I...I just didn't want to do the public part anymore, that's all."

"Why?"

He was as demanding as an interrogator, and as relentless. She looked away, not wanting to go down that road again, and especially not with him. "It was...more difficult than I'd imagined," she finally said. "Constantly traveling, waking up wondering what city I was in. I just grew tired of it."

"Bull."

His emphatic reply had her jerking to face him.

"I know you better than that. You're not a quitter. You wouldn't let the band down by bowing out like that. Something must have happened, something big enough to cause you to give up the dream of a lifetime. Most singers fantasize of reaching the success you did. People don't walk away from it easily. Not without a damn good reason."

"Well, I had a damn good reason," she answered shortly, glaring at him. Abruptly she pushed away from the table. She didn't enjoy being subjected to his analysis or to his half-baked theories. The fact that he was right didn't make it any easier to face it again.

"What was it? Did you hate it that much?"

"Some of it. Not all." Parts of that life had lived up to every fantastic image she'd spun about it. There was no other experience on earth that matched the high she'd received from singing her heart out to sellout crowds. The energy that infused the fans returned to her, propelling her even higher. "It wasn't too bad at first, but as we established a following, things got more...complicated. It seemed like I was never alone. I was with the group practicing, or we were traveling or, later, in meetings with our manager or accountants. At first I was able to return to the valley fairly frequently for short visits to regroup. But then those visits got harder and harder to schedule. When we grew more popular..." She hesitated. Even now the reality felt like a cruel trick of nature.

"It became difficult even to get to the concert we were going to put on. And forget about getting out of it without being mobbed. No amount of planning could keep the crowds at bay. We insisted on the tightest security. But I came to dread every concert. Just the thought of having to brave that crowd as we left to go home at the end of the night was enough give me the shakes."

Trey listened quietly, comprehension dawning as he focused more on what she didn't say. He knew what a single touch could do to her. What must it have been like to be mobbed by hundreds of strangers night after night? He could only imagine that kind of sensory bombardment.

"We were doing a concert in Tucson. It was a full house, and the energy was high. Security wasn't as tight as it should have been, and I think there was a lot of drinking going on in the crowd." She sighed, as if the retelling in itself was tiring. "One young cowboy jumped up on the stage and started waltzing me around." The memory was sharp, as clear as if it had happened yesterday.

"About the time security would have reached us, he swept me up and passed me down to someone in the crowd. It was like a game to them. I was handed around over the heads of the high spirited concertgoers."

His face went taut and still. "They were all touching you."

She gave a shaky breath. "It sounds juvenile, I know, but by the time security rescued me I couldn't go on with the concert. I spent the rest of the night huddled in my dressing room, basket case, because some unruly young men got tanked up enough to be overly brave. It was just a prank to them, but to me ..." Her voice tapered off.

"That was when I faced reality. I'd been fooling myself into thinking I could be a normal person, that I could chase my rainbow just like anyone else. Something like that was bound to happen sooner or later, and it was just the final straw." She looked at Trey then, pain easily apparent in her eyes. "I'm not *normal*, and I never will be. Granny always told me these visions were a gift, but at that point they felt like a curse to me. They represented the reason for everything I thought I'd lost— my mother's love, my music career." She stopped, biting her lip. Granny hadn't seemed surprised to find her back in the valley to stay. It was in the weeks to follow that Jaida realized Granny had known the outcome of her short-lived career all along. In her wisdom, she'd let Jaida discover it for herself.

Trey's jaw tightened. He damned himself for pushing her about this. If she'd looked delicate before, now she appeared positively fragile. Her eyes were huge and haunted, and more than anything he wanted to remove that look from them. He didn't move. He didn't have the right to comfort her, any more than he'd had the right to push her. But still, he found himself trying.

"You're normal in all the ways that count, Jaida." His voice was rough. "You give of yourself at great personal cost. There aren't many who can claim the same."

She gave a slight smile. "I've long since come to terms with what it means to have my gifts, Trey," she said simply. "But I can never live the way most people take for granted. I avoid crowds, and I live where I can pretty much control the number of strangers I come into contact with. I worked out a compromise with our manager. He wasn't happy—he still isn't—but we've settled things pretty well. *Pure Jade* still has the first option on all the songs I write, and at recording time I join them in the studio. It's not what I'd once hoped for, but it's enough."

"Is it enough, Jaida?" His voice was so low it was almost soundless. Though he moved no nearer, he seemed to fill her vision. "In all the time since, you've never wanted more?"

She let out a shaky breath. She could tell him what she knew firsthand about wanting more. Most of it she'd learned since meeting him. But wishing something didn't make the reality go away. And Trey Garrison was at the top of the list of things she shouldn't let herself wish for.

Pining for the moon, Granny would call it. And her feelings for Trey were just as out of reach. She had no doubt that physically she could have him, for a very short time. But emotionally, he was as unattainable as that lunar globe in the night sky.

"I've learned not to want what I can't have."

"Then you've learned more than the rest of us." His breath was on her neck, yet he didn't touch her. "Most of us can't keep ourselves from ... wanting."

The word reverberated in her ear, and she shivered at his meaning. No doubt if she were to verbalize exactly what it was she wanted, he would respond with a total withdrawal. She remained silent. Whatever happened between her and Trey, she would never burden him with her feelings. She knew too well that he carried around a load of guilt too heavy for most people to bear. She refused to add to it.

She swayed a little on her feet, the events of the day catching up with her. His hands came up to cup her narrow shoulders, and she gasped at the now-familiar shock.

"Jaida." His voice was insistent in her ear. He turned her around. "Today ... at the park ..." He frowned fiercely. "I never considered how difficult it would be for you."

"It doesn't matter," she assured him quietly.

"It damn well does matter," he declared tersely. "It should have occurred to me before. I can't imagine that walking around the park with six or seven thousand people was a picnic."

She smiled wearily. "It does take a lot out of me."

"Then let's get you ready for bed now," he said. He gave her a little push toward the bathroom.

"You're right. I'm going to need quite a bit of sleep to get ready to try again tomorrow."

"That wasn't what I meant, dammit!" Trey's face was thunderous. "You look dead on your feet and you're pale as a ghost. I'd be lying if I said I wouldn't use every avenue open to me to find Benjy, but that doesn't mean I'm not concerned about *you*, too." He stopped then, and his jaw clenched.

"It's not your fault," she said quietly. She was touched at his expression of concern, but unwilling to allow him to add her to the burden of guilt he seemed determined to build for himself. "This is my choice, my responsibility." She smiled slightly. "It's a small enough price to pay if we can find Benjy, isn't it?" Turning away, she picked up her overnight bag and went into the bathroom.

Trey was left staring at the closed door. Regardless of her brave words, she'd almost staggered with exhaustion as she'd crossed the room. And yet, she was also right. Knowing what it cost her physically, would he be willing to give up on the slim lead her presence in the park afforded him? The answer was irrefutable. Benjy's welfare came first with him, but that didn't mean he was completely oblivious to what he was putting her through. The knowledge that she had insisted on being part of this was only partially mollifying.

The fact that he was concerned about her didn't alarm him. Although at times she seemed to think otherwise, he was capable of some of the gentler emotions. Compassion and gratitude, to name a couple. But it wasn't those feelings that had him twisted up inside right now. It was his desire to shield her... to protect her.

That scared the hell out of him.

He wheeled around from his post at her door and paced across the plush carpet. Jaida West didn't need protection, and if she did, he wasn't the man to provide it for her. It was in his nature to want to protect his family, his friends. Jaida was neither. So why this concern about what the case was doing to her? Why these feelings of guilt for knowing that at the same time she was useful to him, she was also driving herself to exhaustion or possibly worse?

When Jaida reopened the bathroom door, the bed had been turned down invitingly. Her eyes moved to the man sitting in a chair by it, watching her broodingly. Her steps almost faltered at the fierce expression on his face. She glanced at him warily, wondering what he was thinking. "I... guess I'll go to sleep now," she said tentatively, not understanding what was keeping him in the room.

She slipped into the bed and was startled to have him rise and pull the sheet over her. Her eyes went wide and questioning.

"I'm not an invalid," she said. Her words came out soft, and comforting rather than chiding.

"I know."

They shared another long look, then he snapped off the light switch, plunging the room into darkness. She could still see his shape, darkness against shadows as he returned to the chair he'd occupied earlier.

"I thought . . . don't you have a room?"

"I'll just stay until you sleep. Go to sleep, Jaida." His command was uttered almost soundlessly.

Sleep with him in the room? she asked herself a little wildly. Somehow she didn't believe that was going to be possible. She was too conscious of him. But his presence was comforting. Her body fought with her for the sleep it craved, and she gradually began to lose the battle.

Jaida's breathing had eased to a slow, even rhythm long before Trey stirred from the chair. His own room seemed cold and sterile in comparison with this one, the one where she lay sleeping. But his body was demanding the same kind of peace, a few blessed hours of unconsciousness before awaking to begin the search again. He stared through the darkness a while longer. Then he rose and silently made his way to her bedside.

She'd worked one smooth shoulder free of the covers. He gently drew them back over her. His mind ordered him back to his room. His feet didn't move.

He should have considered how traumatic the day in the huge theme park would be for her. Given her past, he wouldn't have blamed her for punching out anyone who suggested she put herself through that. And yet she'd willingly undergone the experience, and would do so again tomorrow. The woman must lack even the most basic sense of self-preservation to volunteer to use her ability to help others.

Without conscious decision, he unbuttoned his shirt and tossed it carelessly to the floor. His shoes and socks were similarly disposed of, and his hand went to his jeans, then hesitated. Leaving them on, he padded around to the other side of the bed and slowly, gently, lowered himself down beside Jaida.

Chapter 11

In the morning, the indentation on the pillow next to Jaida was mute testament to Trey's presence in her bed. She stared uncomprehendingly at it, her sleep-sodden mind taking long minutes to interpret its significance. He had slept beside her all night. The knowledge that he'd lain there, like a guardian angel come to rest, sent an unfamiliar skitter down her spine. Why had he thought it necessary to keep vigil over her?

She suspected she knew the answer to that. If she'd learned nothing else about the man, it was that he had a strong sense of responsibility. He'd been appalled last night after hearing her matter-of-factly relay the physical reactions she suffered in a crowd of people. It wouldn't take much of a leap for him to feel guilty for what she'd undergone for Benjy's sake.

But regardless of his motivation, her heart refused to slow to its usual steady rhythm. She wasn't used to sharing a bed with a man, any man. And the thought of how close he had been to her during the long hours of the night was enough to keep her cheeks flushed all through the time it took her to shower and change her clothes.

When she'd finished getting ready, Trey still hadn't made an appearance. Taking a deep breath, she knocked at the adjoining door, and obeyed his low command to enter. He was on the phone.

Slow heat suffused her. He wore only a pair of wheat-colored jeans, and his attire, once completed, would be the most casual she'd yet seen him in. But it was what he wasn't wearing that had her gaze helplessly welded to him.

He was shirtless and barefoot. She'd seen him thus only one other time, in the cabin they'd shared, and the memory had haunted her. His shoulders and chest were roped with sculpted muscles. He wasn't bulky like a weight lifter, but his sinewy strength was well-defined by the ripples beneath his skin. His would be the kind of coordinated strength that would allow him to move quickly, quietly, eliminating all obstacles in his path with ruthless precision.

The thought of that powerful body sleeping beside her all night made her throat go completely dry. The idea of lying beside him while she was awake was erotic enough to rob her lungs of breath completely. And then he looked across the room at her, his forest-green eyes alight with awareness, as if he'd divined her thoughts and returned them with blatant interest.

For one charged moment the rest of the world faded away. Trey's gaze licked down her body and back up, bathing her with heat. Her own eyes wandered over him, and remained at his waist, fascinated by the growing ridge behind his zipper.

Knowing she was responsible for his very physical reaction was at once intoxicating and terrifying. With a gasp, she jerked around and made her way to the table, where breakfast awaited. She carefully kept her back to him as she feigned an appetite that had suddenly vanished. The one-sided conversation behind her resumed, Trey's voice sounding harsher than normal.

The food was no more than lukewarm when he finally hung up the phone and joined her at the table.

"You were talking to Mac?"

He stared at her, his expression shuttered. She was taking great pains not to focus on him, pretending a normalcy he was far from feeling himself. He'd awakened in a state of semi-arousal from a night spent beside her. A night spent immersed in the scent of her hair, only inches away from her silky body. As torturous as the time had been, he knew he'd feel compelled to do it again. There was something about the woman that made him feel . . . *protective.*

His brows came together at the completion of the thought. Guarding his emotions was a way of life for him, but somehow the woman beside him had slipped beneath his defenses. He'd never had a noble instinct in his life. A noble man would feel gratitude for the help she was giving to his family, the help that came at such a high physical cost. A noble man certainly wouldn't be considering taking advantage of her shy fascination with his body.

He stabbed at his cold waffle with more force than necessary and answered her belatedly. "I've been on the phone for a while. And considering the time difference, I guess it isn't any wonder that no one was particularly pleased to hear from me."

She did look at him then. "Anything new?"

"Lauren has been given a clean bill of health by her doctor. At least," he corrected himself, "she's been told she can travel."

"She's coming here?"

He shook his head. "No, she's going somewhere safe. Mac has a place all picked out, and he'll be moving her soon. Today, I hope."

"I don't understand," Jaida said slowly. "Her house . . . the estate her house is located on is about the most secure place I've ever seen."

"It is secure," he answered grimly. "But its location may no longer be secret. If we're right believing that Benjy's wasn't a random kidnapping, then we have to consider that someone was watching Lauren, waiting for her to leave the confines of her boss's estate. I've gone to great lengths to make sure that Penning has never found out where she's been living. I can't take the chance of leaving her there when it's obvious someone discovered her whereabouts. Not until I know the identity of the kidnappers."

"You still haven't ruled out Penning?" she asked.

Her even voice didn't fool him in the least. He chose his words carefully. "I know you're sure he isn't involved."

"He isn't." The brief mental foray she'd made into the morass of Penning's mind had been vile and revolting. And very revealing. She wasn't wrong about him; she was certain.

"I talked to the detective in charge of Benjy's case in L.A., and to one of the agents who's been assigned to Penning. There's still no sign that he's altered his routine at all." He gave a short laugh devoid of amusement. "The son of a bitch is actually planning a vacation with his parents when they return in a few days. They've got a place on the Cape."

"I'm sure the agents have checked out the beach house, as well."

He quit pretending to eat and studied her. "Yes," he stated deliberately. "It's empty." It took him only a few moments to divine the direction of her thoughts. When she would have pushed away from the table, he quickly caught her wrist. He watched her shiver at the sudden renewal of current that leaped beneath his touch. "That doesn't mean I don't believe you, Jaida."

"Why don't you tell me what it does mean, Trey?"

His fingers tightened around her wrist when she would have slipped away from him. "I know you're certain Penning isn't involved, but he's still the most likely suspect, Jaida." His voice grew harsh when she looked away from him. "Think about it. No one has tried harder than he has to find Lauren's whereabouts. He'd do anything for that information. Even if you're right, and I hope to God you are, and Penning knows nothing about Benjy, how can we be sure that whoever snatched the boy doesn't know Lauren's history? I can't take the chance that her location could be leaked somehow to her ex-husband, no matter what the odds are of that happening." She turned to look at him and he leaned closer, his intensity scoring his next words. "I've already lost my nephew. I won't risk my sister."

Jaida stared into his eyes, and recognized the light of determination shining there. The tension seeped from her limbs. No one knew better than she did the load of guilt and responsibility this man carried. He had said he believed her instincts about William, and his words filled her with warmth. But he was a careful man, who mapped his strategy with methodical precision. He wasn't one to take risks, not with the lives of those he loved. "Until we find the kidnappers, we'll never know for certain, will we? And Lauren will have to continue to hide until you can assure her safety."

Her words echoed his thoughts. No, not his thoughts exactly, because the fear that drove him wasn't so clearly formulated. Rather, it hovered in the recesses of his mind, haunting his every conscious hour. She could have been making an accurate guess, but he knew better than that. He released her wrist suddenly.

She still surveyed him, a wistful half smile on her lips. The wrist he'd held crept up to her chest, and she covered it with her other hand, trapping the heat from his touch. "Lauren and her son deserve a life free from that kind of fear," she whispered.

His gaze met hers, held.

"Let's go find Benjy."

The day was gorgeous, with sunny skies and balmy temperatures. It was also a record-setting day for park attendance. Music was blasting from dozens of places. Characters dressed in period costumes strolled among the crowds. The White Knight and the Dark Knight, hero and villain of the park, patrolled the area on horseback, shouting challenges at each other.

Trey and Jaida strolled through the crowds without talking. It took all of Jaida's resolve to keep her inner defenses lowered, when every instinct she had screamed to raise her guard against the sensory bombardment from the strangers surrounding her.

Trey's all-assessing gaze continually swept the crowd. His powers of observation were instinctual. Yet today his behavior was subtly different. He took pains to remain close by Jaida's side, and it was some time before the reason was apparent. Finally, when he made a sudden move in front of her and she just narrowly avoided being jostled by a squabbling family of four, his motivation became clear.

He was running interference for her. The knowledge almost stopped her dead in her tracks. She watched him for a time. When people threatened to come too near, Trey would appear in their path, cutting them off. A few times they would look up, indignant, but one glance at the tall grim-faced man had them swallowing their words and melting back into the crowd. His efforts were futile, of course. There was no way he could always protect her from the surge of the hordes. But the fact that he was trying so desperately made her heart melt.

The walls of the stone fortresses that housed some of the park's star attractions were no less impenetrable than the one that guarded this man's emotions. Knowing that he was protecting her in this way made it easy to dream that he cared, just a bit. And that dream sustained her for a time, even as her reserves of energy were depleted by the huge mob of people.

"We should sit down," Trey said. The sun was directly overhead, glaring down punishingly. The attendance at the park had swelled to easily twice what it was when they'd arrived. They'd circled the entire area once and were about to commence again. Jaida had been showing considerable signs of strain. She had her purse on one shoulder and was clutching something in the bag she carried in her other with a death grip. Her face was chalk white. As he watched, she swayed a little on her feet. He quickly led her to a ledge surrounding a topiary and forced her down on it.

He looked at his watch and mentally calculated the hours since she last ate. "You wait here," he ordered. "I'll get you something to eat."

She shook her head fiercely, sensations bouncing inside her mind with almost dizzying speed. They flooded her in a tidal wave of outpourings, leaving her shaking as they ebbed. "He's here," she managed in a raw whisper.

His face went still. "Are you sure? How can you know?"

The sensations she'd been experiencing for the past hour were not something she could put into words. "I'm sure."

He remained unconvinced. "You reacted each time we reached a place he'd been. How can you be certain . . ."

Trey's words tapered off as slowly she withdrew the hand she'd had buried in the bag she was holding. Her fingers clutched Benjy's stuffed elephant. "Now?" The word was murmured like a prayer.

"The schedule." She wet her lips and took a deep breath. "Do you have the schedule of the day's activities and a map of the park?"

Trey quickly unfolded the schedule of events and handed it to her. Jaida tried to focus, the vision of singing and dancing characters whirling feverishly in her head. Her temples were already beginning to pound. "What time is it?" she asked.

He checked his watch. "Five after one."

One o'clock. The words rushed up at her from the schedule. She handed it back to Trey and pointed to the show time with a shaking forefinger.

He reached for her and helped her rise. "Let's go."

He guided her through the park, shielding her as best he could as they dodged the throngs. The grandstand they were headed for wasn't far away. But as Jaida glimpsed the hundreds of people bunched around it, her steps faltered.

Trey glanced down at her with a frown; then, as he looked back at the mob, a grim expression settled over his face. "Here," he muttered, turning around and scanning the area. He gave her a gentle push. "Head over to that fence. I'll be back for you."

She shook her head. "No, I'm coming with you."

"The hell you are, Jaida." His voice was savage. "Do you think I don't know that just the sight of this crowd is making you physically ill? I'll handle this, but I can't protect you from this mob. So go over by that fence and wait for me." Not lingering to ensure she complied, he elbowed his way into the crush of people and was lost from her sight.

She took a step in the direction he'd indicated, then hesitated. Turning back, she looked over the crowd, which had already swallowed him. The sensations rushing through the horde of people were unmistakable. Benjy was hidden inside that wall of bodies somewhere. His presence was pulling her, as inexorably as metal filings to a magnet. What if Trey wasn't able to find him before the show was over? What if the people who had his nephew simply drifted away before Trey ever neared them?

Her teeth came down hard on her bottom lip, as compassion warred inside her with an innate need for self-preservation. The wall of humanity was as frightening as a nightmare come to life. It had been years since the scene in the concert garden. The time hadn't faded the horror. Trey would find Benjy. He had to. They couldn't get this close, only to lose him again.

She wheeled around and walked deliberately away, toward the fence Trey had indicated. Her steps stopped after only a short distance. She turned her head, as if compelled, back to the crowd.

Benjy.

His name shrieked through her mind on a howl of desolate yearning. Her lips trembled in response; her heart raced. She stood uncertainly for a moment longer, her legs shaking with indecision. Then slowly, reluctantly, she retraced her steps and cautiously circled the crowd. She thought she caught a glimpse of Trey's dark head once, before the sight was swallowed by the mob again.

Jaida took a deep breath, trying to fight the nausea rising at the thought of what she was about to do. And then with conscious effort, she walked into the crowd.

Trey used his superior size with ruthless efficiency. Ignoring the complaints and mumbled remarks about his rudeness, he shouldered his way into the middle of the throng. He scanned the sea of faces, looking for one small boy with a mop of dark hair and glittering green eyes. He bent down to look in each stroller, earning himself several gasps and more than a few obscene remarks. But when something finally caught his eye, it wasn't the black-haired little boy he was seeking, but a beacon of pale hair that reflected the bright overhead sun with blinding brilliance.

"Jaida," he muttered with frustration. "Jaida!" he shouted, starting through the crowd after her. His heart iced at the thought of what she was experiencing right now. Damn her, why hadn't she stayed put? He pushed through the people, following glimpses of that white gold hair. The crowd seemed to be surging forward. He fought the rising swell of people, impelled by the fear of Jaida lost in their midst.

"I'm warning you, lady, let go or I'll scream this place down. Are you crazy? Let go!"

Trey stumbled at the sound of the words, his head whipping around in the direction of the voice. Pushing aside the people in his path, he found Jaida on her knees, her hands tightly wrapped around the bar on a stroller. He faltered to a stop.

The stroller was easily recognizable. He'd pushed it himself many times through a park or a zoo. The navy blue canopy was folded down, revealing the padded white and blue striped lining.

And inside sat the most precious sight in the world.

"Benjy." He uttered the name with the reverence of a priest in prayer. The child was oblivious to the wall of people around him. He seemed mesmerized by the glowing halo of hair surrounding his confines. As Trey watched, his nephew clutched some of the strands in his chubby hand, then smiled beatifically.

"Lady, this is your last warning. Do I have to get the police?"

Trey's hand clamped around the speaker's forearm like a vise. "I think that's exactly what you're going to have to do. As a matter of fact, I'll help you."

The woman jerked frantically, but was unable to free herself. "Help, someone help me!" she yelped.

"Get security," Trey snapped to a couple gawking at the scene that was unfolding. Raising his voice, he ordered again, "Somebody get security over here." The next few minutes were a jumble of events. Jaida hadn't moved when she'd heard his voice, and he shot her a concerned look. "Honey, are you all right?" he asked, reaching down for her arm. The strange woman picked that time to shove a fist into his midsection and broke free of him. She got only a few steps before he had her arm again, and by that time several unobtrusively dressed men were surrounding them. Security had arrived.

"Let me go!" the woman screeched when one of the men took her by the elbow.

Trey released her. "Call the police," he commanded the guards. He walked back to the stroller and Jaida. Bending down, he looked into the face of his nephew for the first time in almost a month. Even now, he couldn't believe the search was over. He reached out with one long finger and stroked the baby-soft cheek. "Hey, big guy," he said, his voice cracking with suppressed emotion.

Benjy looked up and his eyes widened with delight. "Tay!" He released the hold he had on Jaida's hair and clapped his hands excitedly. "Tay—Tay—Tay!" He thrust his arms in the air demandingly. "Up, Tay, up!"

Trey reached in and took his nephew into his arms. He hugged the wiggling child fiercely, a flood of emotion filling him. Benjy was here, and he was safe. He was safe. Squeezing his eyes shut tightly, he rested his face against the small, silky head. As many times as he'd dreamed of this moment, he was unprepared for the reality of it.

He opened his eyes, needing to convince himself that the small body he held wasn't the product of yet another dream. The boy clasped his uncle's face in his small hands, and Trey looked down in wonder at the face that seemed a miniature of his own. Then he hugged the boy to him again and threw his head back, letting out a shout of laughter. The world had never seemed more perfect, or life more precious.

"You're going to have to come with us, sir."

The voice in his ear was polite, but firm. So was the grip on his arm. Trey's head snapped around, his shoulders automatically hunching to defend his nephew. Recognizing the man as one of the security personnel who'd appeared, he relaxed slightly. The woman Jaida had found with Benjy was already being escorted away.

"I'll take the boy," another guard said, reaching over for Benjy. Benjy immediately set up a howl, but Trey relinquished him voluntarily. Jaida hadn't moved during the entire scene, and he cursed himself now for forgetting everything for a few seconds except for Benjy.

He pulled away from the man who'd apprehended him, squatting down to where Jaida still knelt, her hands tightly wrapped around the stroller. "Jaida, honey, open your eyes," he commanded in a soft voice. "Look at me, now."

Her eyes slowly opened, but he knew she was barely conscious of his presence. Cursing under his breath, he snapped at the guard still hovering above him, "Get those people back from her!" The crowd seemed to have expanded, as attention shifted from the performance on the stage to the real-life drama taking place in its midst.

The guard hesitated, looking at the other two security personnel standing by. "I'm not coming without her. Now, do as I say and get those people away." Trey's voice cracked like a whip, and after a moment, two of the men obeyed the command implicit in his tone.

Trey covered Jaida's hands with his, talking to her continuously in a soft, soothing voice. He watched awareness flicker in her eyes, their brilliant blue dulled now with pain and something else, something he couldn't even begin to comprehend. Gently he released her fingers from their grip on the stroller. He rubbed them in his, speaking in dulcet tones. He wondered if he was doing the right thing. He didn't want to burden senses already overloaded. He wanted to push that psychic bombardment from the crowd away for her, engrossing her only in their touch, in the chemistry between them.

Long minutes ticked by. Finally, she blinked. "Trey," she said in a faint voice.

"That's right, love, I'm here," he crooned, relief rolling through him. She was starting to come back to him. Tenderly he began to lift her to her feet.

"Benjy?" Her voice was no stronger this time, but fear was lacing it.

"He's all right," he soothed. Triumph filled his voice. "You did it, honey. You found him." A slight smile crossed her face, before her body crumpled and he caught her in his arms.

"Does she need a doctor?" one of the security people asked.

Trey rose with Jaida cradled against his chest. "No," he said tersely, hoping like hell he was right. "Bring that stroller." One of the guards did as Trey bade him, and Trey looked at the one who had been trying unsuccessfully to apprehend him for the past several minutes. "Now, take me to my nephew."

The man obediently turned and led them away. "Mister, you're going to have a lot of explaining to do," he said.

"Get the police here first," Trey said shortly, gazing down into Jaida's pale face. "It's a long story, and I'm only going to tell it once."

Sergeant Mitch Garven hung up the phone and turned to the group assembled in the Kids' Kingdom Security Office. "Well, I spoke to Detective Reynolds of the LAPD. Your story checks out, Garrison. He's faxing us the information we need to finalize the identification, although I can't imagine any kid resembling an adult as much and *not* being related." He frowned and looked at Trey. "He does have some questions about how the heck you managed to track your nephew here, and I admit

I'm curious myself.'' His attention was diverted by the fax machine.

Benjy struggled down off Trey's lap and made his way cautiously over to the noisy machine. He turned back a couple times, as if to assure himself Trey was still there, then proceeded to satisfy his inquisitive nature. Soon he was peering up at the machine, his eyes widening when he recognized the likeness of himself emerging. He ran back to Trey quickly. ''It Benjy!'' he announced, clambering onto his uncle's lap.

Trey scooped him up with his free arm. He had the other wrapped around Jaida, and she was leaning heavily against him. Her eyes were closed, but he doubted she was sleeping. He needed to get her back to the motel quickly. He'd remembered the medication she carried with her, but her purse, along with Benjy's toy, was missing. A security officer had been dispatched to find them both, but hadn't yet returned.

It had taken an interminable time to summon the police, tell his story to the sergeant and then wait while contact was made with the LAPD to verify the story. Through it all he was aware of how much the woman at his side was suffering, while he'd been unable to do a damn thing about it.

The door pushed open then, but the guard who walked through it carried only the small bag with Benjy's elephant inside. ''Sorry, sir,'' the young man said. ''I even checked lost and found, but the purse you described wasn't there. Still could show up, though.''

Sergeant Garven ripped the sheet free from the machine. He studied it for a minute, then came over to where Trey was sitting with Benjy. Squatting in front of them, he turned Benjy's head with a gentle hand and pushed aside the silky, black curls that had grown longer over the weeks he'd been away. He found the lone freckle in back of the boy's left earlobe and got up, satisfied.

''It's Benjy, all right,'' he said with a chuckle, reaching down to ruffle the boy's hair.

Benjy ducked away shyly, hiding his face against his uncle's chest.

The man turned his attention back to Trey. ''I'd still like to have you come downtown later and make a statement.''

"Right now," Trey responded evenly, "all I want to do is get back to the motel with Benjy and Jaida. I need to call my sister as soon as possible." He didn't want to do that here, though. Not with the curious security guards standing around listening, and certainly not before he got Jaida to a bed. "I'll want to be kept informed about what you find out from that woman in there." He jerked his head toward the adjoining room, where the woman had been left with the head of Security and a couple of guards.

"She's got some explaining to do," Garven agreed. "I'm kind of eager to hear what she has to say myself."

"She's not working alone." Jaida's voice was strained and quiet. She didn't open her eyes as she spoke.

"What's that?" Sergeant Garven asked, startled.

"We don't believe the woman was alone," Trey said. "We have reason to believe that she was working with a man."

"Did you see anyone with her today?" The man's voice was sharp.

"No," admitted Trey. "But it would have been easy for him to fade back into the crowd once he saw the way things were going."

"Maybe," the sergeant said dubiously.

He promised to call Trey as soon as he was finished questioning the woman and then Trey gave him the phone number of the motel they were staying at. "I need to get these two back there," he said. Looking down at the boy he held in his lap, he added gruffly, "This little guy wants to call his mama."

The sky was just beginning to turn a dull gray, signaling dawn's approach. Mac and Trey sat on the balcony outside of Trey's room. Inside, Lauren and Benjy slept on one of the beds. Lauren held her baby close, even in sleep. The men had crept outside hours before so as not to disturb them.

"You were able to get here in record time," Trey observed.

"It cost us a fortune, but it was worth it. Lauren would have run here if she'd had to." Mac nodded toward the terrace doors. "You did real good, buddy."

"Jaida did it all," Trey corrected. "Most of the time I felt like I was just along for the ride." He frowned then. He had summoned a doctor to their room, who'd given Jaida a sedative. But he'd been aware even at the time that their efforts would be woefully inadequate. He'd put her to bed and piled her with extra blankets to still the trembling in her limbs. She hadn't seemed to have moved in any of the times he'd checked on her.

"Who would ever have believed that we'd find Benjy with a psychic's help?" Mac said, shaking his head in disbelief. "You know, Raine and Lauren were convinced all along that Jaida would be able to help us." At Trey's silence, Mac turned to look at him. "I know you had your doubts at first. But somewhere along the line you must have changed your mind about Jaida."

Yeah, he'd had his doubts. And he'd made her fully aware of them at every turn. His had never been a trusting nature, and belief in Jaida's abilities took more faith than he'd ever had.

But it wasn't the change in his opinion of Jaida that was really worthy of comment, it was the change in his feelings for her. There was no way he could explain to Mac the strange connection that leaped to life between them every time they touched.

"Did you get the arrangements made for your flight back?" Trey asked.

Mac nodded. "You want them at ꞊ sa꞊ꞓ house, I assume."

"For now," Trey answered. "Let's keep a couple of our men with them at all times, too."

Mac shook his head. "No need. I'll stay with them myself."

"Thanks," Trey said. "I'll feel better if you're there, at least until I return. They'll be comfortable with you." He paused for a moment, then added deliberately, "Make sure you're armed at all times."

The two men exchanged a level glance. "You got it." Mac was silent for a time before he ventured, "How long are you planning to keep them hidden away, Trey?"

"Until I know for sure just who the hell is behind the kidnapping and why," Trey replied tersely. "Jaida is sure the woman wasn't working alone, that a man is involved, too. Once the woman starts talking, we'll have a better idea what's been going on. In the meantime, I can't afford to let the kidnapper have another chance."

"When will you be coming back?" Mac asked.

Trey thought for a moment. "I need to stay here another few days and deal with the police. They'll be interrogating the woman we caught, and I want to be here when she spills the information about her partner."

Trey's certainty that there would be a partner, despite having only Jaida's word for it, didn't escape Mac. Something had changed his partner's feelings about Jaida West. He wondered if it stemmed only from the fact she'd led him to Benjy, or if it was caused by something much, much more complicated.

The sun was high overhead when Mac and Lauren were ready to leave with Benjy again.

"I still don't understand why you can't come with us now, Trey," Lauren said, her pretty face troubled with a frown. "And I hate to rush away like this without even talking to Jaida. We owe her so much!" Her voice choked for a moment as she thought of all the woman had returned to her. She hugged Benjy closer to her. "It just doesn't seem right to leave without thanking her."

"I don't want her awakened." Trey's voice was firm. "The experience yesterday..." He hesitated. Just the memory of what Jaida had put herself through to help them find Benjy made him swallow hard. "It was difficult for her," he finished at last. "The best thing we can do is let her sleep as long as she's able." And hope like hell that sleep alone would be enough to restore her stamina.

Lauren bit her lip, then finally nodded reluctantly. Mac cast his partner a speculative glance. His words a moment ago had held a tinge of possessiveness.

"You'll remember the flight plan," Trey said to his partner.

Mac nodded laconically. Pilots were required to submit flight plans to the airports they were using, but Trey had been worried about leaving a trail in case anyone was interested in their destination. There were ways to change the plan en route, ways that would make them difficult, if not impossible, to trace. "Don't worry, Trey. I've got it covered."

Trey crossed to his sister and encompassed her and his nephew in a hug. "Quit worrying, honey. This will all be over pretty soon. The worst is behind us." She smiled at him, and he held out his hand for Benjy to high-five. "I'll see you again pretty soon, okay, big guy? Take care of your mom for me."

Benjy gave him a toothy grin. From his perch in his mother's arms, the world appeared happy and secure.

"Oh, I almost forgot," Trey muttered, looking around the room. Spotting the bag he was seeking, he fetched its contents for his nephew. "You'll be wanting this, I'll bet."

"El-funt," Benjy crowed delightedly. He reached out and snatched it from his uncle's hand, crooning happily. "El-funt, Mama."

Lauren blinked away tears at the sight. As precious as the toy was to Benjy, it would always mean infinitely more to her. It represented Jaida's help, and the way her son had been returned to her. She looked back at Trey. "You'll join us soon?"

He nodded and hugged her again. "As soon as I can."

Mac shepherded Lauren and Benjy to the door. Trey stopped him with his hand on Mac's arm. "Take care of them," he ordered in a low voice.

The two men exchanged a long glance. "You know I will," Mac promised quietly. Trey watched them leave, then turned and crossed the room, opening the door to Jaida's room.

He walked over to the bed and gazed down at her. Her breathing was still deep and even, but she was no longer huddled like a cocoon in the middle of the bed. Sometime in the past hour she'd shed one of the blankets he'd covered her with, and it lay on the floor at his feet.

He picked it up and folded it carefully. He hoped this was a good sign, that she'd be waking up soon. With a gentle hand he reached down and pushed the heavy mass of pale hair away from her face.

Then, with a feeling of déjà vu, he pulled up a chair and settled in for a silent vigil over Jaida as she slept.

Chapter 12

The room was quiet, the air heavy with late-afternoon humidity. Jaida awoke gradually to a sense of sticky discomfort. She lay still for a minute, blinking groggily, trying to get her bearings. Her memory slowly filtered back to her.

Benjy. They'd found him.

She frowned, trying to recall the exact course of events following the scene in the park, but the rest of that day was hazy at best. Her head felt as if it was full of cotton batting. She knew from experience that the sensation came from around-the-clock, druglike slumber.

Slipping out of bed, she padded past the door to the adjoining room. There was no sound coming from the adjoining room, and she wondered groggily where Trey and his family were. The bright sunlight spilling in at the bottom of the heavy draperies alluded to daytime, but she had no way of knowing how long she'd been asleep. She paused to turn up the air conditioner and headed to the bathroom.

Standing under the stinging spray of the shower, Jaida began to feel somewhat human again. She felt alarmingly weak, as if she were recovering from a long, serious bout of flu. Her head was throbbing, but the pain was at a tolerable level, un-

like the clawing agony she'd been in before Trey had put her to
bed.

She stilled in the act of washing her hair. Unlike much of that
day, she had a remarkably accurate memory of being undressed and placed under a mountain of covers to still her
body's shaking. The memory stood out, starkly real against the
jumbled mess her mind had been after finding Benjy. She'd
been reduced that afternoon to a backdrop, a surreal mural
splashed with dozens of strangers' worries, phobias and desires. She took a deep breath and pushed the thought away. She
didn't *want* to remember parts of that day, or what the experience had reduced her to. It was enough to hold on to the fact
that Benjy was finally safe.

Which meant her usefulness to Trey was at an end.

The ache in her heart kept time with the throbbing in her
temples. Her joy and relief at Benjy's safe return were uncon-
ditional, but they brought with them an irrefutable finality. She
should be eager to return to the peaceful valley to recover. Instead, she dreaded the time as it drew inexorably nearer. Step-
ping out of the shower, she wrapped herself in a towel and
grabbed another for her hair. She walked back into the bedroom, her eyes needing a moment to adjust to the dimness.

She sensed his nearness before she'd taken more than a few
steps. She froze. He was standing silently in the corner of her
room, as if he'd just turned away from the windows. Belatedly
aware of her attire, she dropped the towel she'd intended to use
for her hair, and with both hands secured the one she'd
wrapped around her body. It seemed a fragile barrier beneath
his intent regard.

Without taking his eyes from her, Trey reached out and
pulled the cord to open the draperies, immediately brightening
the room. He examined her face. She still looked fragile.
Twenty-six straight hours of sleep hadn't eliminated the delicate mauve shadows beneath her eyes. But there was a hint of
color in her cheeks now. He wondered if it was a sign of her
return to health or a reaction to his presence. The latter possibility was provoking.

The sight of her in that damn towel was provoking, too. Although his brain hadn't sent them a conscious signal, his feet

started moving toward her. He bent down and picked up the spare towel she'd dropped.

"Need some help with this?" he asked.

Jaida remained frozen, her mind slow to interpret his intentions. And then it was too late. By the time her head was shaking in negation, he was behind her, blotting the dampness from her wet hair.

The water had turned it a dark, molten gold. He imagined it shedding beads of liquid gold across the thick, white towel. Bending closer, he inhaled deeply. Gardenias. The fragrance suited her somehow. It evoked images of long, hot, Southern nights spent in an old-fashioned four-poster with a lazy overhead ceiling fan doing little but stirring the humid air.

Deliberately, he slid one hand up her arm and cupped her shoulder. Almost as if he had summoned it, the familiar scene appeared in his mind. He could see them together, the black sheets beneath her back, her slim body twisting under his. Trey closed his eyes, savoring the vivid image.

Jaida gasped and jerked away from him. He watched her with heavy-lidded eyes. For one brief, heart-stopping second she imagined that he had read her mind and shared the erotic image that had reappeared there. It would account for the half dangerous, half hungry look on his face.

Then reality reasserted itself. She was the one prone to random snatches of surreal visions, not he. Still, she couldn't help sneaking a peek at her rumpled bed, rechecking the color of the sheets. White. Letting out a shaky sigh, she banished the sensual picture from her mind.

"I need to get dressed," she said shakily. She was experiencing an almost desperate need to be alone again.

"I brought you something to wear." He motioned to the chair near her bed, and she noticed for the first time the dress draped across it.

"I have clothes."

"Not for where we're going." He walked across the room toward her with slow, measured treads.

"Where we're going?" She repeated his words in a thready voice as she tracked his movement toward her.

"You need to eat," he replied, stopping in front of her. A small smile tilted his hard mouth. "A lot, knowing you. I had some spare time in the twenty-six hours or so you were sleeping. I scouted a restaurant I think you'll like.'' He had had time to do some shopping, also. He'd told himself it was because she wouldn't have brought anything appropriate to wear to the pricey restaurant. He had had to pick something up for himself, as well. But as soon as he'd bought that sapphire-blue dress he'd seen in a store window, he'd known he was a liar. He'd purchased it because it gave him pleasure to look at it, touch it and imagine her wearing it. Imagine himself taking it off her.

Her gasp interrupted his thoughts.

''Twenty-six hours!'' She shook her head dazedly. ''Fifteen or sixteen is usually enough. I've never slept around the clock like that, not even—''

She didn't complete the sentence, but she didn't need to. He knew she was alluding to the concert that had turned into a nightmare for her, the one that had destroyed her dreams of singing in public.

''You've never experienced anything as traumatic as what happened in the park when we found Benjy, either,'' he said, his voice harsh. ''Do you think I don't know what that scene did to you? Why in hell did you put yourself through that? I told you to stay put while I searched the crowd.''

She swallowed. She didn't want to think about that day, the impulses that had forced her decision. It had been the hardest one she'd ever had to make in her life, and she wasn't proud of the amount of time it had taken her to reach it. In the end, there hadn't been much of a choice after all.

''I had to go,'' she finally answered quietly. ''You might not have found him—there were so many people....''

He saw the anguish that swept briefly over her face and cursed himself for putting that look there. He reached out and caught a long, damp strand of hair and trapped it between two fingers. Deliberately, he began winding it around his index finger. ''I sounded ungrateful just then. I'm not. We owe you so much—if it wasn't for you, we would never have found Benjy in time. But, honey, you've got to start thinking of yourself. I won't pretend to know exactly what it cost you to go into that crowd, but dammit, I know what you were like when it was over.''

She dropped her gaze, avoiding the intent look on his face.

"Why do you do it?" He sounded genuinely puzzled. "Why in God's name do you put yourself through this kind of pain to help strangers?"

Strangers. The word echoed in her mind. He hadn't been a stranger to her, not since the first time he'd touched her. She hadn't understood him, hadn't trusted him right away, but she'd never denied the immediate and violent reaction she'd had to him. Perhaps she didn't need to explain that to him. He'd shown her time and again that he was affected by it, too, and strangely compelled by it.

Belatedly, she answered his question. "Why do I even exist if I don't use my gift to help others? It's cost me so much in my life, and it would seem futile if it didn't mean something." She caught her breath, distracted for the moment by his thumb rubbing the moisture from the ribbon of hair he'd twined around his finger. "It's rare when it becomes ... so intense."

Frowning, he corrected her. "You need to take prescription pain medication every time you have a vision. Don't tell me that's not intense."

She smiled slightly at the concern in his voice. It was foolish to be warmed by it, but she was nonetheless. "I choose to use my gift to help others. And when I'm successful, like when we found Benjy, there is nothing that can compare with that kind of joy or satisfaction."

He remained troubled despite her answer. She needed to be protected; she couldn't be trusted to take care of herself. What would stop some unscrupulous person from learning of her talents and taking advantage of her? If her gift ever became widely known, she'd be the target of every con artist in the country. Someone needed to watch over her, to make sure she didn't often put herself in the kind of situation she'd thrust herself into when she'd entered that crowd. He could appreciate what she had done for his family, but her disregard for her own emotional state was maddening.

Suddenly aware of the direction of his thoughts, he disentangled his fingers and stepped back from her, shaken. It wasn't the first time she'd elicited his protective instincts, but each time was equally troubling. He'd always had a strong need to protect his family. But Jaida wasn't family. So why did she spark the same urge to look after her?

He wasn't sure he wanted to examine the answer to that question.

"Where's Benjy? Is Lauren here yet?" she asked.

"She's been and gone, honey." At her disappointed face, he added, "Lauren was upset she didn't get to speak to you before she left, but I didn't want you disturbed. You needed to sleep. Mac flew her and Benjy to a safe house in the Rockies. They'll stay there for a while. You'll have a chance to talk to her later on the phone."

"What about the kidnapper they arrested? Has she told the police anything—"

"Jaida."

His voice was soft, but purposeful. She caught her breath at the look in his eyes. She'd often seen them impenetrable, unreadable, but the light in them now was all too easy to interpret.

"Do you really want to continue this conversation wearing that towel?"

She looked down quickly, newly reminded of her state of dishabille. She could feel heat suffuse her cheeks. It grew hotter at his next words.

"Because if you do, I'm not sure just how much longer you'll be wearing it."

His face was taut, a mask of frustration. His eyes glittered like hot emeralds, and the look he was painting her with made her bones weaken.

"Get dressed," he suggested finally. "I'll be back." He strode quickly from the room.

As the door to the adjoining room closed behind him, Jaida dropped to the bed. She was inexperienced, but not so naive that she'd had any difficulty reading the look he'd worn. It filled her with elation and wariness simultaneously. Everything womanly inside her responded to the blatant promise in his eyes. The caution that had been part of her nature for so long seemed to dissolve each time he got near her. A man like Trey would be a practiced, experienced lover, capable of satisfying a woman completely. She knew that instinctively.

She sat still on the edge of the bed, apprehension filling her. She just didn't know what a twenty-seven-year-old virgin would be able to offer him in return.

* * *

"We'll order right away," Trey told the white-jacketed waiter. He inclined his head toward Jaida.

"The seafood Alfredo over fettucine noodles," she decided aloud. "And a small ladies' fillet. With a baked potato, please, and no dressing on the salad."

The waiter was too well trained to display his surprise by more than a flicker of an eyelash. "Very well, madam," he said, his pencil flying furiously. "Will there be anything else?"

"Not until dessert," Trey told him, amusement in his voice. He placed his order and ordered a bottle of wine for the meal, as well.

When the waiter disappeared, Trey returned his attention to Jaida. She was looking almost recovered from her ordeal, a process he hoped the meal would complete. But nothing could detract from her appearance. She'd pulled her hair into a chignon at the base of her scalp. The look was coolly elegant, and one he'd often admired on the women he'd dated.

He didn't like it at all on her.

He was used to seeing her with that sheaf of hair tumbling over her shoulders and down her back. He preferred the look. He liked to think that at any moment he could reach over and bury his hand in its washed-silk texture, or fantasize about having it spread across his chest. Right now his fingers were itching to find just how many pins he'd have to dispense with to send the mass of hair cascading.

The thought made his loins grow heavy. So did her appearance. He'd bought clothes for women before, and he had an eye for color and sizes. The dress he'd purchased for Jaida was a perfect frame for her unusual coloring and highlighted her exquisite figure. The straps were narrow pieces of material that defied gravity and left her shoulders and arms completely bare. He traced the neckline with his gaze. It delved to the top of her breasts, hinting at the delicate cleavage below. Although not snug, the dress draped her curves enticingly, ending several inches above her knees.

She had had the attention of every man in the room when they'd entered, and he'd been torn between the desire to cover her with his suit jacket and the urge to take her back to the hotel room. He'd done neither. Instead, he was sitting across

from her, suffering from the constant arousal that had been
simmering in him since they'd shared the cabin.

"What's the matter?"

"Hmm?"

"Is there something wrong?" she asked again. "A moment
ago, you looked, so . . . fierce." Her voice tapered off, and she
wished she hadn't spoken. That intense, hooded regard was
focused on her now, bathing her with heat.

"No," he answered belatedly. "There's nothing wrong."

"Is it the woman we had arrested?" she insisted. "You never
told me if she's given the police any information that would be
useful."

Trey shook his head. "So far all they know is that her name
is Maria Kasem. She's refused to tell them anything more. I'm
hoping to talk Garven into letting me speak with her tomorrow."

"I could help."

"No." His answer was immediate and so emphatic she
blinked. "I know what you're offering, but you're not coming
to the precinct with me, and you're not going to talk to Maria.
And you most definitely are not going to touch her."

Her chin went up at his autocratic tone. "It isn't your decision to make."

Too late he recognized that he had angered her with his orders. But he wasn't about to back down.

"You need rest between your visions. You've told me that
yourself."

"I've had rest."

"Not enough," he disputed with finality. "And you know as
well as I that what happened at the park was more intense than
you're used to. Your body and mind need time to recuperate,
and that's just what you're going to give them time to do."

"We'll see."

It was apparent from her airy drawl that she didn't consider
the matter closed. His mouth flattened. He'd been wondering
earlier what would keep her safe from unscrupulous people
who would use her gift for their own ends, but perhaps a bigger fear was who would protect her from herself. She didn't
seem to have an ounce of self-preservation.

The wine arrived then and was presented to Trey for his approval. He signaled the waiter, and the man poured two glasses, setting one in front of Jaida, then him.

She eyed hers warily. "I don't usually drink."

"One glass won't hurt you," he said. He watched with a slight smile as she sipped cautiously from her glass. She probably shouldn't have more than one, anyway. With her strange metabolism there was no telling what effect an excess of alcohol would have on her. But he wouldn't let her drink to excess. He'd hoped that a little wine would relax muscles that were probably still much too tight and relieve some of the strain she'd been under. But instead, the strain on him was increasing.

The wine moistened her lips, making them glisten in the table's candlelight. He imagined himself leaning across the table and licking the moisture away. She'd taste of wine and the sweetness that was uniquely Jaida.

She looked up from her salad a few moments later to see Trey stabbing at his with fierce intent. For once she had a few seconds to watch him unobserved, and she savored the opportunity. The black suit and white shirt he was wearing provided a perfect foil for his dark good looks. Complete with a subtly patterned tie, he appeared remarkably similar to the man who had first approached her in the meadow in Arkansas.

He'd become so much more now. She'd known from the first time she'd seen him that he wasn't what he seemed. A master at pretense, he had from the beginning been able to shield his thoughts, while wielding that polished charm. That ability had made her wary and angry by turns. She would have done well to continue viewing him with only those two emotions. But the possibility of maintaining a distance from him had vanished the first time he'd touched her. She somehow knew that the flame that sprang to life under Trey's touch was not something she'd ever experience with anyone else. She accepted the fact stoically.

It was not quite as easy to accept the fact that the man who evoked such a response would soon disappear from her life.

* * *

"I'm not tipsy," she insisted, preceding him into his motel room. "And I'm not the least bit tired. We should have gone for a drive or something."

He smiled. No, she wasn't tipsy, as he'd teasingly suggested, but the small amount of wine had flared color to her cheeks. Regardless of her protests, he'd brought her straight back to their rooms. It wasn't late, but he didn't want her to exhaust herself.

He changed the subject to distract her. "I have to get up early tomorrow, if I want to catch Garven at the precinct."

She was immediately disarmed. She had failed to consider that Trey had probably gotten by on very little sleep since Benjy was found. "Wouldn't he have called you if Maria Kasem had named her accomplice?"

Trey undid the knot from the tie and pulled it from his shirt. "I'd certainly hope so. I told him to. It appears she's keeping quiet, at least for the time being. I don't know what she's hoping to gain."

He kicked off his shoes and undid the top two buttons on his shirt. Her mouth went dry. He was still fully covered, but his actions were as seductive as if he were doing a striptease. His open buttons revealed a wedge of muscled chest, with an intriguing thatch of black, curling hair.

He paused in the act of unbuttoning his cuffs. Frowning, he took a step toward Jaida. "What's wrong?" She was completely still, her gazed fixed on him.

She backed hastily away. "Nothing."

He surveyed her for a moment, noting the way her gaze kept slipping away from him and then sneaking back. Masculine satisfaction curled inside him. Deliberately, he finished unbuttoning his cuffs, then rolled them back on his forearms. She was watching him raptly, and his eyes drooped to half-mast. He strolled toward her.

"Are you sure you're feeling all right?"

She moistened her lips with the tip of her tongue and shook her head dumbly. Her head screamed a message to her feet, but she remained rooted to the floor.

"Because your face is flushed." He used the tip of his finger to trace across her cheekbones. "Right here." His finger trailed lower, until it rested against the pulse pounding at the base of her throat. "And your pulse is racing . . . here."

Jaida swallowed hard. It didn't seem fair that he was able to call forth her reaction to him so effortlessly. Then she made the mistake of looking in his eyes again, and what she saw there scorched her.

Desire. Raw and unbridled, it simmered in his green gaze as it rested on her. Their eyes remained locked as his finger continued its liberties and wove a meandering path across her shoulder, and followed the narrow strap of her dress down to its neckline. Her breathing grew more labored as Trey traced an invisible line across the top of her breasts. Oxygen was in short supply when his finger dipped, for one leisurely moment, into the cleavage exposed.

He cupped her shoulders with his hands, enjoying the prickling sparks of electricity that jumped between them. "It's like fireworks going off beneath my hands every time I touch you," he said huskily. "You feel it, too, don't you, Jaida? You have from the first. That's why you pulled away from me that day in the meadow." She was trembling, and automatically he caressed her shoulders.

"Yes." Her response was little more than a whisper. She watched a satisfied smile tilt his lips, and he skated his hands slowly down her arms. It was frightening to be held like this, to feel the current skitter crazily between them. She tensed involuntarily, wondering for a moment if his touch would elicit another vision or bring her yet another peek into his feelings, his past. But nothing existed except the chemical reaction between the two of them. The sensations he was causing within her seemed too strong for anything else to interfere.

Beckoned by the open neck of his shirt, her hand moved of its own volition. It hovered timidly, until Trey rasped, "Touch me." He guided her hand inside his shirt, and her fingers curled in the crisp, dark hair on his chest. Exhilaration filled her at the shudder that escaped him then, warring with the sensuous wonder of touching him as she'd been longing to do. He unbuttoned the rest of his shirt quickly, pulling the tails from his pants.

Unbidden, both her hands came up to explore his muscled chest, rubbing and kneading it rhythmically. His fingers went to the zipper hidden in the back of her dress. In the next moment he was dragging the narrow straps from her shoulders, freeing her breasts.

The dress hadn't allowed for a bra, and the air-conditioned air in the room was cool on her sensitized nipples. He watched them grow even tauter under his gaze, then his arms snaked around her and brought her into contact with his torso. He caught her gasp in his mouth.

Hungrily he kissed her, without the restraints he was usually so careful to keep in place. A woman like her should scare the hell out of a man like him. He'd lived his life with his guard raised, yet she could read him with a touch. He should have been running in the opposite direction, but the connection between them was too rare, too tempting, not to stay.

He lifted his head, desire clawing at him. The look of drugged wonder on her face did nothing for his control. "Do you remember what I told you the last time I kissed you?"

She blinked eyelids that seemed weighted. Yes, she remembered. She remembered everything about him. "You said when it was over..."

"We'd finish what was between us," he grated. "Now's the time, Jaida. If it's not what you want, too, this is your chance. Walk out that door, back to your room."

He must have thought he was giving her a choice, but she knew there really wasn't one at all. He had been right all along. The feelings between them were too strong to deny. She'd be a fool to believe that he felt anything but passion for her.

She'd be a bigger fool to walk away from it.

He waited, but she didn't move. She stood there, breasts bare, watching him with eyes that managed to look both anxious and beguiling. When she spoke, her soft drawl made her words seem even more provocative.

"I'm not going anywhere."

Chapter 13

Jaida's words had Trey releasing a pent-up breath, one he hadn't been aware of holding. Then he drew her into his embrace again, not quite gently, and shuddered with the exquisite sensation of her skin touching his own. He wanted to believe that he hadn't been lying, that the choice had indeed been hers. But he'd spoken the truth that night in the cabin. This thing between them was unavoidable.

Her gasp distracted him then, as she reacted to the sparks leaping between them. He knew without a doubt that she felt them, too, that she always had. This woman had been entwined in his life since the first day in the meadow, the first time that he had touched her. Their fates had been sealed irrevocably from that day, as had this night. This long-awaited night.

Impatiently he tugged at her dress, which had draped at her hips. His movement sent the dress to form a pool at her feet. He released the pins from her hair, five of them, and her hair tumbled over her shoulders.

He surveyed her then through slitted eyes. With that pale hair and light skin, she looked like an ice princess, all haughty and cool. That appearance was in direct contrast with her personality, he knew, and the contradiction was driving him crazy.

Deliberately, he traced a finger down one breast to encircle the hardened nipple with a feather-light touch. Primitive satisfaction filled him as he watched her shiver and gasp. It was his nature to retain control of every situation, to be unwilling to relinquish it. Now, at this moment, he had no doubt of his capability to do just that.

Jaida forced her eyes open, when they wanted nothing more than to remain closed in a helpless response to his touch. What she saw when she opened them almost made her weep.

Desire, the strength of which weakened her knees, was evident on Trey's face. But so was a primordial male satisfaction. She knew he was firmly in control of his emotions, and she had a sudden urge to flee. Even as his mouth went to her neck, she was aware of being at a great disadvantage. He was still wearing his pants and shirt. The clothing represented, to her, the guard he kept over his own emotions. Others would be stripped of their defenses, appear vulnerable, but not Trey. Never Trey. And though she knew better than most what made the man the way he was, his continued defenses now made her angry in a way she didn't totally comprehend.

The cord along her neck was nibbled, and she flinched slightly at the stinging kisses he dropped there, to be soothed immediately with his tongue. Her eyes fluttered to half-mast and she became aware of the care he was taking to avoid touching her anywhere else. Despairingly she wondered if making love to her was something he could do without reciprocating any answering emotion other than need. She didn't question if it was love she felt for Trey; love seemed a far too weak description for the flood of emotion that overwhelmed her each time she felt his touch. She only questioned how fate could be so cruel as to give this man such power over her emotions, without providing her with a like control over his.

He bracketed her body, resting his forearms against the wall on either side of her. Still he kept a few inches between them, and that distance represented emotional miles to her. Her throat was sealed with a necklace of hot, moist kisses, and her head fell back to rest against the wall. Her lips parted slightly, and it became more difficult to concentrate on her morose thoughts under the wicked distraction of his mouth.

He moved lower, skirting her breasts, concentrating on the smooth, pale skin of her waist and stomach. He sank to his knees, and she felt the hot kisses trailing down the outside of one thigh, the flick of a tongue across the back of her knee. Her eyes remained closed, her neck arched, her breathing growing ragged. He forged a matching path with his lips on the inside of her leg, and her knees parted to allow him greater access without her direct volition. His mouth scorched a path up her inner thigh, before pressing a kiss against her center, at the apex of her thighs. She jerked in involuntary response to that bold kiss. She could feel his heat through the thin, silk panties she still wore, and a strangled cry escaped her.

Jaida reached for him then, doubts swirling away. Her fingers dug into his shoulders, and he obeyed her unspoken demand, rising to fix his mouth over hers. Her lips opened beneath his, and her kiss evoked a response of its own. Without thinking, Trey closed the gap between them, pressing her close against him. He wasn't aware of the action of her hands until he felt her fingers smoothing over his chest, and he shuddered in response. He shrugged out of his shirt and it fluttered, unnoticed, to the floor. Her hands were stroking over his shoulders and down his biceps, making an exploration out of their journey. His muscles tensed as he attempted to counteract his body's natural reaction to her touch, a reaction that had seemed predestined from the start.

At first he'd been curious about the chemistry that leaped to life between them when they touched, and at times he'd evoked it deliberately, stoking the flames, savoring the uncustomary reaction. Fires were springing to life everywhere they touched. As gratifying as her response was, his own was just as involuntary, just as out of control.

Out of control wasn't a natural state for Trey Garrison.

He shook his head slightly, trying to clear it, unfamiliar with the fog of desire that had every other thought fading away. His mind wasn't obeying his command to focus; Jaida's touch was making a shambles of his carefully erected defenses. When her mouth went to his chest he groaned and took a step back. He wasn't consciously aware of his own attempt to recreate that distance between them, or of his failure to do so. Jaida followed him step for step, matched him stroke for stroke. His hands came up to delve in her hair, and he cradled her skull in one large palm, unconsciously guiding her lips to the places on his chest that would give him the most pleasure. The scrape of her teeth across one tight nub on his chest may have been by accident or design, but the effect had his breath hissing out between his teeth. He clutched handfuls of her long, blond tresses and rubbed them against his chest, closing his eyes in sybaritic pleasure. This was too much like the fantasies he'd had about her for days. But it was more than the fantasies, much more.

Reason edged further away. His hands stilled in her hair, sanity flickering feebly from a great distance. He'd anticipated this moment from the first time he'd touched Jaida. But in the recesses of his mind he was aware that this was going to cost him far more than he'd ever given another woman. Then she tilted her head to look up at him, her deep-blue eyes dazed now with passion, and that distant warning in his mind was effectively silenced.

Gathering her up suddenly in his arms, he walked the short distance to the bed and followed her down on it. Propping himself up on one elbow, he leaned over her, his gaze all-encompassing and intent.

Jaida quaked beneath that experienced gaze but sent one hand around his neck, fingers delving into the close-cropped hair at his nape. She understood despite her inexperience that he would want to regain his flagging control. Something deeply feminine inside her knew that to allow him to do so would be a mistake. So she gave in to the overpowering urge to touch him, to stroke his chest, with its light padding of muscles.

Trey held still under her gentle touch for long moments, unable to separate the sensations racing through him. The constant electricity between them sent flares of current firing under his skin, through his blood, mingling with the pulsing of arousal.

She knew the exact moment that he gave up his silent battle. A great sigh shuddered through him, and he pushed closer against her wandering hand, seeking a firmer touch. His hands went to her breasts, and the intimate caress caused her fingers to falter.

She had no intention of turning back, couldn't have forced herself to do so. She wasn't afraid of Trey; he'd never hurt her physically. But she couldn't control the naturally feminine fear of a woman about to lie with a man for the first time. He was so much bigger, and much stronger. Could he help hurting her?

He bent his head and took her nipple in his mouth and she gasped at the warm, wet suction. Her fingers went to his head and slid through his dark, thick hair, holding him closer to her. An involuntary whimper escaped her when he raised his head, but his hand came up to soothe the breast he'd abandoned, as he turned his attention to its twin. The aching longing in the pit of her stomach exploded, sending tendrils of sensation throughout her body.

His knee was urging her legs apart, before sliding upward to press lightly against her center. Jaida bucked against the pressure, which provided momentary relief from the unfamiliar ache lodged there. But soon it wasn't enough. Her hands skated desperately over his broad back and made contact with the dress pants he was still wearing.

She tugged at them frantically, ineffectually. Had she been able to think, she would have been embarrassed at the prospect of undressing Trey, tantalizingly frightened at the thought of his nudity, but right now the barrier between them was unbearable. He withstood her fumbling efforts for a few moments, but then the back of her hand brushed against the ridge behind his zipper, and he groaned.

She abruptly stilled at the sound. He raised his head and looked at her, his eyes smoldering slices of emeralds. "Touch me," he demanded huskily when she made no further movements. "Do it, Jaida." He took her hand in his and drew it down to rest against the zipper of his pants, pressing it against the bulge of hard male flesh there. She made a sound that was shocked discovery, and it mingled with his second groan.

He shaped her fingers against him, and she obeyed eagerly, lost in wonder. Her hand remained there after he released it, exploring his hard length. This was totally new for her, the freedom to touch and explore, and it seemed safe somehow through the barrier of his clothes. She wondered how he would feel in her hands, with nothing between them, but couldn't bring herself to work the zipper.

Trey remained motionless, enjoying her gentle touch. He rocked his hips once, forcing a firmer caress, but soon it wasn't enough. When one of her hands crept to the waistband of his pants, he couldn't summon the patience to wait. He reached down and unfastened them himself, drawing down the zipper, lifting his hips and kicking them off. He removed something from his pants pocket before disposing of his maroon briefs. Then he rolled back to lie on his side to face her.

Jaida's eyes were drawn inexorably, irresistibly, to his masculinity. And this time he didn't have to beg for her touch. She reached for him, and was shocked at the feel of his heated, pulsing length. Shyness was forgotten as she explored him in fascination, running her fingers over the veins and ridges of his desire. He was silk-encased steel, and her fingers faltered at the thought of him inside her. She hadn't guessed that he'd be so large, so powerful, and for the first time realized that he couldn't help but hurt her.

Trey reached an arm around her waist and brought her close to him, so close that her breasts flattened against his chest. He rubbed against her, enjoying the sensation. Then he sealed her mouth with his again, his tongue delving deep, tangling with hers. His hand swept across her bottom, lifting her to fit against his arousal. Their kiss grew more desperate, more demanding. His fingers skated just barely beneath the elastic of her panties, before delving inside to caress the silky cheeks.

His mouth twisted against hers, his hunger fed by her answering demand. He pushed the panties off her hips and broke away from their kiss to feast his eyes on her uncovered secrets.

Jaida felt blistered by his searing regard, but made no pretense at modesty. The time for modesty was long past. And it was difficult not to respond to the blatant admiration in his eyes.

"You're beautiful," he rasped. He brushed a gentle hand across the pale-blond hair at the juncture of her thighs, and she flinched in surprise. He spread his fingers to cup her femininity, and his accompanying kiss succeeded in distracting her from his bold caress. He fitted his knee between both of hers, enjoying the feel of his hair-roughened leg between her silky-smooth ones. He parted her femininity and found the small bud of desire hidden there. Using her own dampness to moisten her, he rubbed sensuous circles around the sensitive bundle of nerves and felt Jaida writhe against him.

She broke away from his kiss. "Trey!" Her cry could have been a plea or a protest. But her hands went to his shoulders, her fingers clenching unconsciously on the muscled expanse. He left a trail of fire as his lips scorched a path to her breast and drew her nipple into his mouth. His devilish fingers continued to work their magic, and the dual assault had her writhing against him.

The smoldering embers of desire combusted, sending tendrils of fire racing through her veins. There was a direct connection between the sensations at her breast and between her thighs, and she was helpless to fight the tidal wave of feelings. They were as wondrous as they were new, and a little frightening in their intensity. Jaida moaned as her muscles tightened. Trey's actions grew firmer, her response wilder. She was reaching for something, something she didn't quite understand. Unconsciously, she began to fight that terrifying feeling.

"No." Trey's voice was in her ear, guttural and viscerally sexy. "Don't fight it. Let it happen. Let go. Jaida! Just let go, love." His hand moved more firmly against her and abruptly she shattered, crying out his name against his lips. Her body tightened, then bones and muscles dissolved, and she was jetted over a precipice of pleasure.

Awareness returned very gradually. Trey caressed her face, pushing away the damp hair at her temples. Her eyelids fluttered, and her gaze when it met his was unfocused. That look in her eyes beckoned tender feelings that had been buried in him long ago, feelings that would be better left hidden. But that didn't stop him from giving her a gentle kiss, one that couldn't quite hide the need that still raged within him.

He released her and let her shoulders rest against the mattress. She was only half aware of his actions to protect her, before he was back, leaning over her, coaxing her legs apart and moving between them. Panic flared briefly as she struggled against the drugging effects of her climax. His shoulders were broad, and above her he looked overwhelmingly strong and powerful. He took her hand in his and guided it to his manhood, where it was poised at the juncture of her thighs. She swallowed convulsively. He couldn't help but hurt her; he was too big, his control too frayed. She didn't dwell on the possibility of pain, though. She craved his strength on top of her, his body touching every inch of hers, pressing her deeper into the mattress. She wanted him, fiercely, totally. She wanted him to be a part of her, to fill her where she was damp and aching. And she wanted this to be enough. When he was gone and she was alone again, she didn't want any regrets.

She curled her fingers around his hard length and urged him closer. One hand moved to his hip, the other to his shoulder. Trey didn't wait for any other signal. He could feel her readiness in the slick, moist heat that greeted his entrance. His back teeth clenched as he inched into her, feeling her tight inner muscles stretch to accommodate him. His muscles bunched as he retreated a little, then he entered her completely with one long, smooth stroke.

Jaida couldn't prevent a wild cry from escaping her. That brief, tearing pain was sharp, but immediately faded. It was a dizzying welter of other sensations that had elicited her cry. She could feel him, tense and still, his body quivering as he rested his weight on his strong forearms. He was throbbing inside her, but remained unmoving.

"Jaida." His voice was raw, and full of regret. She refused to listen to that note, refused to allow him to feel it. She clutched at his shoulders and raised up to kiss him, trying to force him to surrender his flagging control. There was a moment when she was unsure of her success, before his weight pressed against her and his mouth ground against hers. She stroked his chest, his back, down his sculptured biceps and, daringly, across his hips.

"It's all right now." His voice was dark velvet in her ear, and she shuddered wildly when he nibbled at the skin beneath the lobe. "It's going to be fine." She didn't understand the meaning behind the words, but she responded to his soothing tone. Something began to flare within her again, something raw and frightening, and it warred with her response to his stinging wet kisses. She abruptly stilled, trying to regroup, afraid of losing herself completely to another body-shattering experience. But he wouldn't allow her to hold back. One hand slid beneath her and lifted her into his next thrust.

She tensed, but the anticipated spasm of pain was absent. Instead there was fullness and heat and the slick glide of flesh.

She felt him stretching her with each movement, and an answering pressure was building inside her.

Trey's other hand crept between their bodies and pressed firmly, a seductive temptation to succumb to the racking pleasure anew.

"No," Jaida whimpered, her head twisting on the pillow. "No more."

"Yes." His voice was low and hypnotic and totally entrancing. "Again, Jaida. Take more. Let go." His fingers touched her, practiced and inexorable. He rocked his hips against hers, over and over. His breath was coming in great gusts, blackness forming before his eyes. When he heard her cry, felt her body's release, he grasped her hips and lunged into her, again and again. There was a moment of awareness, just before his explosive climax, that this act had tied him to Jaida in a way he didn't want to admit. And then the shock waves of release flooded over him, and conscious thought ebbed away.

"You should have told me."

His words filtered through Jaida's haze of drowsy contentment. She lay on her side, facing away from him. His body was curved around hers, his arm across her waist, keeping her close. She didn't know how long they'd been lying like this, his other hand smoothing rhythmically through her hair. She caressed the arm at her waist. The meaning of his words was clear, and she'd known they'd be spoken.

"You might have stopped." She hadn't wanted to chance the possibility that he would regain his famed control and leave her. If this was all she would have of him she'd been determined to have it all, while she could.

Her whispered response had his hand stilling in her hair momentarily. She couldn't possibly know how impossible that feat would have been for him. "No," he refuted wryly. "But you should have said something, Jaida. I could have hurt you. Badly."

She turned her head to look at him over her shoulder. "You didn't," she assured him softly. He urged her body to face him, and she willingly complied. A soft kiss was pressed to her lips.

"Are you sure?"

She nodded.

He wasn't completely satisfied with her answer. Control was something that he prided himself on, but it had been noticeably absent in this instance. He knew that realization should bother him.

The first to lose control loses. The voice from his past hissed across his mind.

"Trey? Who was Colonel Lambert?"

He looked at her with stunned surprise. An instant later shock turned to an all-too-familiar wariness, and she could have bitten her tongue in half. She was pressed against him, her breasts against his chest, their legs entangled, and his random thought had passed to her so instantaneously she'd spoken without thinking. His body was completely still against hers, and she knew he had retreated in all ways but the physical. She could have wept at her clumsy probing.

Odd, but he'd almost forgotten the way that weird, mystical link between them could work. He doubted he'd ever get used to having her take these psychic peeks into his mind. Everything inside him recoiled from her ability.

"I'm sorry," she mumbled, trying to slip out of his arms. She hadn't felt so mortified since she'd been nine and the horrified looks on the faces of her mother's guests had told her better than words that she'd just mentioned something unacceptable. She wanted to do nothing more right now than hide.

His arms tightened automatically around her, preventing her escape. The shocked dismay he'd felt a moment ago at her question was nothing to his emotion at witnessing the look on her face now. He'd embarrassed her; no, worse than that, she was humiliated, in a way he'd bet she hadn't been since that witch of a mother of hers had made her feel like a freakish act of nature. He couldn't forgive himself for putting that look on her face.

What, after all, was a few answers from him? Especially after all she'd given to him, offered freely, without reservation. A couple of answers was no more than she had a right to. The fact that it was more than he offered most of the women in his acquaintance was another fact he didn't think about.

"Shhh, come back here." He restrained her feeble attempt to slip away from him and dropped a lingering kiss on her lips.

"I'm sorry," she mumbled again, as soon as he raised his lips. "You don't have to answer. I wasn't trying to, honest. I never try. It just came through and I asked without—"

"It's okay, Jaida, really," he assured her, trying to inject a note of humor in his voice. He wasn't going to let anything taint the time she'd spent with him here in this bed. When she remembered them, he wanted her to think of the pleasure they'd found with each other, pleasure he had the experience to know wasn't going to be found elsewhere. "I just get tired of talking about myself all day long, that's all."

His joke surprised a gust of air from her. "Yeah, Garrison, you're a real chatterbox."

He smiled involuntarily, as much at her relaxed drawl as at her words. Still, it took him several moments to gather his thoughts. He really wasn't familiar with this kind of give and take. "I guess you can say that Colonel Lambert saved my life." He could read her reaction in the way her gaze flew to his. "Not in a dramatic sense. He didn't pull me out of a flooded river or anything. But he saved me from the path I was heading down, just as surely as if he'd tossed me a life jacket." One of his hands went to her spine and rubbed up and down the delicate vertebrae there. "You'll find this difficult to believe, but I used to have a whale of a temper."

She didn't have much difficulty believing that. Once she had become convinced that his cold exterior was a facade, it hadn't been hard to realize that his rigid control hid emotions that burned much too hotly.

"I was mad...at just about everybody. Everything. And I let the world know it." *Mad* seemed an insipid word for the rage he had carried around inside him for so long. Rage at his mother, for being weak and ineffectual, for dying and leaving him and Lauren at Hank's mercy. Rage at a father whose biggest concern was drinking himself into a stupor, and who used his kids for punching bags whenever he was sober. Rage at a social system that had taken him and his sister out of that house, then made it impossible for them to stay together. When Lauren had been adopted, his whole reason for being was gone. And he'd gone about making the world pay for that.

"I was fifteen when I met Colonel Lambert. He walked up on me while I was inside his car, trying out my new skills at hotwiring." The colonel had been remarkably calm as he'd pointed out to the sullen-faced tough that he'd been trying to join the wrong two wires. Trey shook his head in remembered admiration. "He gave me two choices. I could answer his questions or wait for him to call the police."

He slid her a sideways gaze. "I didn't like answering questions any more then than now, but I chose that option. The police were already way too familiar with me and my escapades." Certainly they'd turned him over to the social agencies on enough occasions. He'd never known what the man had heard in his short, surly responses, or what he'd seen in the teenage hood who'd spent most of his last eight years on the street. What the man had offered next still had the power to stun him. "After we talked, he was quiet for a while, and then he gave me two more choices. Be taken to the police station or go home with him. I was big for my age, and cocky as hell. I didn't doubt my ability to take care of myself. I went home with him." His gaze grew pensive, faraway. "I lived with the colonel and his wife, Cora, for three years. They made me go to school, something I'd never done with any regularity. The colonel taught me . . . a lot."

Respect. The knowledge came flowing through her fingertips, where they were pressed against his chest, swirling through her mind with utter certainty. Jaida didn't doubt that Colonel Lambert had been the first man in his young life that Trey had respected. And that he'd been the one to teach Trey about control.

You did your job much too well, she said silently to the colonel. No one could accuse Trey these days of not keeping his emotions under control. She'd often damned that rigid front of his, and despaired of ever reaching him on any level.

But perhaps she was doing the colonel a disservice. The events from Trey's childhood must have started that wall he kept around his emotions. Each disappointment, each loss, had been another block in the fortress. The colonel had merely given him a socially acceptable way of dealing with the world.

Because he looked as if he was regretting his uncustomary verbosity, she kissed his chin to distract him. Conversation was forgotten. She didn't want to argue, and she didn't want to talk. She only wished to fill the remaining moments she had left with him with memories such as these. When the time came for him to leave her she would have nothing else, but she'd have this.

An intuition totally unrelated to her gift told her that time was coming quickly.

Trey stared hard at Sergeant Garven's ruddy-complected face. "What do you mean, Maria Kasem is gone?"

"I mean she's gone. She's been extradited to California. Two guards were sent for her, and they left about an hour ago. I was going to call and let you know."

"Damn!" Trey bit out the curse.

"It wasn't as if she was cooperating with us, anyway," Garven said fatalistically. "Maybe LAPD will have better luck with her, especially with the Feds involved."

Jaida tossed Trey a concerned look. He'd been visibly unhappy at her insistence on accompanying him this morning. Only her threat to take a taxi to the precinct alone had him grudgingly concede to bringing her along. Even then, she had spent the entire ride listening to his warnings, as he forbade her from even attempting to see the kidnapping suspect.

This news washed away all Trey's concerns about her involvement today. But it seemed to frustrate him just as much. "You say you didn't get any more information from the woman?" Jaida asked Garven.

"Nothing she gave willingly. We ran a check and found she had a rap sheet. Prostitution, bad checks, that sort of thing. She even did a few months' time on the last bad-check conviction."

Jaida swallowed. This woman had had Benjy in her care for a month, and all they knew about her was her name and that she was an ex-con. No wonder Trey was frustrated.

"Tell you one thing, though," grunted the sergeant. "If anyone can convince her to talk, it'll be the Feds. Kasem was definitely shook up at the news they were waiting for her. Maybe when they get done leaning on her, she'll feel a little more talkative."

There was nothing more the man could tell them, so Trey and Jaida returned to the motel.

"Now what?" she wondered aloud.

"I'm going to call L.A.," he responded. "I'll talk to Detective Reynolds there and tell him I want to be notified if Kasem gives them any information. It's the least he can do," he muttered. "He was sure worthless while we were tracking Benjy down."

After a moment, Jaida went back to her room and picked up the phone there. Trey had been checking daily with the lost-and-found office at Kids' Kingdom, inquiring about her purse. After a brief conversation, she hung up the receiver with a sigh. Still no luck. There was no use in holding out any more hope. If it was going to be turned in, she had a feeling it would have been. She'd already canceled her credit cards and made arrangements to have replacements issued, but she called the credit companies anyway. There was no record that someone had tried to access her accounts. She then made a call to Arkansas, but as she'd half expected, there was no answer. When she hung up the phone, Trey appeared in the doorway.

"Who were you talking to?" he inquired.

"I was just trying to reach Granny, but there's no answer at the cabin. I'm not surprised. She had been planning to visit her sister Nora and her husband. That's probably where she's at."

"Have you checked today with the lost and found?"

She nodded. "No luck, I'm afraid."

Trey frowned. "I'll replace the money that was in your purse, of course."

She immediately bristled at his words. "That won't be necessary."

"Yes, Jaida, it is." His voice was firm. "You've already put yourself through enough. There's no way we can repay you for finding Benjy, but I can make damn sure you don't incur any personal expenses along the way."

She stared at him, her chin squared. They hadn't mentioned compensation since the day he'd been determined to pay her off and send her home. She'd told him then she wouldn't take anything, and if he knew what was good for him, he wouldn't bring the subject up now, either. Especially now, when this experience had become so much more than a missing-person case.

Especially now that she was in love with him.

She had to turn away then, afraid of what he'd see in her face. She knew what was in store for her. Trey was grateful for her help in finding Benjy. And in spite of her inexperience, he'd given every sign of a man satisfied by their lovemaking last night. But she didn't try to fool herself into believing that it meant anything more special to him. Although he'd been concerned about her last night, and gentle once he'd learned she was a virgin, she didn't dare allow herself to hope for something that didn't have a cotton ball's chance in a windstorm of coming true.

She thought she was prepared for what it would be like back home in Arkansas alone and without him. No doubt it would be worse than she even expected. But she was determined to return to the valley with her pride. There would be no uncomfortable scenes when it was time for them to part. Despite his gratitude for Benjy, Trey owed her nothing. She wouldn't be able to bear it if she suspected he felt otherwise. Gratitude wasn't an emotion that would be enough from this man. Not nearly enough.

She'd rather return home shrouded in her tattered pride than make demands on him he couldn't hope to meet. When the time came for them to part ways, she'd do it with nonchalant dignity if it killed her.

Lost in her morose thoughts, she was startled by his presence behind her. He took her shoulders in his hands, and she was jolted anew by those tiny pinpricks of electricity that accompanied his touch. She'd awakened this morning, a slight achiness the only thing to remind her that she would no longer feel like the only twenty-seven-year-old virgin in the country. She'd been unable to summon any regrets.

"Are you tired?" The words were spoken into her ear, low and sensual. He pushed her hair back over her shoulder and kissed her lobe.

She shook her head, then stopped to arch her neck under his wandering mouth. "No."

"You didn't get much sleep last night." She didn't need his words to remind her of the hours they'd spent exploring each other. By the time she'd fallen into an exhausted slumber, the sky had already begun to lighten.

"Neither did you," she reminded him in a shaky voice. He made a sound of agreement, his mouth otherwise occupied. Her breathing grew unsteady.

It was a moment before she identified the ringing coming from his bedroom. Trey stiffened for a moment, then, cursing, straightened. He strode through the open door to snatch it up.

It was a few more moments before Jaida recovered. It took a concerted effort to calm her pulse, but she made the attempt before she joined him.

When she walked through the doorway, she was pleasantly shocked by the look of frustrated possessiveness in Trey's hooded gaze. The next moment it was gone, and his face was blank as he listened to the caller. After a few minutes he hung up, his expression remote.

"That was one of the FBI agents who has been tailing Penning. He was calling from Logan International Airport. Penning went there to pick up his parents, and they're on their way to the Cape."

"Will they be followed?"

He nodded. "The Feds are unwilling to give up, even now that Benjy's been found. They're still hoping to get something on Penning to put him away, which suits my purposes just fine. I doubt they'll be allowed to spend much more time on the case, though. Benjy is safely home, and there's nothing linking Penning to his kidnapping."

She watched him pace to the French doors. "Now what?"

He turned toward her, his look thoughtful. "Well, there's no use hanging around here. Kasem is gone, and so is the chance to talk to her. I wouldn't mind going back to Boston, though. I can't help but hope the agents do find something they can hang on Penning, something that would put him away for a good, long while." That would certainly solve a big problem of his. The evidence Lauren had stolen from Penning's house the night she'd escaped him wasn't enough to put him away. But if the FBI had other reasons to jail the man, Lauren and Benjy would be safe once again, to live a life finally free of fear.

He eyed Jaida. "How about it? Are you up for a trip back to Boston?"

An almost giddy sense of relief filled her at his words. There was no reason for her to accompany him; Benjy had been found and returned home. The only other possible interpretation of his invitation was that he wanted her with him, at least for a while longer.

"It's been...let's see—" Trey made a show of looking at his watch. "All of four hours since you last ate. You must be hungry."

She shook her head. His face was easing into an expression that was all too easy to read, one that had her bones dissolving.

"No?" He stalked toward her. "I am," he informed her. Reaching her, he caught her in a loose embrace and lowered his head. "In fact, I'm starved."

She returned his kiss with lips that wanted to tremble. She was certain waiting wasn't something he did gladly, but she felt as though she'd just been handed a reprieve. A few more hours, perhaps a couple of days, seemed very precious and much too short.

It was more than she'd dared hoped for.

Chapter 14

Trey and Jaida caught a flight back to Boston early the next morning and checked into a motel there. He put in a call to Colorado, and when he'd finished talking to Mac and Lauren had held out the phone to Jaida. Distance hadn't been able to dim the emotion in Lauren's voice. Any discomfort Jaida might have felt in light of Lauren's repeated thanks was lost in the sheer joy of knowing she'd helped reunite Lauren and her son.

Trey rented a car and announced that they were going to the beach. But their first stop was the boutique in the hotel. It had been so easy to pretend they were a normal couple, one with some sort of relationship, some sort of future with each other. Trey had piled swimsuits that met with his approval into her arms, an act that was both arrogant and seductive. She'd been unrelenting in her own choices, putting back the ones that were too daring. But she'd reluctantly admitted that he had chosen well. The suit she'd eventually bought was one of his selections, blue again, a fairly modest two-piece.

She remembered reading once that most men's favorite color was blue, and that certainly seemed to hold true with him. His own purchase had been made with far less care. The black trunks were plain, but she'd known that they would show off his hard, lean body to perfection, and she'd been right.

The only thing that marred her sheer happiness at spending a carefree day with him was noticing the careful way he kept sweeping the area with his gaze. While they drove to the motel, and again when they went to the beach, his eyes went frequently to the rearview mirror.

He was watching for anyone who might be following them.

The certainty put a chill in her blood. But she didn't mention it until they'd found a small space on the crowded beach and sat down on the beach towels they'd purchased.

Rummaging around in her tote for some meganumber sunscreen, Jaida asked him nonchalantly, "So, who were you expecting to find in back of us on the trip here?"

Trey merely looked in her direction. She couldn't see his eyes behind the dark-tinted glasses, but she knew if she could, they would be unreadable.

She squirted a dollop of lotion in her palm. "Is it the second kidnapper? Is that it? You think he's hanging around to take his chances with us?"

He was silent so long she didn't think he would answer. When he did, his voice was flat. "It's possible. It's hard to know what he would do next. He might have fled as far away as possible, knowing his partner had been arrested. He has no reason to believe she hasn't given the police information on him. With a possible APB out on him, he'd be stupid not to go into hiding."

"But you don't think he did, do you?"

"There's no way to tell. Since we don't know the motivation for the kidnapping, we can't guess at his next move. But," he said, his voice hardening, "we're his best bet for finding Benjy again, if that's still what he wants to do. That's why, when we do go home, we'll have to be a little ingenious about not leaving a trail. I'm probably being paranoid," he added, noting her ashen cheeks, "but I'm also not going to take any chances."

Jaida made a production of applying more lotion to her leg. It wasn't his plan that had had the blood rushing from her face; it was his casual mention of their parting.

When we do go home ... The words could have another interpretation, a much more cozy one—if she allowed herself to pretend that they would be leaving here together. But that scenario was as farfetched as the one about little green men taking over the earth. When they left, it would be separately, to their individual homes. And she wasn't quite sure yet just how she was going to survive that.

"Here, let me," he offered, taking the tube of sunscreen from her unsteady hand. He squirted some into his palm, then rubbed it with both hands to warm it. Then, with much more thoroughness than the act called for, he proceeded to apply it to her arms and then her stomach. He stopped to replenish the supply before focusing on her shoulders and chest. When he reached the tops of her breasts, where they curved above her swimsuit, he used utmost care. His hands left a lingering heat in the wake of their rhythmic circles.

"Have you spent much time at the ocean?"

His casual words, so at odds with his intimate touch, rendered her momentarily mute. His emerald eyes were lambent, and she responded helplessly to the heat in them.

"No...I...that is, I've been to the ocean before, of course. When I was a child." He removed his hands then, finished with his task. Her skin immediately felt the loss of his touch.

"Did your grandmother take you?"

She giggled helplessly, unable to picture Granny in a bathing suit. "No, not Granny. Why, I only remember her leaving the valley once, and that was a long, long time ago."

"What made her leave the valley then?"

He'd met with this careful silence before, and knew it meant he'd touched upon a memory that wasn't pleasant for her. He wished he could retract his words. He didn't want her troubled by anything right now, and certainly not by some ghost from her past better left buried. He of all people should know what it was like to fight to protect your privacy.

But eventually, despite her pensive frown and prolonged silence, she did answer. And her words were couched in her customary candor. "I've told you before that my mother never really wanted me with her, but there was one time, when I was eight, that I did go to live with her and her new husband. David was her third, I think. Or maybe her fourth." She shook her head slightly. "It doesn't matter. But unlike her other husbands, he professed to be delighted at the thought of a ready-made family. He insisted that I come to live with them in Memphis after the wedding. Marilee went along with the idea, but I doubt she was too thrilled about it.''

She stopped then, contemplating the ocean. The rhythmic wash and flow of the waves on the shore were soothing. The waves rushed in and wiped several feet of beach clean of marks, of flaws. Time was a little like that, she mused. The years had a similar way of easing painful memories, if not totally erasing them. "I was so excited to be going.'' She smiled a little, thinking of the eight-year-old she'd been. "I was sad to be leaving Granny, but I was eager, too. So eager that I never told anyone that there was something about David that made me uncomfortable. Whenever he touched me...'' She stopped and shook her head. She hadn't had the words as a child, but he'd made her flesh crawl. She hadn't understood then the meaning of the snippets of emotion she would pick up from his touch. "I soon learned to avoid him, but after I moved in with Marilee and him he made that impossible. It seemed as though he was constantly finding reasons to stroke my hair or my arm, to hug me a little too tight, a little too often.''

She glanced at Trey and his face was hard. "Granny is precognitive.'' She made the remark as casually as she would tell her grandmother's age. "I was an adult before I understood exactly why Granny left the valley that time. But I don't doubt that she saw something so horrible, so frightening, in my future...'' Her voice trailed off. All she remembered was her joy at seeing her grandmother so unexpectedly, her confusion at being sent to her room, at the raised voices downstairs. "A couple of hours later my things were packed and Granny and I were on our way to the bus station to buy a ticket back to Arkansas.'' She added, almost as an afterthought, "My mother and David separated not long after that.''

Trey became aware of a pain in his jaw, and only then realized how tightly he was clenching it. It took conscious effort to release the tension there, and even more effort not to reach over and haul Jaida into his arms. "He didn't hurt you?'' The words were raw, torn from him.

Her gaze was on the tide again, and she shook her head. "I know now that he would have eventually. That was what

Granny must have seen. It was the only thing that would have made her leave the valley.''

He brought her hand to his lips, where he pressed a quick kiss in her palm. ''You owe your grandmother a lot.''

''I owe her . . . everything,'' Jaida agreed softly. ''She raised me, and took care of me, and never once made it seem like I was a burden. She is my family—all that's ever mattered, anyway.''

''I'm glad you had her,'' Trey murmured. With her hand still clasped in his, it wasn't difficult to tell he was thinking of his own childhood, his and Lauren's. He surprised her, and himself, by saying, ''When Lauren was adopted by that couple, the only thing that made the pain of her loss better was to imagine this wonderful life she was having. I'd weave this fairy-tale existence for her, because I couldn't deal with not knowing for sure if she was all right, if she was happy.''

''And was she happy?''

''I think so. She says she always felt there was something missing in her life when we were separated. I think she lived in fear of doing something that would disappoint her new parents so much that they would send her away. She doesn't talk about them much, but I'm sure she misses them. She had to break contact with them when we made a new life for her, away from Penning. They were very much in favor of her marriage, and great admirers of her husband. They would have told him immediately if they knew where she was.'' Resentment crept into his voice. ''The one time she told her parents of Penning's abuse, she was told to stop making her husband angry. She couldn't turn to them for assistance when she wanted to leave. She had to rely on herself.''

''And you,'' Jaida reminded him softly. ''You were the one to help her escape him.''

''Yes. But Lauren had already been making plans of her own before I ever found her. She'd hidden some things away, the bloodstained clothing I told you about, hoping to be able to use it to buy her freedom. When she discovered she was pregnant, she knew she couldn't wait much longer to leave him. That's about the time I found her.''

''Does Penning know about you?''

He shook his head. "Lauren said she never mentioned me to him. And although her adoptive parents knew she had a brother when they decided to adopt her, I doubt they said anything to him about it, even if they still remember my existence." He said the last words without rancor. The couple had been enchanted with four-year-old Lauren, but less so with him. He'd been wise beyond his years, with a chip on his shoulder and ice in his heart. He hadn't wanted to be adopted, but given a choice it would have been better than being separated from Lauren. He hadn't been given a choice.

A vision wafted across Jaida's mind, settling over it like a filmy blanket. A vision of a small girl, screaming as she was led away, and several adults holding back a young boy who was fighting with unworldly strength to go to his sister. She could feel his shattering pain, and the bleakness that had permeated his existence for so long afterward.

She swallowed convulsively. "I think you needed her as much as she needed you. I'm so glad you found her."

He knew then that she'd seen something, some scene transmitted through their touch, and immediately released her hand. He couldn't get used to that ability of hers, didn't *want* to get used to it. He'd spent too many years fortifying the walls around his feelings ever to be comfortable with a woman who could so easily circumvent them.

And yet…there was a bond between them he couldn't deny. Their physical relationship had only strengthened it. He might have been able to convince himself that making love with her had been unavoidable and was a natural progression from their proximity and mystical connection. But finding she was a virgin had changed all that.

She hadn't asked, hadn't demanded anything from him, but he was still edgy. Edgy the way a man got when he knew he'd received more, far more, than he was comfortable returning. And rather than running in the opposite direction, he was greedily taking every moment with her he could get, while successfully putting off offering her anything in return.

It was late afternoon when Trey announced it was time to go and they made the trip back to the hotel. Jaida knew without being told that he wanted to get back to phone the agents watching Penning. The contacts were always there, hovering in the background, nebulous reminders that what she had with Trey was fleeting. The contented day they'd spent had been soothing in its ordinariness. But there was nothing ordinary about the circumstances that had brought them together, or the ones that were, for the moment, keeping them together.

The phone began ringing almost as soon as they entered Trey's room, so Jaida took the opportunity to slip into her own room for a shower. After she'd finished and dressed again in shorts and a tank top she wandered back into Trey's room. He wasn't on the phone. She heard the shower shut off and realized he was in the bathroom. Moments later the door opened and Trey sauntered out, drying his wet hair with an extra towel.

Jaida's throat went dry. He was attired in nothing but a towel, which looked startlingly white wrapped carelessly around his hips. Each step he took made the knot on the towel seem a little more precarious. A stripe of hair angled upward above the covering, and his wedge of chest seemed even broader than usual above it.

"You were quick," he said. He dropped the towel he had in his hand and slicked his hair back with careless fingers. She'd never seen him less than perfectly groomed, and she stared in fascination. Lack of clothing made him seem bigger, more dangerous. It was as if clothes were part of the camouflage he donned in his presentation to the world of an urbane, civilized man. Now, at moments like these, she was reminded of just how much of a facade that was. He moved with the lean grace of a jungle cat. The tensile strength alluded to in the play of muscle under sleek skin was compelling, and she tried in vain to look away.

"That was one of the agents on the phone," he offered, walking to the dresser. "Not much to report. The Pennings have had no visitors so far, and the beach on their property is private." His eyebrows rose at her in the mirror when she remained silent. "That's good news."

At his reminder, she managed to pull her gaze away from him. She seemed incapable of speech while she was watching the hard muscles move beneath his smooth expanse of shoulders. "Yes." She cleared her throat and tried again. "Yes, it is."

Masculine satisfaction curled inside him. She was uncomfortable, and he was the source of that discomfort. Despite the times she spent in his arms, she was still naively, innocently, transparent. His near nudity shouldn't make her nervous; the towel covered more than his trunks had earlier. But she wasn't experienced enough to take a moment like this in stride. Just as she wasn't experienced enough to hide her reaction to him.

He turned deliberately away from the mirror, and caught her eyes on him. Sauntering toward her, he said, "Something tells me your mind isn't on the agent's phone call."

"Yes, of course it is," she stammered.

He stopped only a few inches from her, close enough to inhale the fragrance of her damp hair, to see the hint of moisture collecting above her curved upper lip. "I don't think so," he disagreed. Her hair had left damp streamers across her shirt, and he traced one of them where it wandered over her shoulder.

The world narrowed to include only the two of them. He seemed closer, although Jaida wasn't aware of him moving. His mouth was very close to hers. She could feel his breath brushing her lips, making them tingle.

"I know you well by now," he said in a husky voice.

The words were spoken so close to her mouth she imagined she could feel his lips forming each syllable. "You think so?" she whispered, entranced by his rapt gaze.

"I know what you're thinking about. I know what you want."

His words were evocative, with meaning, and she moved helplessly closer. "Tell me," she whispered against his lips.

He brushed her mouth with his and then dragged his lips up her jaw, where they paused below the lobe of her ear. "You want..."

He breathed the words and then paused. She waited in painful anticipation.

"Dinner," he completed.

So caught up was she in the spell he had woven, it took her a moment to interpret his meaning. When she did, she pushed at his shoulders and whirled away from him in embarrassment.

He chuckled behind her, and she stilled, her ears straining at the sound. She turned her head slowly and stared, bemused, at the sight.

Trey Garrison was laughing. His hard face was alight with amusement, and his eyes...on anyone else she would swear the look in his dark-green gaze was teasing. She felt as though she'd stumbled across something rare and precious. Never would she have expected the sight to fill her with simultaneous desires to laugh and weep. She had a feeling that such moments were all too unusual for him.

She wanted to prolong it, to return it. And so she said lightly, "You know, you're absolutely right. I *am* famished. I think I'll go down to the restaurant. You can meet me there if you want." She turned and strolled toward the door.

He was behind her before she'd gotten more than a few steps, drawing her back against his chest. "Boy, if that isn't typical." His voice was mock aggrieved. "Mention food once and you're out of here."

"You shouldn't have reminded me of how hungry I am."

"Honey, I'm hungry, too."

The words were growled in her ear, and suddenly Jaida found herself swept into his arms.

"Very hungry," he continued. "But I had something a bit more...private than the restaurant in mind."

She pretended to give that some thought. "You mean like room service?"

"Exactly," he affirmed. "This is my room, and I am a full-service kind of guy."

He strode rapidly across the room and dropped her on the bed. The next instant he was propped over her, his eyes still crinkled in amusement. Jaida reached out and traced the shallow laugh lines fanning out from his eyes. His playful demeanor was something she knew he rarely indulged in. Somehow she thought that of all the memories she would carry of him, this one would always be the sweetest, and the most painful.

Jaida's wistful expression had the smile fading from Trey's lips. Her moods were like quicksilver, always showing on her expressive face. He didn't know what she was thinking, but knew beyond doubt that her thoughts were bittersweet. He couldn't help feeling responsible for that. His lips touched hers with a gentleness he would have denied, a yearning he couldn't put a name to.

Her mouth twisted sweetly under his for only a moment, before her lips opened to invite a deeper, more intimate kiss. Gentleness was left behind as the familiar need roiled inside him and his tongue pressed into her mouth to tangle with hers. He pulled her shirt from the waistband of her shorts and his hands swept inside to knead the smooth skin at her waist. The silkiness there was intriguing, and his fingers stroked reflexively.

His tongue flicked at the sensitive roof of her mouth, and she shuddered against him. He could feel desire take a deep, hot hold in the pit of his belly. Her responses fueled his own. He wanted her responses, all of them. He wanted to feel her skin damp and her pulse pounding. He wanted to feel her writhing against him, her hands clenching on his skin. He needed to hear those little cries she made when the passion became too strong to control. He wanted to feel the tension that tightened her limbs before she melted like honey beneath him, around him. He wanted it all—needed it again, needed *her* again. He wondered if it would be enough this time. He wondered if it would ever be enough.

Her teeth nipped at his lower lip and his mouth crushed against hers, in a deep open-mouthed kiss that held just a hint of desperation. He pushed her top up and cupped her breasts in their lacy confines. His fingers danced against her nipples, coaxing them into taut, sensitive points. Pulling his lips from hers, he moved down and took a nipple in his mouth, dampening her bra. He grazed it with his teeth, and one of those delectable little cries came from her.

He stopped suddenly, pulling away and lifting her with him to strip her of the shirt and bra. Then he pressed her back on the bed. He moved between her legs and rubbed his torso against her soft breasts, savoring the sensations as they flattened against him, the nipples pricking him. She was so exquisitely feminine that she had his hormones screaming at her touch.

Her hands smoothed over his back, their movements a little frantic. The hint of desperation from her fired his own, made him burn a little wilder. He bent to suck strongly from her breast, drawing it deeply into his mouth, tongue batting at the nipple. He was dimly aware of her ragged breathing, of her nails digging into his shoulders.

The snap of her shorts opening and the zipper being drawn down seemed unnaturally loud. He paused in his task to taste the soft skin on her belly, his tongue delving into her navel. He pulled her shorts and panties over her hips, dragging them down her long, silky legs. She cooperated by kicking them off, and Trey took the opportunity to slide further down her body.

He pressed his mouth against the heat of her, at the juncture of her thighs, and a strangled cry escaped her. She was warm and damp against his mouth, and he cupped her bottom when she would have tried to tighten her legs against him, against the unfamiliar caress.

Shock held her rigid for an instant as he nibbled at her most sensitive flesh, teasing the taut bundle of nerves there. Carefully he entered her with his finger, her tight, moist channel clenching immediately around it.

"Trey," she moaned. He controlled her movements, tilting her hips up toward his mouth. Her hands slid down and tangled in his hair. But she wasn't pushing him away. Her fingers clenched and pulled him nearer.

He couldn't get close enough. He wanted to absorb her, absorb himself in her scent and feel and touch. He wanted to have it all, and he wanted it to be enough this time. Enough so he' never want again, never need again. He pleasured her with exquisite care, his own pleasure climbing at her tortured gasps, the sound of his name on her lips, her body writhing against his mouth.

He heard her repeat his name, a mindless litany as the pressure built in her and abruptly crested. She convulsed against him and he drank her reaction. Her response triggered something in him, something usually kept tamped down and tightly controlled. He slid up her body and entered her with a long smooth stroke, swallowing her gasp.

He wouldn't let her relax, wouldn't allow her body to melt against his in satisfaction. He wanted more. He wanted her to climb the precipice again. He wanted her with him, all the way, wanted her cries in his mouth; needed to be inside her when the shock waves of pleasure exploded again. He wanted it to last forever, for nothing else to matter but he and the woman who held him deep inside her.

But what he wanted didn't matter. Already he could feel the prickling at the base of his back, could feel his manhood grow tight and heavy. Blackness was swirling before his eyes and his movements became faster, harder. Their bodies were slippery with perspiration, and they slid against each other, a perfect counterclockwise movement. His hands went to her thighs, drawing them around his hips. She kept them there, tightening them reflexively and drawing him deeper, ever deeper.

She bucked beneath him once more, and then her gentle scream sounded against his mouth. He had one long, heat-filled instant to savor her response, before his body slammed against hers once more and he joined her in the bone-shattering climax.

The hours passed like liquid, the minutes flowing together indeterminately. They dozed a little, woke, made love again and then lay there for a time contentedly. Finally her fabled appetite drove them to dress and go out for dinner. When they returned, it was after midnight. He slipped out of his shirt and shoes, before indulging himself by urging her to the floor, to sit between his outstretched legs. Then he spent long minutes pulling her hairbrush through her pale-blond hair, brushing it until it shimmered in the darkness. She leaned her head back, and it flowed over his bare chest, just like it did in his dreams, like it always would in his dreams. He rose and undressed her slowly, leisurely, and made love to her the same way, with absorbed concentration. They slept entwined, and if his constant touch through the night brought her unbidden glimpses into his past, she didn't say.

And he found that the prospect of that didn't bother him nearly as much as it should have.

Midmorning the next day, Trey was seriously contemplating the appealing idea of joining Jaida in the shower. The phone's ring put an end to his plan and an edge to his voice.

"Trey Garrison," he growled into the receiver.

"Mr. Garrison, this is Detective Reynolds, LAPD."

"Yeah."

"We've got Maria Kasem here, and Mr. Garrison, I think she's ready to tell us what she knows."

The words had him jackknifing in bed. "What have you got?"

"You were right—she didn't act alone. And she's given us the other guy's name. Tony Franken. You know him?"

"No," he answered, "I've never heard of him." He hadn't really thought that he would, and he found his patience rapidly eroding.

"Well, I'll be running a check on him. Kasem seems to think he did some prison time, so I should be able to get my hands on his sheet. I'll get a picture, too, and we can run it by your sister. But I haven't been able to contact her at home. You know where she might be?"

"I know exactly where she is," Trey told him, his mind racing. "But I don't want you calling her with this. At least, not yet." He wanted to be at Lauren's side when she got this information, and by the time the detective finished gathering the information on Franken, Trey would be.

"I'm going to make arrangements to fly to meet Lauren today," Trey said. "I'll call you when I get there, and you can tell me what else you find out. Be prepared to fax a picture, if you get one."

"Of course," the detective responded, annoyance coloring his voice. "But why don't you just tell me where you'll be? Then I could—"

"I'll call you, Detective," Trey interrupted. "Sometime this afternoon. Have the information ready by then." He hung up the phone, having already dismissed the man from his mind. He was probably being overprotective, but he needed to be with Lauren when she saw the man's picture. Confronting the person who had snatched Benjy away and stolen a month of his young life was bound to be an emotional moment.

It would be much more if she *did* recognize the picture.

It was a moment before he was aware of Jaida's presence in the room. He looked up to see her framed in the bathroom doorway, swathed in a towel. He frowned now in immediate concern. She was very pale, and the hands clutching the towel were shaking. But it was her stillness that alarmed him the most. Other than the trembling in her hands, she was completely, utterly, motionless.

"Are you okay? You're not sick, are you?"

"You have the name of the other kidnapper."

The way she said it wasn't a question, and he knew she'd heard much of the conversation. Her voice soothed his earlier concern for her. It was steady, and not weak at all.

"Maria Kasem finally coughed up the identity of the man. I guess when threatened with life in prison, she got lonely at the idea of going solo. She gave us his name, and Reynolds is running a check on him right now." He hesitated for a second, then looked squarely into her eyes. "I have to go."

The softly spoken words hung in the air. Their gazes met, clung. Her face, usually so transparent, was blank, as still as the rest of her. She seemed to become aware of her unsteady hands and clasped them instead, at her back.

"Of course you do." Again her voice was level, inflectionless. "You'll want to be with Lauren when she tries to identify the man. Do you think you'll have difficulty getting a flight so soon?"

He hesitated before answering, his mind puzzling over her matter-of-fact attitude. "No, I don't think so. I'll want to take some precautions, of course. I don't want anyone to be able to follow us."

She offered him a cool smile. "Of course not. And I'm going to really shock you and let you make my ticket back home on a *plane*."

He missed the rest of her sentence, focusing on the words that seemed to ring with an ominous sound. "Back home?"

She nodded. "I'm anxious enough to get back to Arkansas that I'll even fly. I'm going to pray to all the airport gods to spare me from getting sick this time, but at least I can be home in a few hours."

"You're in a hurry to get home, then," he said slowly, his eyes fixed on her.

"I'll want to check on Granny, of course, although she'd hate the thought of that. She's visiting her sister and her husband in the next county. I may decide to go over there for a few days to say hello."

He was silent for a moment. "You'll want to know how this all turns out, won't you?"

Her eyebrows arched. "Of course. Call me. I can't wait to hear that Lauren and Benjy are completely safe once and for all. Now, I'm sure you'll want to leave as soon as possible. I'll go pack."

He watched with narrowed eyes as she walked through the adjoining door to her room. The door closed behind her with a gentle, irrevocable click.

Minutes ticked by, and still Trey sat on the edge of the bed, staring. He wondered why that closed door seemed to represent so much more.

And he wondered why his gut felt like someone had just tried to do surgery without benefit of anesthesia.

Chapter 15

Jaida busied herself with meaningless chores around the cabin. After unpacking and doing her laundry, she swept the spotless floor, then polished the already gleaming furniture. Those tasks done, she mixed a pitcher of lemonade that she wouldn't drink and made a large dinner for one that she wouldn't eat.

The cabin was almost eerily silent without Granny. Jaida had rarely been here alone. She had called Granny first thing when she'd arrived home, and it had been soothing to hear her voice. Her pointed questions, however, hadn't been soothing at all, and Jaida had brushed them aside feebly. She wasn't up to Granny's insightful comments right now.

The plane ride home had been interminable. She'd watched, with an odd sort of calm, as Trey had taken over at the airport. After checking the flight schedules, he'd gone from window to window, making arrangements. He used cash to buy tickets to places they wouldn't be traveling, using, she suspected, fake names.

He'd returned, his face once more a determined, emotionless mask, and given her her instructions. "Your flight leaves right before mine, but I have to go across the airport to reach my gate." He handed her three different sets of tickets. "The flight to Little Rock is on top. I want you to wait until the very last boarding call before you make a move for that plane." She'd taken the tickets and nodded her understanding.

"Here."

She'd frozen at the sight of the money he was holding out to her. "I don't want it." Her voice had been strained, harsh. That instant had come very close to shredding her carefully comprised composure.

"Take it," he'd ordered. "Your purse is gone, and so are your money and credit cards. You're going to need a way to get from Little Rock home, and I sure don't want you to have to make arrangements for a bus. Not in the state you'll be in after the plane ride."

She'd known he was right, but had made no move toward the money.

"It's for expenses, Jaida." His words reminded her of what she'd once told him when they'd discussed a fee she didn't want, wouldn't take. Slowly she'd reached for the money, and had taken extraordinary care to avoid touching him.

It hadn't mattered, though. She took a deep breath, remembering the way he'd drawn closer, as if he couldn't help himself. He'd raised a hand and caught some of her long hair between his fingers. His face had drawn nearer, and he'd whispered her name.

For one heart-stopping moment she'd thought he was going to kiss her, and after a first foolish leap of her heart, she'd panicked. She'd been very much afraid that if he kissed her, if he so much as touched her, the steady, calm facade she'd strived for would shatter, and she'd be left a trembling, pleading mess.

The image of her begging, clutching him with needy hands, crying pitifully while he watched, his face a mask of distaste, had had her spine stiffening. She'd pulled away from him with a jerk.

He had regarded her with enigmatic eyes and she'd wondered if he had expected the scene she'd just imagined. She'd allowed herself one last, thirsty look at him before she'd whispered goodbye. And then, with all the dignity she could muster, she'd turned and walked away.

She hadn't looked back. Oh, how she'd longed to look back. But she knew if she allowed herself the indulgence, she'd see nothing more than the back of him, striding away from her, heading out of her life. She'd spared herself that.

She'd forced herself to concentrate on the nightmare of the plane ride. No one had boarded after she did. She was late enough to earn herself reproving frowns from the plane attendants. When she'd found her row, she'd stopped short and swallowed hard. The three passengers that she was going to have to crawl across to reach her seat had eyed her with suspicious, long-suffering looks. She'd steeled herself once again, reached for her tattered guard, and plunged through them.

Jaida shuddered at the memory. Coupled with her persistent nausea on the trip, it had been enough to keep thoughts of Trey if not forgotten, at least at bay.

It was a couple of hours before sunset when she'd finished scraping the remainders of her meal into the garbage. Washing the few dishes took less time than she would have liked. She'd stood staring at the cabin rooms, their emptiness evocative of the way she felt inside. Making a swift decision, she'd strode to her room and repacked her suitcase.

Her great-aunt Nora and her husband, Bob, would be delighted to have Jaida visit. Somehow she didn't think Granny would be surprised at all to see her. A couple of days away would give Jaida some time to reconcile with the fact that she was once again alone, in a way she hadn't been before.

And it would give her time to figure out a way to live the rest of her life without Trey Garrison.

Trey sat on the couch of the borrowed mountain retreat, with Lauren's hand clasped in his. Benjy had just been laid down for an afternoon nap. After initial resistance to sleep, he'd insisted on Trey being the one to tuck him in. Trey had obliged willingly. He'd needed the time alone with Benjy, as well. He'd never understood how it was possible for one small creature to arrive on the scene and so naturally hold all the adults' hearts in his hand. It was a long time before he would lose the memory of the terror they'd been through when they'd lost him.

Afterward he spent a fruitful fifteen minutes on the phone to Detective Reynolds. Then he turned on the fax machine to await the copy of the mug shot the detective would be sending them.

"You have something to tell me," Lauren prompted him gently. Her green gaze, so like his own, was steady.

He nodded. "Yeah, honey, I do. I talked to Reynolds twice today, and Maria Kasem spilled everything she knows. They have the name of the other kidnapper. Reynolds is getting ready to fax us a picture of the guy."

"What's his name?" she asked.

Trey watched her. "Tony Franken." She blinked once. That was all. Her eyes remained on him, but she faded away. She wasn't seeing him anymore. She wasn't seeing anything.

"Oh, God," she whispered, her voice raw with anguish. She began to rock in her seat, faster and faster in rhythm with her mindless litany. "OhGodohGodohGod..."

He grasped both her shoulders in his hands. "Lauren," he said urgently. "Do you know this guy? Who is he? How the hell do you know him?"

Her lips were trembling. "Oh, Trey, oh, Trey, what are we going to do? What are we going to do? He'll find us—I know he will—I've always known it—"

"Tell me!" Trey ordered her. "Who is Tony Franken, Lauren?"

She pressed a hand to her mouth, as if to still the trembling there. "He works for William. Ever since I met him, Tony was one of the men who followed us everywhere." She gave a big gasp for air. "He was the one guarding the house the night you helped me escape."

Trey folded his sister's shaking body into his arms, calming her with his strength.

"You know what this means, Trey. William has found us. Just like I always feared he would. We'll never be safe again, never, never..."

"Yes," Trey promised tersely, "you will." The words were a vow. "Calm down and listen to me. Lauren?"

Taking a few deep gasps of air, she eventually pulled away and faced him.

"Good," he said soothingly. He took one of her hands and squeezed it reassuringly. "According to Maria Kasem, Franken didn't talk much about his past, and apparently she's not the type to ask questions. But when she met him, he wasn't working for Penning—he was a baggage handler at O'Hare.

They lived together for about eight months in Chicago. One day about two months ago he never came home from his job. She didn't see him for about a week, and when he did return he was all excited about a plan he claimed was going to make them rich."

Lauren closed her eyes tightly, as if to shut out Trey's next words. "Oh, no."

"I'm afraid so, honey," he said grimly.

"He must have seen me returning from a business meeting with Jack." Jack Saunders was a former client of Trey's, and Lauren's boss. After Benjy's birth, she'd wanted a place of her own. Jack offered her a job and the use of the guest house on his property. She'd accepted both. He ran his computer-analysis business from his home. Her duties as his personal assistant ranged from the secretarial to the very occasional business trip.

"He saw you and recognized you immediately, I'm sure," Trey agreed. "And why not? You very likely cost him his job with Penning."

Lauren's eyes met his and she nodded slowly. "When William found out I was gone, he must have been...enraged." Not a very descriptive word really for her husband's probable reaction. She shivered. Even now, years later, it was hard not to react when she thought of her husband.

"The fact that Franken is walking around on two good legs leads me to believe that he didn't stick around for Penning to find out you were gone. He must have been so scared that Penning would blame him—"

"He would have," Lauren asserted.

Trey nodded. "So he took off before Penning could take his rage out on him."

"People who disappointed William were punished," she whispered.

"At any rate," Trey continued grimly, "it was sheer bad luck that had him working at an airport you were passing through. He followed you to L.A., probably hoping to get into Penning's good graces again by finding out where you lived and letting him know."

"This doesn't make sense, Trey," Lauren cried softly. "If he wanted to make an impression on William, he'd have taken me and never mentioned Benjy. With all the time he spent with

William, he would surely have known how he felt about children."

"And he would just as surely have known about how your in-laws felt about them."

Lauren stared at her brother. "Oh, my Lord." Her voice was almost soundless.

"Kasem said finding out about Benjy delighted Franken. He hadn't been eager to contact William again, even with the news of your whereabouts. He couldn't predict his reaction, especially when Penning found out about Benjy. But it probably didn't take him long at all to figure out how to turn the situation to his advantage. Everyone knew how desperately William's parents wanted grandchildren. Leo Penning could be counted on to pay big bucks to get his hands on his only grandchild."

"And Franken is still out there." Lauren raised her visage to his, dry eyed. "We're not safe while he's free," she said simply. "What's to stop him from telling Leo or William about us? What's to stop him from searching for us? We'll have to hide the rest of our lives, living in fear..."

"No," Trey said firmly. "I won't let that happen. Since Franken is the guard who let you escape William in the first place, he's got no credibility with the Penning family. He probably fears for his life at the thought of contacting them right now, because without Benjy, he's got nothing.

"Don't worry," he reassured her softly, tightening his arm around her. "I'm going to make sure we never have to worry about Franken again. Or your bastard of a husband." He didn't ask himself how he was going to accomplish that feat. His mind was already working overtime on the problem, and he didn't doubt that he'd find a solution to this mess.

The lives of his sister and his nephew depended on it.

A couple of days spent with Granny had kept Jaida's loneliness at bay for a time, but the cabin seemed no less empty when she returned. She made a trip back into Little Rock, because Dixon Falls didn't have something as elaborate as a courthouse and she needed to get her missing driver's license replaced. The woman in the picture on the front of the new one looked as forlorn as she felt. It would be an unwelcome reminder for the next five years of just what, or who, had put that despair in her eyes. While she was there she went to the pharmacy and had her prescription for the pain medication refilled. Then she returned home.

She spent the afternoon completing every task she could think of in the cabin, before starting on Granny's garden out back. Weeding was a chore that kept her body, if not her mind, occupied.

She hadn't attempted to return to her songwriting. It was too soon, her separation from Trey too raw. Right now she feared that if she even tried to set pencil to paper, the emotions would spill forth like water from a levee. And that was something she definitely wasn't ready for.

She'd thought she'd been prepared for their parting, thought she'd known what to expect in his absence. But this...God, this felt as if a giant vacuum had gone through her and removed every bit of feeling, every scrap of anything that mattered, leaving nothing in its wake but a giant void. But no, that wasn't quite right, either. Because a void was an absence of feeling. And the pain of being alone was too intense, too sharp for that.

She knew she'd done the right thing, though. Trey was an intensely private man. He'd spent his whole life building walls around his emotions. How could she expect him to be comfortable with her, with someone who could read him through a casual touch?

She made dinner, and surprised herself by finishing the entire meal she'd prepared. She took the return of her appetite as a good sign. Perhaps she had underestimated the soothing impact of seeing her grandmother again.

The knock on the door came while she was lingering over washing the few dishes she'd dirtied. Peering out the window, she noticed a stranger standing on the porch. She used an unfamiliar caution when she opened the door, leaving the chain on. She might not be a security expert, but she had a normal amount of sense. The cabin was isolated enough to warrant being careful at any time.

"How ya doin'?" The man on the other side of her door greeted her with a half smile. "I been having some car trouble. Left it down at the bottom of your lane there." He jerked his head to indicate the area behind him. "You don't happen to know of any good mechanics nearby, would ya?"

Jaida looked at the man carefully, but he seemed harmless enough. The frustration in his voice was reflected on his blunt features. He was solidly built, although only a few inches taller than she was, with hair the color of walnuts, slicked back from a square forehead.

"I'm sorry." She shook her head. "But the nearest mechanic is Ernie, in Dixon Falls, and he usually closes late afternoon and goes fishing. There's no telling when he'll be back."

The man checked his watch and grimaced. "Just my luck," he mumbled. Squinting back at her he asked, "And how far to the nearest town of any decent size?"

Jaida's eyes followed his to the gold watch on his wrist and remained glued there. The face of the watch was black, with a small diamond indicating where the twelve would be. It wasn't the watch's face she was focused on, however; it was the thick gold band encircling his wide wrist. It glinted as a ray of fading sunlight strayed across it. Her attention caught, she noted the large bones in his hand and arm and the black hairs that curled over the watch band.

After a moment she said, "That would be Little Rock. I could make some calls there if you want. Surely someplace has a tow truck."

His smile this time looked more like a grimace. "How far's that? Fifty miles or so?"

Jaida felt a spark of sympathy for the man's plight. "I'm afraid it's more like sixty-five."

"Well . . . shoot. That'd be one heck of a bill, now wouldn't it?" He scratched his head. "I guess I'll take my chances a while longer and see if I can get a bit farther down the road. The car's been cutting out on me while I'm driving, but it always starts again. I was just thinking about getting it seen to before it decides to quit for good. But it looks like I'm going to have to keep going and hope it gets me another sixty-five miles."

Jaida eyed him doubtfully. "It's going to be dark in a couple hours. Maybe you should have me call that tow truck after all."

The man began to back away from the porch. "Naw, I think I'll chance it. Unless I get to the car and find it don't start at all. Then I'll be back. Thanks for your time." He edged away.

Jaida watched him for several minutes, until he disappeared around a bend into the trees. She closed the door, troubled. There was something about the man that bothered her. Something about his appearance. She leaned her back against the door. Something hovered in her consciousness, just out of reach. She tried, and failed, to summon it. Her feeling of unease increased.

Shaking her head wryly, she pushed away from the door and headed for the kitchen to finish the dishes. The solitude was certainly telling on her if she was going to obsess over a poor guy with car problems.

She washed up her dishes quickly. The cabin had been fitted with most modern appliances at her insistence years ago, but Granny had resisted putting in a dishwasher. She claimed she enjoyed washing the dishes, and Jaida hadn't pushed the point. It would have taken quite a bit of remodeling to fit the appliance into the old kitchen anyway, and even at the time she'd understood the importance of immersing oneself in small tasks that calmed.

She picked up the towel and began to dry the utensils she'd cleaned. The dinner knife gleamed brightly, reflecting her features, and in an odd association she abruptly remembered the light glinting off the stranger's gold watch. Her movements stilled. While she'd tried to summon the memory that teased her about that sight earlier, now it was flashing across her mind without invitation. And it left goose bumps rising on her arms.

The wide gold watchband encircling a thick wrist... the forearm lightly dusted with black hair... the fingers clutching the back of Benjy's shirt, yanking him back up on a bed...

Jaida gasped and the knife clattered as it dropped to the floor. That was why the sight of that watch had teased at something familiar to her. The slightest flick of imagery she'd had about the other kidnapper had been brief and not very helpful. She'd never seen the kidnapper's face. Only his arm.

His wrist encircled by a wide gold-banded watch.

For one fleeting moment she wondered if she was losing her mind. Why else would she insist on linking a hapless stranger with car trouble with Benjy's kidnapper, based on a *watchband?*

Feeling foolish and no less nervy, she moved to the front window of the cabin. The familiar scenery was like a balm. Her truck was parked where she'd left it, at the top of the lane. It could never pass for a driveway, or anything other than what it was . . . a narrow path through a heavily wooded area, leading unexpectedly to the clearing where their cabin sat. Every spring the rains would turn the lane into a muddy, rutted mess. The summer months would bake the ruts deep and solid, and they would provide a bone-numbing jar each time she hit one.

But her mind wasn't on the condition of the lane right now. She was peering into the trees, trying vainly to discern whether a stranger's car sat on the road half a mile in the distance. It was ridiculous, she knew. The lane took a sharp bend a hundred yards from the cabin and disappeared into the trees, the first of four curves it would take before leading to the road. The dense foliage provided the cabin with a natural privacy barrier and shielded it from the intrusive sounds of civilization. It would be impossible to see what lay beyond that first bend, and yet still her eyes strained.

After several minutes Jaida turned away from the window, feeling foolish. There was nothing to see out there but dogwoods gathering shadows in the approaching dusk. There was no movement out of the ordinary. The solitude must be working on her more strenuously than she knew. That was ironic, really. There had been a time in her life, after the ill-fated concert in Phoenix, that this same solitude and privacy had beckoned her, soothed her. Since she'd returned alone it seemed to underscore her loneliness.

And now it was seeming a bit sinister.

Impatiently, she shook off her uncustomary nerves. She wasn't going to stand at the window and obsess over what was likely an unfortunate incident for a guy who just wanted to get home. For a swift moment she allowed herself to yearn to hear Trey's voice. She got as far as the phone, her hand reaching for the receiver, where it hovered and then dropped. She forced herself to go to the kitchen and start cleaning out cupboards that didn't need to be straightened.

The one element of pride she'd managed to hang on to when she and Trey parted was that she hadn't begged and she hadn't asked him to stay. Calling him now would seem contrived, a mere excuse to hear his voice, and there was a grain of truth to that, as well.

But she wouldn't allow herself to wallow in her misery, and she wouldn't let herself try to force Trey into admitting feelings for her that just didn't exist. She had no doubt that she could make him feel something; she hadn't misread the pure masculine possessiveness that had shone in his eyes each time he'd looked at her in their last days together. She knew well that a deep streak of protectiveness ran in him, too. He felt it for Lauren and for Benjy. But she wanted more, much more, for herself.

And she wasn't likely to get it from him.

That knowledge sent pain lacing through her heart. It seemed like life's cruelest ironies that she had spent her life avoiding physical contact and avoiding intimacy. She'd doubted her ability to respond as a woman as her mind grappled with the thoughts and emotions that would rush to her from her partner's touch.

Trey had been different. From the beginning there had been an awareness between them that she couldn't fight and hadn't known how to deny. At first she'd been dismayed by the unexpected sparks that flared at their most casual touch. She'd been even more dismayed at how easily he could make her respond to him as a woman. Jaida had been half-fearful that if she ever responded to him physically, the combination of her psychic gift and that awareness would combust and literally destroy her.

Instead, for the first time she'd found a man who could still her intaking stimuli and immerse her totally, completely, in him and in her own responses as a woman. The first time that happened she hadn't known whether to be glad or frightened. She still didn't.

The last cupboard was straightened, and she contemplated whether she should spend the next hour scrubbing the woodwork to an even greater shine. She rubbed at her aching spine, wishing it were just as easy to rub away the feeling of impending doom that still hovered over her. Unconsciously, she moved to the front window again.

There was nothing to see out front, and it was growing too dark even to try. She turned away from the window, a frown on her face. She'd never been afraid to stay alone at the cabin before, and she wasn't afraid now...exactly. The source of her unease was probably already in Little Rock, happily ensconced in a motel room while an all-night garage worked on his car. But as ridiculous as it seemed, she'd be a lot more comfortable if she knew that for a fact.

Her gaze landed on the telephone. It wouldn't hurt to call Granny and tell her she'd arrived home safely. She picked up the phone and started to dial. When it didn't respond, she disconnected, ready to try again. Only when she failed to get a dial tone the second time did the realization hit her.

The phone was dead.

A long moment passed while Jaida held the receiver to her ear, listening to its silence. That silence seemed to grow into something else, something much more malign. It oozed out of the dead receiver and encompassed Jaida in a blanket of dread.

Her fingers clutching the phone seemed suddenly numb, and she was unaware of her actions as she replaced it on the table. Without thought she went to the front door and turned the dead bolt, checking to make sure the chain was still on. Then she moved from window to window like an automaton. She made sure each was secured, and pulled the rarely used blinds and curtains. The kitchen door didn't open to the outside. Instead, it led down to the cellar, where Granny kept the vegetables she canned each year. There was another set of stairs leading from the cellar to the outside, but they were covered with thick double doors, secured from the inside with a solid wooden bar.

She returned to the living room, her arms clutching her middle. She attempted to reassure herself. Phones went dead sometimes. This one had a few years ago. That had been in a windstorm, however, and right now there wasn't even a breeze rustling the leaves on the trees shrouding the lane. The night air was completely still, as if, like her, it was waiting for something.

The logical, reasonable voice in her mind was warring with the part that seemed, for the moment, to be paralyzed with fear. Her ears picked up a sound outside, and all her senses strained, as though to transmit energy to her hearing. But the sound wasn't repeated. This cabin was surrounded by wildlife, and at night it wasn't unusual for a raccoon, possum or skunk to come sauntering close to the cabin looking for food.

She heard another sound, this coming from outside the back of the cabin. Calling herself ridiculous, Jaida went to the bedroom window and peered out. She saw nothing. Without thinking, she turned off all the lights, except for one dim lamp in the corner.

She was definitely spooked, and it had all started by the appearance of the man who had seemed completely harmless and unfamiliar—*except for the wide gold band encircling that thick wrist*— and now she was letting the coincidental loss of phone service spook her into imagining things. She sank into a chair, wrestling with her runaway nerves.

Minutes ticked by. She was never sure how long she sat there. Long enough for darkness to fall completely. Long enough for night noises to begin outside, each sounding threatening, despite its ordinariness. Her gaze traveled unseeingly around the room before landing on her keys. Her focus sharpened. The truck was right outside. She could unlock the front door and run to the truck, turn it around and speed away from the cabin, away from . . . what?

She crossed to the table and reached for the keys, clutching them reflexively. Somehow they made her feel better.

Until she heard the noises.

Her temporary peace was shattered at the foreign sounds coming from the side of the cabin. She listened intently for a moment, almost expecting that she had imagined the sounds. But these were real.

She heard the alternating tapping and rasping sounds. They came over and over, first one set, then another. It was long minutes before she could identify them. It took even longer for the realization to sink in.

Someone was outside, taking the cellar doors off their hinges.

Chapter 16

The sun was setting over the Rockies, majestic purple peaks backdropped against brilliant orange and red. The scene was lost on the two men sitting together on the deck. They were engrossed only in their conversation.

"So there's been no sign of Franken?" Mac asked.

Trey shook his head. "Not yet. Hell, he could be anywhere. He could have left the country before Maria Kasem ever named him as her accomplice. If he's smart, that's what he would have done."

"Smart isn't necessarily a trait of a kidnapper," Mac remarked.

"Maybe not, but he was clever enough to steal the drug to inject Lauren with, stage the kidnapping and leave the scene without any of the bystanders able to remember who had strolled off with Benjy."

"He got lucky. Most likely when Lauren collapsed a crowd gathered, and he and Kasem were able to fade away."

"The same way he was able to fade away at Kids' Kingdom at the first sign of trouble," Trey said grimly. "There are APBs out for his arrest all over the nation, but he's proven damn good at eluding the police and the FBI throughout this whole case."

Mac studied him. "He evaded the police, but he couldn't evade Jaida, could he?"

"No." Trey's voice dropped. "He couldn't evade Jaida." He didn't welcome his friend's reminder of the woman who had saved his nephew. But it didn't take Mac's mention of her to summon her image. He'd already lost too much sleep thinking about her. Every time he lay down he'd be tortured by the memory of that one image—or was it a vision?—of her lying naked on black, silk sheets. He shifted restlessly in his chair.

"When did you last speak to her?" Mac inquired.

Trey scowled at him and didn't answer. Their roles had neatly been reversed. He'd always been the one to effortlessly charm the women, and on more than one occasion had lectured Mac on softening his abrasive edges. But the charm that Trey had used with such effect in the past hadn't had much effect on Jaida. The easy way she had said goodbye had puzzled and, yes, angered him. She'd acted so casual about the whole thing, and dammit, their relationship was anything but casual. He'd been worried about Lauren and in a hurry to get back to his sister, to be the one to tell her about Franken. But, dammit, he hadn't planned to go back to Colorado alone.

He hadn't given it much conscious thought, but he'd assumed Jaida would accompany him. She had effectively laid that plan to rest. With her cool little smile she'd said she understood completely, and matter-of-factly started making plans to get back to Arkansas. And on a plane, no less. The easy way she'd gone about getting ready to return home, without a question of lengthening their time together, had effectively squashed his half-formed plans.

It had also made him mad as hell.

He wasn't used to being in the position of chasing after women, and he hadn't cared for the experience. And he certainly wasn't used to that unsure feeling he'd been left with at the airport, that of something infinitely precious being snatched out of his grasp.

How the hell had she managed that cool little scene? His guts had felt like they were being ripped in two, and she had strolled off without a backward glance. Just the memory made his jaw clench. She'd left as easily as if they'd spent a weekend away, casual sex between two strangers, and he knew damn well it had been more, much more than that. She'd been a virgin; she couldn't pretend that their time together hadn't meant something to her, not when he'd been the first man she'd trusted enough to make love to.

Maybe it had frightened her, this bond that had grown so intense between them. It sure as hell had scared him, still did. But now she'd had more than enough time to contemplate what they'd had. He wasn't going to allow her much more time alone.

"Have you talked to her since you got back?" Mac probed.

"No," Trey answered shortly. After a time he explained grudgingly, "I called twice today. This morning there was no answer. I called again right before you got here, but the line was no longer in service."

"That's odd, isn't it?"

He didn't know about odd, but it was damned inconvenient. He needed to talk to her, needed to reestablish the almost mystical connection between them. He wasn't going to give her the chance to forget him; he was going to make damn sure that was impossible. "She lives in the Arkansas Valley, in a cabin in a wooded area off the beaten path. I'm not sure how dependable the phone lines are."

"Isolated, huh?"

"Very," Trey replied. "She lives with her grandmother, but Jaida thought she would be gone visiting relatives when she arrived home." He frowned for a moment, something about the thought of Jaida being alone in that cabin bothering him.

"Maybe she went to visit her relatives, too," Mac said. "But I'd think she'd be interested to know that Lauren identified Franken as a former employee of Penning's. She's got to be thinking the same thing we are, that there's still a possibility that Franken will try to snatch Benjy again. She's probably going crazy wondering what's going on—"

"God Almighty."

Mac gave his partner a strange look. For a man with accomplished finesse, he was being unbelievably obtuse. "What I'm saying is you need to contact her. Hell, I know there's something going on between the two of you, and you're crazy if you just let her go."

If Trey had been listening he might have been amused at his partner's machinations to push him at Jaida. But he hadn't been focusing on Mac's words. A thought was forming, one so horrible in its implications that he didn't want to contemplate it.

His chair clattered over backward as he strode into the house. He snatched up the phone in the kitchen and redialed Jaida's number. When the recording informed him the line was out of service, he slammed the receiver own.

Mac joined him. "Calm down. Maybe the line will be fixed in the morning."

Trey turned to face his friend slowly. "I don't think I ever mentioned it to you, but Jaida lost her purse that day in Kids' Kingdom, when she found Benjy."

Mac was taken aback at the man's seeming non sequitur. "Yeah, that's tough. But I'm sure she can replace the stuff, right?"

"Maria Kasem claims Franken was with her in the park, but that he took off when Jaida started making a scene. What if he didn't?"

"What if he didn't what?"

"Take off," Trey said impatiently. He thought of how he'd found Jaida in the midst of the huge crowd, people pressing in from all sides. He hadn't been paying attention to anything besides her. Her and the precious little boy who was taking such an interest in her moon-glow hair. "He was there," he muttered. The pieces started to snap into place like an automated jigsaw puzzle. "He might have faded back into the crowd at the first hint of a scene, but he didn't go far. He stayed close enough to watch what went on without having to worry about getting caught. He saw the whole thing...me finding Jaida, the security guards taking us all away...and Jaida's purse lying on the ground."

Finally his friend's words started to make an awful kind of sense to Mac. "Her wallet was in her purse?"

Trey nodded grimly. "Driver's license . . . address." He saw understanding flicker in his friend's eyes. Self-castigation filled him. "I never thought of it. Not once. Goddammit!" His fist came down on the counter with the force of a sledgehammer striking steel.

He wasted no more time. He marched through the house, past Lauren, who had come to check on the noise, and into his bedroom. His sister and Mac followed him. Without a hint of his usual fastidiousness, he began throwing clothes into his suitcase and slinging orders at Mac.

"Get hold of the sheriff in Jaida's county," he said. Mac nodded. "Tell him to get out to Jaida's, and fast. Rouse Mc-

Intyre, tell him to get our plane ready. Have him file a flight plan to the airport nearest Dixon Falls, regardless of size. I'll need a vehicle once we get there.''

"You got it.''

Lauren's gaze went from one man to the other. Trey's face was terrible; the only other time she'd seen that expression was when her baby had been kidnapped. Her voice quavered. "Trey, what is it? What's wrong? Is it Jaida? Is she in trouble?''

Her brother's face remained stoic, but his eyes were anguished. "I hope not.'' The words were harsh, fervent. His gaze met hers. "I sure as hell hope not.''

Time had long ceased to have any meaning to Jaida. She assumed it had been hours since the noises began, but how many, she couldn't be sure. The only thing she was certain of was that the threat that had hovered on the brink of her consciousness since late afternoon had materialized.

She'd spent the time in a numbed state of disbelief. There was no question in her mind that the stranger who had come to her door was the same man outside at this moment trying to break into her house. She was certain of it, just as she was certain of his identity. Somehow Benjy's kidnapper had traced her here. She was alone, she was isolated and there was no way to summon help.

She could rely only on herself.

The realization had a curiously calming effect on the fretful jumble of half thoughts and fears in her head. She had no options, no recourse. She couldn't try for the truck now. The creak of the heavy front door would give her away and she wouldn't make it halfway to the vehicle before he came to investigate.

That meant that she stayed here, in the dim light in the living room, and waited. Each minute was nerve-racking. If she allowed herself to, she could have easily lost control, focusing on the noises coming from outside, imagining with each renewed sound how much closer the man was to getting inside. But after the first long minutes of panic, she firmly banished those thoughts. She had other things to worry about right now.

Like how to stay alive.

Jaida had no illusions. Benjy's kidnapper had come here to learn from her the boy's whereabouts. And once she had seen the man, she'd be able to identify him, so her fate would be sealed. Once he had the information he sought, she would be expendable.

She used most of the time she waited searching for a weapon. The results of her search were dismal. There were no firearms in the cabin, of course. There were several lethally sharp kitchen knives, but she seriously doubted her ability to use one on the man. She'd have to get very close to utilize such a weapon, and she simply could not take the chance of touching him. If he attempted to fight with her for the knife, his thoughts and emotions might transfer to her at his touch. She was unsure of her ability to protect herself if she found herself immersed in the twisted, evil workings of his mind.

Her attention finally landed upon Granny's selection of nonornamental canes. One of them could more accurately be described as a walking stick. Made of rough-hewn oak, it was solid and heavy. The handle was a round brass knob attached to the top. It would have to do.

She grasped it tightly and padded soundlessly over to the lamp. She turned the switch off, plunging the room into darkness. Then she moved stealthily into the kitchen. The most obvious place to hide would be in the corner the kitchen door would make when it opened. But she would have to push the door out of the way to get at the intruder, and she couldn't be sure that the precious seconds that would take wouldn't tip him off to her presence. So she chose, instead, to stand back on the right side of the door.

She would be immediately visible when he entered the kitchen, but she was going to have to hope that she could strike before he would see her. She had no doubts that he'd be armed, and once he saw her, she wouldn't have much chance, regardless.

He was in the cellar now.

Jaida swallowed hard and hefted the walking stick into the air, fighting panic. She couldn't allow fear to overcome her, not in these final moments when she was going to need every bit of wit and cunning. But the seeds of terror, earlier sown, threatened to spring forth, crowding rational thought aside. Her mind frantically sought a point to fixate on and immediately landed on one.

Trey. His name screamed into her mind, and she mentally clutched it as she would a talisman. It had taken him a long time to come to trust her, to depend on her ability to help him find Benjy. She would never betray that trust now and put that little boy at risk again. For Benjy's sake, she had to escape the madman in the cellar. She would focus on Trey, on the strength and courage that were so much a part of him, traits that had drawn her to him, made her love him.

She took a deep breath, feeling the terror ebb a bit, even as she heard the first step of the man on the cellar stairs. She fixed her thoughts on Trey, and a curious sense of comfort flickered through her veins. It was the same sensation she'd felt whenever she'd been held by him, protected by him. For the first time since they'd parted she sensed his presence so strongly, could almost feel the strength of his will. It was a curious experience, oddly consoling, but she had no more than a minute to wonder at it.

The waiting was over. The kitchen door was making its telltale creak as it was pushed open; the man was closer than she'd thought. He was through it before she had a chance to react.

He must have sensed her presence almost immediately. When Jaida sent the solid piece of oak swinging through the air at him, he was already turning toward her. He didn't have time to get out of the way, though. His arm came up, a gun pointed at her, before the oak caught him squarely in the side of the head.

The gun flew out of his hand, clattering on the kitchen floor. It went off with a sound that tore through the night. The man crumpled to the floor in a heap in the doorway. Jaida stood over him, hands trembling on the heavy stick. Adrenaline and fear pounded through her, each vying with the other for supremacy. She wanted to run, but she was rooted to the spot. The man didn't move.

Had she killed him?

The thought filled her with dread and nausea. She knew she needed to use the opportunity to flee, but first strained to hear any sound of his breathing. She lingered for a moment, before satisfying herself that she could hear the thready sound of oxygen being drawn in.

Abruptly, self-preservation reasserted itself and she began to inch away from the body. She needed to get to the front door. Once she had it opened she could be on her way to freedom.

She hadn't taken more than a step before fingers clamped around her ankle. Jaida screamed and raised the stick again.

The man was attempting to use his grasp on her to help him up, and bile rose in her throat.

Evil. It rushed at her, transmitted by his touch, attempting to encompass her in its grasp. His thoughts were fuzzy, but his deadly intent wasn't. He'd killed people before and they hadn't mattered—they'd only been a means to an end. One more wouldn't matter; *she* wouldn't matter.

The vision was upon her suddenly, curling from his subconscious like smoke under a door. *The shot had been placed in the center of the forehead, and ugly laughter had sounded as he was praised for his accuracy. The boss had smiled at the way Weber had landed across his feet, begging for mercy like the dog he was . . .*

Jaida screamed again, almost gagging from nausea as the scene in the man's mind engulfed her. She was still reeling from her unwilling foray into the bloodbath, when another brief flick from the man's thoughts reached her.

Now he was lying at this bitch's feet, just like a dog, just like Weber had, and she'd pay for that; he'd make her pay. He'd have killed her anyway, but now he was going to do it slow and take his time with her. Before he was done this bitch would be praying to be delivered to the fires of hell. . . .

The hand grasped her more tightly and the man raised his head, using his other elbow to lever himself from the floor. Jaida struggled against the pervasive shroud of the man's emotions and intentions threatening to suck her in. Her breath came in sharp little pants. Without conscious thought her hands brought the stick down again, this time striking the man across the shoulder and back. The hand on her ankle weakened; he slumped to the floor, but didn't completely let go of her. His thoughts were growing weaker, like a transmitter whose battery was wearing down, but Jaida was still unable to free herself completely from them. She had to get away from him—she had to—before she was sucked in for good into that vapid morass of a mind. The pain was starting behind her eyes, clawing over her shoulders and down her spine. She brought the stick down once more on his wrist, stumbling away when his fingers finally released her, not only from a physical grip but from the more deadly mental one.

The freedom from the vision was dizzyingly relieving, but her limbs, earlier frozen, had returned to life. She ran drunkenly across the dark cabin, bumping into furniture that had remained in familiar locations all her life. At any moment she expected to feel that hand on her again, to be vacuumed back into that sick mind. She had to avoid that, had to, had to....

She struggled with the dead bolt and chain for endless seconds before she finally had the door open. Then she was racing down the front steps, avoiding the lane, heading for the wooded area surrounding it. Bushes tore at her clothes; tree branches reached for her throat and face. Bringing her hands up to protect herself, she barreled on. She didn't try to remain quiet. The sounds of her pell-mell flight into the woods reverberated with the snapping of twigs, the pounding of her steps, her ragged breathing.

She didn't care about the noise; she didn't care about the darkness surrounding her. All she knew was that she had to get help. She had to get help before the man reached her again.

Sobbing, she put on a burst of speed.

Spotlights beamed across the area in front of Jaida's cabin. The lane was filled with four sheriff's cars, and Trey could see several men caught in the lights. He left his rental and sprinted up to the man nearest him.

His uniform identified the man as a deputy, and his scowl said Trey's presence wasn't going to be accepted readily.

"Who're you?"

"Where's Jaida?" Trey demanded.

The younger man tucked one hand into his belt and let the other hover menacingly over his firearm at his side. "I'll ask the questions 'round here. Who are ya, and whadda ya want?"

"I'm the one who called your office. Now, where the hell is Jaida? Is she here? Is she all right?" When it didn't seem as though answers would be forthcoming from the suspicious deputy, Trey brushed past him, intent on searching for Jaida himself. She had to be here; she had to be safe. The fear that had threatened to swallow him the entire flight across country was rising again, panic rearing its head.

"Here, now, hold up, I'm talking to you. Sheriff?" the deputy called. "Sheriff, you better come over here."

Trey ignored the man's call, just as he ignored the portly-looking sheriff making his way over to him. His gaze scouted the area frantically, before landing on the porch. Relief filled him. In a few strides he was across the lane and taking the porch steps two at a time.

"Jaida."

She stiffened, pausing in midsentence. Turning from the deputy she'd been talking to, she watched in disbelief as Trey moved toward her, like a specter from her dreams. She was afraid to answer, afraid to move, as if to do so would dissolve this mirage before her eyes. And then she was caught up in his very real arms, her head bent back to receive his very real kiss. The connection was there, crackling and urgent. His mouth was hard, bruising her lips, and she responded suddenly and totally without reservation. She let go of the blanket someone had placed over her shoulders and it slid to the ground as she wound her arms around Trey's neck. He hugged her tightly, but it wasn't tightly enough. She could never get close enough to him.

"Trey." She sighed against his lips.

There was a nervous throat clearing from the deputy on the porch, and another voice angrily demanded, "Miss West, are you all right? See here, mister, this is a crime scene, and the perpetrator is still on the loose. Y'all can't just go barging in here and—"

Trey raised his head. Now that he had convinced himself that she was in one piece, his gaze moved down her body, cataloguing the scrapes and bruises that marred her skin. That gorgeous hair was a mass of tangles, and her clothing was torn and dirty. His jaw tightened at the evidence of her trauma, and his eyes chilled.

"He came here," she whispered, the words shuddering out of her. "And I couldn't get away. I couldn't call for help. I had to fight him off, and then he touched me and I saw..." Her breath hissed in an almost painful gasp. "Oh, God, Trey, I had to hit him again and again, and I couldn't get away...." She took a deep breath and he rubbed her back soothingly, pressing her face against his chest.

"I thought I'd killed him," she murmured, her voice muffled against him.

His hands were all the comfort she could ever wish for. "I wish to hell you had," she heard him respond. And at his words, the horror of the past few hours finally began to recede.

Chapter 17

They'd taken turns answering the sheriff's questions until Trey, seeing the exhaustion on Jaida's pale face, finally put an end to them. "Let's wrap it up, Sheriff," he said flatly. "Jaida needs some rest, and you have enough to keep you busy for the next several hours."

The stout officer studied him with shrewd brown eyes. There was a long silence as the man contemplated Trey's words, before nodding slowly. "Mebbe you're right. Beggin' your pardon, Miss West, but you do look all done in. We'll clear out of here for a while—give you time to rest—and be back at first daylight. Won't do us any good to search for your intruder till then, anyway. Whoever he was, he 'pears to be long gone from here." Leveling a look at Trey, he continued politely, "Of course, we'll check out the information you were able to give us."

Trey nodded, not at all offended that the man wasn't going to take him at his word. He had to respect the man for doing his job thoroughly. His office had dispatched several cars out here at Mac's call, and one of the officers had met Jaida, panting and stumbling on the road. It was a faint relief that since he hadn't been here to protect her, these men had come to her aid with admirable speed.

The fact that he hadn't been the one do so would haunt him
for the rest of his years.

After directing them not to disturb the crime scene in th
cabin, the sheriff gathered up his officers and the cars headed
back to town.

Trey tightened the arm he had around Jaida's waist and
turned her gently toward the cabin. They mounted the step
without a word, but he noted her visible hesitation before the
crossed the threshold.

Lights were blazing in the living room and kitchen, and Trey
stood still, his gaze sweeping the area. Furniture was slightl
akilter, giving the room an askew look. Even from this dis
tance he could see that there was some blood on the floor in th
kitchen area. He had assured himself earlier of the extent of he
injuries, so the sight didn't fill him with anything other than
grim satisfaction. That feeling faded, however, when he no
ticed the chunk of plaster missing from the wall. There was a
small, unmistakable hole in the center of it.

She noted the direction of his gaze. "He had a gun," she ex
plained unnecessarily. "It flew out of his hand when I hit him
the first time, and it went off." She surveyed the damage in the
wall silently for an instant, and her voice held a note of de
tachment. "He must not have been able to spot the gun in the
dark. Or maybe he wasn't thinking clearly enough to look for
it. The sheriff found it under the table."

Her lack of expression about the matter was his undoing
Shock was starting to set in, as she was beginning to realize jus
what had happened here. What could have happened. She was
safe, but he felt an overwhelmingly primal instinct to assure
himself of that fact, in the most primitive, satisfying way pos
sible. His arms tightened around her as he fought for control.

She welcomed his embrace, desperately craved it. Only his
touch could stamp out the horror of the past few hours. She
needed this and more. She wanted to lose herself in the pas
sion again, and convince them both that the nightmare was
over.

She raised her face for his kiss, and his lips crushed hers with
a desire she fully reciprocated. The overpowering emotion in
him transmitted to her, and she stiffened in discovery at the
voyeuristic peek into his thoughts.

Her hands became urgent. She started to unbutton his shirt
and then, frustrated by her lack of progress, pulled the tails

from his jeans and smoothed her hands up his waist. Their gasps mingled as the current flickered to life beneath her touch. With fingers unusually clumsy, Trey unbuttoned her blouse and dispensed with her bra. Her brief feeling of satisfaction was interrupted by his mouth on her breast, and she cried out brokenly. His mouth was hot, wet, compelling. He caught up a handful of her gauzy skirt and raised it above her thighs.

The night air was cool, even in the cabin, and Jaida gasped as it rushed across her thigh, her breasts. Somehow she managed to get his shirt open, and her hands clutched his chest. A rumble sounded beneath her fingertips as he responded to her touch, and then time seemed to catch them and speed up to an almost dizzying level. He was moving her backward, his chest hair brushing across her breasts, his mouth fastened over hers. Jaida felt the table at the back of her hips.

Then Trey's hands were under her skirt, knowing and seeking. Her panties were pulled down, his hand moving between her legs. She was lifted a little, so that she sat on the table's edge, and he moved between her opened thighs.

Their hands battled each other's as they sought to release the button and zipper on his jeans. He allowed her to finish the task as he guided her legs around his hips. She'd barely freed his manhood from the heavy jeans, her fingers exploring his rigid length urgently, when he uttered a hoarse plea. "Now, Jaida. I want to be inside you now." The words were rasped across her lips, urging them open even as she moved to respond. Her hand guided his pulsing length to the part of her that was warm, damp and aching. Then he entered her with a heavy thrust that drove the breath from her chest.

Her eyes opened dazedly, and the eroticism of the scene encompassing her was more than she could bear. The expressionless mask was gone from his face. His eyes were tightly closed, a sheen of perspiration dampening his brow. Passion sharpened the planes and angles of his countenance.

His hands went to her hips. Then he thrust again, this time reaching deeply inside her, and reality flickered away. There was only sensation. Her arms crept around his shoulders. Her breasts were flattened against his chest, his mouth hard and demanding on hers. He began to thrust with heavy power, his hips hammering into hers. His breathing was harsh, the sound mingling with her soft moans.

The savagery of their desire was too acute to last for long. He could feel her body tighten and he increased his rhythm, pounding into her with heavy force. He felt her legs crawl higher, until they were clenched around his back. When he heard the keening cry escape her lips, he gave one last long, heavy roll of his hips and then shuddered against her as he convulsed.

They clung to each other, unable to let go. Each soothed the other as the quaking rippled through them, as muscles slowly relaxed. Long minutes stretched before Trey could gather the strength to move. He slipped out of her carefully and scooped her into his arms. Then, deliberately, he made his way to her bedroom and followed her down onto the bed.

He finished undressing her with silent, efficient movements, the intense concentration on his face almost making her weep. Then he rose and swiftly divested himself of the rest of his clothes.

She watched in the darkness, a little amazed at the desire that had overtaken them, so savage and sudden that neither of them had fully disrobed. In the next second he was under the quilt with her, his weight causing them both to sink down into the feather tick mattress.

She turned to him immediately, unwilling to relinquish his touch for even an instant. He gathered her close, and rubbed his face against her tangled mass of gold hair. One hand caressed her spine soothingly.

"How did you know to come here?" she murmured drowsily. Even as she spoke the words, she knew his answer didn't matter. She'd needed him, and then he'd been there. His hard arms were holding her close, and his still thudding heartbeat was sounding in her ear. She'd never felt safer. "I need to tell you. That man . . ."

"Sh-h-h," he whispered. "It can wait until morning. Sleep now, honey. Just sleep."

He held her long after she slipped into slumber, listening to the deep, even cadence of her breathing. He needed the continued physical contact. The realization of how easily he could have lost her tonight kept his adrenaline flowing, and sleep at bay. He didn't mind. It was enough to hold her like this, to feel those now-familiar sparks everywhere their skin touched.

It was enough knowing that he wasn't going to let her go again.

* * *

Jaida offered the last pancake to Trey, then slipped it onto her own plate when he shook his head. It didn't bother her that he watched her eat with indulgent satisfaction, nor did it bother her that she'd devoured more breakfast than he had, although he was close to twice her weight. When she got to the point that he could no longer scoop her easily up into his arms or carry her to bed, *then* she would be bothered.

Earlier he'd relayed everything that Kasem had told the federal agents about the scheme to snatch Benjy and present him to his paternal grandparents, hoping the elder Pennings would reward them well for their efforts. She considered the information as she cut into the pancake.

Her eyes met his, stunned to see the now-familiar look of lambent desire shimmering in them. Slowly, provocatively, she licked a drop of syrup from the corner of her lips. Warm satisfaction curled inside her as his eyes slitted, following her movements with fixed interest. His voice was husky when he spoke the words that shattered her self-congratulation.

"If you're trying to get me back in bed, honey, I'm more than willing. But I have a feeling your local sheriff is going to be making an appearance soon, and I don't really think you want him walking in on us, do you?"

She frowned thoughtfully, not at his words, but at the memory they'd elicited.

"About the sheriff," she began uncertainly. "I'm afraid I've done something that isn't quite . . . well, legal."

He cocked one elegant eyebrow questioningly, and she was distracted for the moment by the achingly familiar sight. She'd never thought to see him make that arrogantly lovable gesture again, hadn't thought she'd be held by him, make love to him again. Emotion welled up inside her, scattering her thoughts like wisps of clouds.

When she didn't elaborate, Trey responded, "Somehow I can't see you as the next candidate for the chain gang. What did you do? Ignore a parking ticket?"

"Not exactly," she mumbled, her gaze skirting his. "That man who broke in here, he was the other—"

"Kidnapper," Trey finished for her. "I know, honey. It took me a while to put it all together in Colorado. Maria Kasem identified him. His name is Tony Franken."

"He worked for Penning," she whispered.

"He used to, yes. He was one of William's bodyguards, until, I suspect, he fell out of favor because he was on duty when Lauren escaped. Then he must have fled for his life."

"He won't rest until he has Benjy again."

"That's why he was here," Trey said tersely. "He hoped to get Benjy's new location from you. He must have grabbed your purse from the park." And then he must have hightailed it to Arkansas, Trey thought grimly, fighting renewed fury at the idea. All the time they'd spent hoping Franken was still in the vicinity of the park, or even later, thinking he might have followed them back to Boston, had been time wasted. Because the bastard had probably been near here the entire while, biding his time until he could make his move on Jaida.

His fist clenched involuntarily, his anger directed as much at himself as it was at Jaida's attacker. Jaida, seeing the action, reached over and covered his fist with her hands.

"Don't," she said softly. "Don't blame yourself."

"I should have figured it out sooner. In the excitement of finding Benjy, capturing Maria, I didn't think of the significance of you losing your purse with all your ID."

"Neither did I," she remarked.

His mouth twisted. "The difference is, sweetheart, that I'm trained to think of things like that. I failed to protect you, failed to consider you'd *need* protection. And you were almost killed as a result. That's pretty damn unforgivable."

And his was an unforgiving nature, she knew, hardest on himself. He'd spent his life blaming himself for failing Lauren and then her son. He was a man adept at an emotionless facade, but behind the front he maintained emotions that burned hotter, more intensely than did other people's.

"Stop it," she said sharply, startling him. "You may be perfecting the art of walking on water, but you're not God and you're not infallible. No one else expects you to be, so quit beating up on yourself. Let go of that damn load of guilt you carry around and stop feeling responsible for the world. You're not, you know. We're all responsible for ourselves, and when we can help each other, well, then that's great. But we can't always be there and we can't always help. Accept that and go on."

He eyed her with bemusement. "Have you been talking to Lauren?"

"No, not since Boston. Why?"

He shook his head, wondering at the similarity between this conversation and the one he'd had with his sister, before he and Jaida had even started their search. "The two of you have a lot in common," he muttered.

"As terrifying as last night was," Jaida said, "I think we can turn it to our advantage. That man, Franken, wasn't just Penning's bodyguard. He was a...I don't know what you'd call him, a hired gun, maybe. Trey..." She hesitated, shuddering at the memory of the deadly scene that had transmitted to her at Franken's touch. "I think Franken is the one who pulled the trigger that time, killing the man who died at Penning's feet."

She had Trey's full attention now, and she took a deep breath before delivering her next words.

"And I think I know how to find him."

Chapter 18

"Explain," Trey ordered Jaida tersely.

"Last night, I didn't escape from Franken right away. He grabbed me...just my ankle," she hastened to add when she saw Trey go tense. "He was dazed from the blow, but I still picked up on a scene from his past. It matched with the one I saw when Penning touched me."

"Can you describe it for me?"

She hesitated. "There were four of them. Franken, Penning, another man and the one who got shot. Weber," she added after a moment.

Trey leaned forward urgently. "You know the victim's name?"

"It was all part of the scene I picked up from Franken. They were in someplace big, shadowy, cavernlike. A parking garage, maybe."

He surveyed her, his mind racing. "That means Franken's worth to us just multiplied. Not only did he kidnap my nephew—"

"He can also explain the source of the bloodstained clothing Lauren stole from Penning," Jaida interjected.

Trey nodded. "If you're right and Franken can connect Penning to a murder, we'd no longer have to worry about him finding Lauren."

"She and Benjy would finally be free to live in peace."

"If," Trey said grimly, "Franken could be persuaded to turn state's evidence on his former boss. And if the man can ever be found." Remembering her earlier words, his gaze lifted to hers.

She managed to look both stubborn and incredibly guilty at once. "This is where we get to the kind of illegal thing I was telling you about. Last night one of the deputies found a black, leather glove lying on my kitchen floor. They were going to take it in as evidence, but I sort of said...I told him..."

"You told him..." Trey urged when she didn't go on.

The rest of the words came out with a rush. "I said the glove was Granny's, one of a set. That she used it for gardening...." Her voice trailed off. "It was all I could think of." She snuck a peek at him. He was eyeing her expressionlessly.

"I wonder what kind of time you can get in Arkansas for withholding evidence," he finally asked aloud.

She glared at him. "Don't be obtuse. Franken dropped it. He was wearing a pair when he was in the house. I was pretty fuzzy by the time the sheriff got here, but when they talked about finding a glove I operated on pure instinct. Don't you see? I can use that glove to lead you right to Franken."

"No." The word cracked like a whip. He rose from his chair so quickly it teetered behind him. "Not again. I'm not going to let you undergo that again. Not now that I know what it costs you."

"What's it going to cost Lauren if I don't?" she countered. "What's it going to cost Benjy? They can't go home again until Franken is apprehended. They can never live a normal life until Penning is out of the picture. How else is that going to happen if I don't go through with this?"

He stared at her bleakly. She was presenting him with a Hobson's choice, forcing him to choose between two equally distasteful decisions. What kind of man would he be if he let her hurt herself to help him, to help Lauren?

"You really don't have a choice, you know."

Her words, delivered in that airy drawl of hers, fueled his temper. "I don't?"

She shook her head. "I can find him, with or without you. I want it to be with you, of course. I don't really wish to encounter Franken alone again."

"There's no way you're getting near him again," he snapped.

"If you say so," she said simply. She returned to the process of cutting off another piece of pancake, soaking it copiously in syrup, and lifted it to her lips.

The seconds ticked by, stretching into minutes.

"You've already made up your mind," he accused. "You're determined to do this."

Intent on savoring her last bite, she merely nodded.

He muttered an obscenity. Turning on his heel, he went to the window. She used the time to finish her breakfast.

"There would be no need to come with me," he said finally. Frustration was rife in his voice. "You could pinpoint his location and I could go alone."

"You know it's not always that easy. Look how many times he moved around with Benjy. We may get lucky and find him on the first try. We may not. You'll need me with you in case I have to try again."

"No." He shook his head emphatically. "You can wait for me—" He broke off. Her slight smile lit his temper and his imagination. "I can read you like a book, Jaida."

"How interesting. Maybe my skills are rubbing off on you."

He ignored the gibe. "You'd follow me if I set off by myself, wouldn't you?"

"Would I?"

"Damn right you would." He glowered at her. He knew the woman well enough to be painfully familiar with her stubborn streak, and when she wore her most angelic expression his blood ran the coldest. Like right now. He might not have her ability, but he knew how her mind worked. She probably had it all planned out.

"I'll be safer with you," she observed logically. "We don't know whether Franken is going to come back here again."

The truth of her words made sweat bead on his forehead. She was right. There was no way she'd be safe here or anywhere in the area. Franken could still be lurking. He wasn't going to leave her alone, vulnerable again. He couldn't trust anyone else to take care of her, to protect her the way he could.

"Damn." He walked back to the table and glared at her. "I can't concentrate on finding Franken and wondering whether you're safe at the same time."

"It would be a shame to divide your concentration like that," she agreed.

His face lowered to hers, and his teeth were clenched. He'd been outmaneuvered, and finding himself without choices did nothing for his temper. "If you come with me, you'll do as you're told. That's the way it has to be, Jaida. Promise me, now."

She smiled angelically. "Trust me."

After the sheriff and one of his men had been and gone, Jaida had Trey bring her the glove from beneath the counter. "That's where I had the deputy put it last night," she explained, striving to keep the nerves from showing in her voice. Her hand trembled as she took the glove from him, distaste showing on her face as soon as she touched it. And then slowly, as if forcing herself, she slipped her hand inside it.

He almost warned her not to, actually took a step toward her, as if to stop what would come next. But there was no way to stop the visions that engulfed her, no way to save her from an ability that came from within. He watched her helplessly as she used her gift again, hoping fervently that this time the cost wouldn't be too high.

The physical change she underwent was frightening. Her eyes were wide, unfocused. Her face went absolutely bloodless and then her whole body began to quake.

He crossed to her and unwrapped her fingers from the glove, pulling it off her hand and flinging it aside. In the next moment she bolted from the room, and he followed her into the bathroom, holding her while she emptied her stomach—her body's reaction to the vileness she'd just immersed herself in.

He glanced at her now concernedly. He wrapped her in two thick afghans to still her shaking and brought her medication. She refused to take more than one tablet, unwilling to sink into the stuporous slumber her body craved. It was long minutes before she spoke. "He didn't go far," she said, her voice a raw whisper. "And he's going to try again."

* * *

The city limits of Little Rock were ahead of them, and Trey glanced worriedly at Jaida. She'd barely uttered a word during the drive, answering his questions monosyllabically.

"Jaida, are you sure you're going to be all right?" he asked for the dozenth time. "Because I've got to tell you, you're scaring me to death."

She wished the pain in her temples would abate enough to let her think so she could gather the words to reassure him. But the vision had been too strong, too repulsive, and her reaction was only going to strengthen.

"I'm fine." The weakness in her voice mocked her words and, by the frown between his brows, did little to convince him. "We're getting closer, that's all. It's going to affect me."

He looked swiftly at her. "You mean he's in Little Rock?"

She nodded and leaned her head on the headrest, letting her eyes slip shut. "Keep driving," she mumbled. "I'll tell you where to turn." The chill was creeping from her skin to her insides now, getting stronger with each passing mile, with each of her mumbled directions. And with each rerun of the cruel twisted scene she'd experienced in the vision, the ice encasing her grew a little thicker.

Trey eyed the seedy establishment grimly. "Open your eyes, honey," he said to Jaida, his voice gentle. "Is this it?"

She forced her eyelids open and gazed unfocusedly at the rundown bar that was identical to so many others in this part of town.

The Loose Goose. Its name didn't strike a chord with her, but she knew the place nonetheless. She knew it because it had figured in the last vision. She recognized it from her physical reaction, the chills that seemed to rack her from within. "He's inside," she said almost soundlessly.

Trey went still. "Franken? Now?" He should be grateful that Jaida's suffering would soon be at an end, but he hadn't expected to find the man this quickly. He'd hoped to have time to leave her somewhere safe, somewhere she could sink into the slumber her body was demanding, while he pursued Franken.

"I'm going in," he said, reaching a sudden decision. "You stay here. I mean that, Jaida. Don't move from this car. You gave me your promise," he reminded her urgently. "I'm holding you to it.'' Without another word he opened his door and slid out, hitting the button for the door locks.

He squinted in the smoky interior of the bar, giving his eyes a few seconds to adjust to the light. The bartender glanced at him as he made his way slowly in, but none of the dozen or so occupants even looked at him. Spotting his quarry, Trey walked to the back of the bar and slid in beside the man drinking alone in the last booth.

"Get the hell out of here," the man snarled.

"How are you doing, Tony?" Trey asked softly. He noted with satisfaction the white gauze bandage covering one side of Franken's head. At least Jaida had made the bastard suffer last night.

The man stiffened and slowly put the glass of beer on the table. Staring hard at Trey, he said, "I don't know you, man. And I don't know who you're looking for, but my name ain't Tony."

"Amnesia is a funny thing," Trey observed. "You never know when the memory is going to come back. Should we see if I can jog yours a little? Tony Franken, former associate of one William Penning of Boston. You did time for assault twelve years ago. But that time will seem like a vacation compared with what's in store for you now. Kidnapping is a federal offense, you know." He bared his teeth. "No chance for parole."

Franken eyed him. "You a cop?" One of his hands dropped casually below the table.

"Don't even think about it," Trey advised, shifting so his jacket gaped. The gun in its shoulder harness was plainly visible. "Let's keep both of your hands on the table, shall we?"

The man swallowed, then did as he was told.

"Wise choice. Now, to answer your question, no—I'm not a cop. I'm Benjy's uncle."

Trey's words got a definite reaction from the man beside him. Sweat appeared on his brow and he licked his lips nervously.

"I'm the one man," Trey murmured, his eyes alight with purpose, "who has the most reason to want to see your guts spilling across this table."

"You're not going to kill me," the man blustered. "Not here. Not in front of witnesses."

"You're right about that, Tony," Trey said almost regretfully. "I'm not going to kill you. No matter how much you de-

serve to die for putting my nephew and my sister through hell,
I didn't come here to shoot you. I came here to offer you a
choice.'' Trey outlined the man's options in succinct terms.

Franken's reaction was immediate. ''You're crazy, man. I'd
rather take my chances with prison than turn on Penning. At
least in prison I'll be alive.''

''You obviously misunderstood your choices,'' a second
voice said. Franken's eyes grew wide as Jaida slid into the other
side of the booth. She didn't spare Trey more than a glance. She
knew that her presence in the bar infuriated him. But she'd
been drawn here by forces far stronger than the promise she'd
given him.

''You see, Tony, we're not offering you the chance to go to
prison for kidnapping.''

The man looked from her to Trey suspiciously. ''That's not
what he said.''

''No, that would be too easy. Instead, I think we'll just call
William Penning and tell him where you are. I think we'll tell
him…'' She frowned thoughtfully. ''We'll say that you're ready
to tell the police that he ordered the hit on Weber. You did the
shooting, of course, but it wouldn't be the first time a criminal
cut a deal so the government could get a bigger fish, now would
it?'' The man's jaw dropped.

''When we describe the murder scene, how the others praised
your marksmanship, how Weber died at Penning's feet, begging for his life, I think we can convince him that we could only
have heard the story from you.''

''I never breathed a word of that,'' Franken cried. Looking
around, he lowered his voice and grated, ''I never told no one
about my work for Penning, and I ain't about to start now.''

''You're missing the point, here, Tony,'' Trey said repro-
vingly. ''It doesn't matter whether you told anyone. All that
matters is that Penning will believe that you did.''

''My life won't be worth a plugged nickel if Penning gets told
that,'' the man whimpered.

''I wonder what would happen if Penning found out you
were all set to deliver a son, one he never wanted and didn't
know about, to his parents, hoping for a huge payoff,'' mused
Jaida.

Franken was sweating copiously now.

''And then there's always the information we could give him
about how you stole from him, Tony,'' she went on.

Her words garnered Trey's avid attention, as well. For the first time he noticed the fine tremors that still shook her, the precise enunciation she was using. His gaze dropped to the hand she held in her lap, the one encased in a black leather glove.

"Do you think he'll believe that you helped yourself to things around the house, things you could pawn later? I'll bet he's always thought that Lauren took her jewelry with her. He'll be interested to know that you gathered it up yourself after she escaped. It was your... severance pay, isn't that what you thought?"

"You can't tell him any of that," Franken pleaded. "He'll kill me for sure. You'd be signing my death warrant as soon as you made the call."

"It's up to you, Tony," Trey said almost gently. "It's your decision. Which way will you feel safer? With Penning free... or with him in prison?"

"You still look pale," Trey said critically. "Are you sure you got enough to eat?"

Jaida wrinkled her nose at him. She was lounging comfortably on the couch in his apartment, the picture of contentment. "My appetite hasn't recovered from the plane ride. After that landing at LAX, I may never eat again."

His teeth shone. "Now, that I'd have to see to believe." He surveyed her, looking for signs of stress, but other than her lack of color she seemed to be all right. The past week had been grueling for her. Once Franken had been convinced that his best hope of staying alive was to tell what he knew about his former boss, events had progressed quickly. Granted immunity from prosecution for his own involvement in the crimes in which he implicated his former boss, Franken had become a fountain of information. The FBI agents had been almost gleeful at the opportunity to arrest Penning, on charges ranging from racketeering to murder. And given the physical evidence Lauren was able to supply that linked him to Weber's death, one charge, at least, seemed certain to stick.

"Will Lauren have to testify?" she asked quietly.

"I hope not. Franken's testimony and the bloodstained clothing may be enough to tie Penning to Weber's murder. The prosecutors are going to do their best to keep her out of it."

"Thank God Penning didn't make bail," she said soberly. "Lauren won't have to worry about him finding her any longer."

"As soon as he's in prison for good she can start the divorce proceedings," Trey said, satisfaction filling his voice. That would mark the beginning of his sister's new life. She would finally be rid of the constant fear that had haunted her. She and Benjy would be free to live in peace.

"What will happen to Kasem and Franken?" she asked.

"Franken still faces charges for kidnapping, and with Kasem's testimony he doesn't stand a chance of getting off. I understand she's going for a reduced charge. She's hoping to convince the jury that her involvement was under duress. All in all, the three of them aren't going to be causing any trouble for quite some time."

He fell silent then, enjoying the sight of her on his furniture, in his home. She looked right here, as if the dark cloth covering of the couch was made to showcase that light hair. Primitive possessiveness flared, swift and intense. He hadn't questioned his instinct to bring her with him, or the one urging him to keep her here. He'd lived his life by following that instinct. It had never failed him yet.

Jaida gazed about his apartment. The space was huge and perfectly decorated in navy, burgundy and gray. It had been designed with chic comfort in mind, and the effect was restrained elegance. It was such a perfect foil for Trey that Jaida was certain he had designed it himself.

Just as he'd designed a reason for her to travel back to L.A. with him. There had been no real need for her to accompany him to L.A. once the loose ends had been taken care of in Boston, and his excuse that Detective Reynolds might need to talk to her had been blatantly transparent. It had suited her own purposes to accept his explanation at face value, especially since remaining with him was what she wanted most in the world. But the question that had been hovering on her tongue for hours finally slipped out. "Why am I here, Trey?"

It was amazing how well she was beginning to read him. Not that he let even the merest flicker of an eyelash show that she'd disconcerted him. But his face lost that half-indulgent look it had been wearing and became the expressionless mask she'd first become accustomed to.

"You needed to give your body time to recuperate," he said evenly. "You can't be trusted to take care of yourself, Jaida. Don't argue," he admonished, when she opened her mouth to reply. "I've watched what the visions do to you physically, and in the past few weeks you've undergone them over and over. You've never been under this kind of stress before, so you have no idea the toll this whole experience has taken on you. I'm going to make sure you allow yourself time to fully recover."

"So once I've recovered I can go back home?"

That question sparked a hint of temper. She was doing it again, making plans to leave him, even while lying in languorous comfort on his couch. It was just like the time he'd had to fly back to Colorado and she hadn't given him a chance to talk her into coming with him. No, then, too, she'd announced her own plans, and just as cool as you please had walked away, leaving him with his guts in knots. But not this time.

He rose from his chair and stalked toward her. He sat down very near her, so close she was pressed between the pillowy arm of the couch and his warm, hard body. He slid one hand to the satiny skin beneath her jaw, and when he felt the pulse hammering there, he allowed himself a tiny smile.

"You can try to pretend, but you can never hide this, Jaida." The prickles of electricity beneath his fingers warmed him. "You can never hide your reaction to me." He covered her lips with his, forcing an even deeper reaction from her, from both of them. Her response was immediate and helplessly complete. He pushed up her top and filled his palms with her lace-covered breasts. Their mouths twisted together, their breathing growing ragged. Long minutes later he raised his head a fraction, savoring the sight of her sprawled half beneath him, her lips swollen, nipples straining against their confines.

"You don't want to go back to the cabin," he muttered, dropping a kiss on the top of one flushed breast. "You don't want to leave me, any more than I want you to go. You love me, Jaida. A woman like you doesn't make love to a man otherwise. You couldn't." His mouth was at her neck now, drawing her pulse into a more fevered beat. "Tell me," he demanded gutturally. "Tell me you love me."

She offered the words freely, relishing the chance to say them out loud. "I do," she whispered. "I love you, Trey."

The words had barely escaped her before his mouth covered hers again, thirstily drinking the words from her lips.

"Then stay. Marry me, Jaida."

Her eyelids flickered dazedly. "Marriage? Trey, you don'
want to marry me."

His face was only a fraction from hers, so close she could see
the intent in his eyes. "Honey, you're supposed to be psychic
You, better than anyone, should know how I feel."

"I do." The ache was in her voice, tearing at her throat. His
brows came down at the raw emotion. "I knew how you felt the
moment you took me in your arms when you raced back to the
cabin the night Franken broke in. And I also know how you fee
about my...gift." She saw the agreement on his face and could
have wept. "You've spent your life shielding your thoughts and
feelings from the world. You hate it when I touch you and read
something."

"No," he said bluntly, "I don't like it. I can't deny that it'
going to take some getting used to. But I do know your ability
works different with me than it does with anyone else. You re
spond every time I touch you, and your own emotions get in the
way, don't they? The closer we get, the more difficult it be
comes for you to concentrate on anything except what I make
you feel."

His hand was caressing her nape now, and the shivers racing
down her spine were proof of his words. "There's the trade
off," he whispered. "I may not always like the power of you
gift, but I damn sure like the effect my touch has on you, the
effect it has on both of us."

She evaded his lips when they would have sealed hers. "I'
not normal, Trey. I made my peace with that a long time ago.
can't live in a city, constantly raising my defenses so I can walk
down a crowded street. I can't sustain the kind of shield i
would take."

He listened to her, more to the wistfulness in her tone than
to her words, and something inside him softened. "We can live
anywhere you'll be comfortable," he promised. "The Arkan
sas Valley isn't the only remote spot on the map. If you want the
mountains, I can live with that. Beachfront?"

She flinched slightly at the stinging kiss he pressed against the
spot beneath her earlobe, before he soothed it with the tip of his
tongue.

"We can do that, too. Just say that you want to stay. Say
you'll marry me."

She cupped his hard jaw wonderingly. She'd spent long years coming to terms with what her ability meant—a lack of love, of intimacy, in her life. To be offered it now, from this man, was a rare gift indeed.

"Yes," she said simply. She couldn't say more—her throat was too full. But the one word was enough to make his green eyes glitter with suppressed emotion. He sat up, scooped her into his arms and walked swiftly from the room.

Once there, he let her slide slowly, intimately, down his body. That sense of familiarity was back; the overriding sensuality of finally having her here, in his bedroom, was threatening to engulf him. He rapidly divested her of the rest of her clothes, his progress hampered by her hands dispensing with his. He backed her up to the bed, reached beyond her and yanked off the comforter. Then almost gently, he laid her down, his jaw tightening as he took in the picture she made.

He followed her down, raising himself on one elbow above her. With one forefinger he traced her lips, her delicate jaw. "I love you, Jaida," he said hoarsely.

She smiled, a slow, secret smile, against his fingertip. "I know," she whispered.

Her reply surprised a gust of laughter from him. "Think you know everything, don't you? But you don't. You're not the only who can have visions. I've had one myself. Over and over, of you, me, on this bed. Like this. Just like this." Her eyes widened in surprise at his words, and then that Mona Lisa smile crossed her lips again.

He watched her through slitted eyes. She was as exquisite as any work of art. Her hair spilled across the sheets, the pale color shining like diamonds on a bed of velvet. The black sheets were a perfect foil for her silky body.

He lowered his head to kiss her. This was one vision that was going to last forever.

*   *   *   *   *

The Calhoun Saga continues...

In November
New York Times bestselling author

NORA ROBERTS

takes us back to the Towers and introduces us to
the newest addition to the Calhoun household,
sister-in-law Megan O'Riley in

MEGAN'S MATE
(Intimate Moments #745)

And in December
look in retail stores for the special collectors'
trade-size edition of

THE
Calhoun
Women

containing all four fabulous Calhoun series books:
COURTING CATHERINE,
A MAN FOR AMANDA, FOR THE LOVE OF LILAH
and *SUZANNA'S SURRENDER.*
Available wherever books are sold.

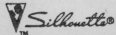

Silhouette®

Look us up on-line at: http://www.romance.net

CALHOUN

MILLION DOLLAR SWEEPSTAKES
AND EXTRA BONUS PRIZE DRAWING

No purchase necessary. To enter the sweepstakes, follow the directions published and complete and mail your Official Entry Form. If your Official Entry Form is missing, or you wish to obtain an additional one (limit: one Official Entry Form per request, one request per outer mailing envelope) send a separate, stamped, self-addressed #10 envelope (4 1/8" x 9 1/2") via first class mail to: Million Dollar Sweepstakes and Extra Bonus Prize Drawing Entry Form, P.O. Box 1867, Buffalo, NY 14269-1867. Request must be received no later than January 15, 1998. For eligibility into the sweepstakes, entries must be received no later than March 31, 1998. No liability is assumed for printing errors, lost, late, non-delivered or misdirected entries. Odds of winning are determined by the number of eligible entries distributed and received.

Sweepstakes open to residents of the U.S. (except Puerto Rico), Canada and Europe who are 18 years of age or older. All applicable laws and regulations apply. Sweepstakes offer void wherever prohibited by law. Values of all prizes are in U.S. currency. This sweepstakes is presented by Torstar Corp., its subsidiaries and affiliates, in conjunction with book, merchandise and/or product offerings. For a copy of the Official Rules governing this sweepstakes, send a self-addressed, stamped envelope (WA residents need not affix return postage) to: MILLION DOLLAR SWEEP-STAKES AND EXTRA BONUS PRIZE DRAWING Rules, P.O. Box 4470, Blair, NE 68009-4470, USA.

SWP-ME96

As seen on TV!
Free Gift Offer

With a Free Gift proof-of-purchase from any Silhouette® book,
you can receive a beautiful cubic zirconia pendant.

This gorgeous marquise-shaped stone is a genuine cubic
zirconia—accented by an 18" gold tone necklace.

(Approximate retail value $19.95)

Send for yours today...
compliments of ▼ *Silhouette*®
TM

To receive your free gift, a cubic zirconia pendant, send us one original proof-of-
purchase, photocopies not accepted, from the back of any Silhouette Romance™,
Silhouette Desire®, Silhouette Special Edition®, Silhouette Intimate Moments®
or Silhouette Yours Truly™ title available in August, September or October at your favorite
retail outlet, together with the Free Gift Certificate, plus a check or money order for
$1.65 u.s./$2.15 can. (do not send cash) to cover postage and handling, payable
to Silhouette Free Gift Offer. We will send you the specified gift. Allow 6 to 8 weeks for
delivery. Offer good until October 31, 1996 or while quantities last. Offer valid in the
U.S. and Canada only.

Free Gift Certificate

Name: _____

Address: _____

City: _____ State/Province: _____ Zip/Postal Code: _____

Mail this certificate, one proof-of-purchase and a check or money order for postage
and handling to: SILHOUETTE FREE GIFT OFFER 1996. In the U.S.: 3010 Walden
Avenue, P.O. Box 9077, Buffalo NY 14269-9077. In Canada: P.O. Box 613, Fort Erie,
Ontario L2Z 5X3.

FREE GIFT OFFER   084-KMD
ONE PROOF-OF-PURCHASE
To collect your fabulous FREE GIFT, a cubic zirconia pendant, you must include this
original proof-of-purchase for each gift with the properly completed Free Gift Certificate.

084-KMD

Your very favorite Silhouette miniseries characters now have a BRAND-NEW story in

CHRISTMAS KISSES

Brought to you by:

LINDA HOWARD

DEBBIE MACOMBER

LINDA TURNER

LINDA HOWARD celebrates the holidays with a **Mackenzie** wedding—once Maris regains her memory, that is....

DEBBIE MACOMBER brings **Those Manning Men** and **The Manning Sisters** home for a mistletoe marriage as a single dad finally says "I do."

LINDA TURNER brings **The Wild West** alive as Priscilla Rawlings ties the knot at the Double R Ranch.

Three BRAND-NEW holiday love stories...by romance fiction's most beloved authors.

Available in November at your favorite retail outlet.

Silhouette®
TM

Look us up on-line at: http://www.romance.net

XMAS96

You're About to Become a

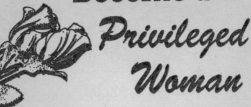

Become a

Privileged

Woman

Reap the rewards of fabulous free gifts and benefits with proofs-of-purchase from Silhouette and Harlequin books

Pages & Privileges™

It's our way of thanking you for buying our books at your favorite retail stores.

PROOF OF PURCHASE
Offer expires October 31, 1996
SIM-PP171

Pages & Privileges ™

TM

**Harlequin and Silhouette—
the most privileged readers in the world!**

For more information about Harlequin and Silhouette's PAGES & PRIVILEGES program call the Pages & Privileges Benefits Desk: 1-503-794-2499

Silhouette®

TM

SIM-PP171